Having Faith

A Novel

Anne Miller

Having Faith

Copyright © 2022 by Anne Miller

Published by The Scenic Route Publications

Anne Miller
Milleranne1284@yahoo.com

ISBN: 978-0578316222

Library of Congress Control Number: 2021922573

This is a work of fiction. All of the characters, names, incidents, or-ganizations, and dialogue in this novel are either the products of the author's imagination or are used fictitiously.

Printed in the United States of America

Dedication

This novel is dedicated to all the mothers that are, to the ones that are soon-to-be, and especially to all of those who longed to be but the good Lord had different plans. Everything happens for a reason, even if we don't understand it at the time.

Acknowledgments

First and foremost, as always, I'd like to thank God for blessing me with this incredible gift of writing and the courage to use it.

To my family: my mom, Geraldine, whom I believe is watching over all of us from heaven; my dad, Howard; my brother, Robert Miller; and my sisters, Mary Raymond and Donna "Jane Q" Rosseau as well as my dear friend Lisa Masnova for being there for me during this past year.

To "Ralph" for all of your car knowledge. I wouldn't sound half as intelligent without it. To James Paul for creating my new and improved website for me. And to Sandra Moore, your insight was invaluable in the making of this story; thank you for taking the time to answer all of my questions.

To all the members of the Upper Peninsula Publishers and Authors Association whom I've had the chance to meet, and especially Tyler Tichelaar and Larry Alexander for using your many talents to bring this sequel to life. I hope we can do just as well on the third book in this series.

To Missy from Flutterby Photography for taking my photograph for this book.

And last, but certainly not least, to all of my fans who have been eagerly awaiting this sequel. I hope it lives up to all of your expectations.

Chapter One

THIS WAS A BIG ONE. Adrian could tell. She felt it from the curl of her toes to the sweet sensation that slowly possessed her body.

She glowed from within. Energy surged through her as if she were a live wire. It left her mind so blissfully intoxicated that she couldn't have formed words even if she had wanted to.

The roar grew so loud it sounded as if the earth had cracked in half. The thrill became so intense Adrian couldn't hold back any longer.

It was like free-falling out of an airplane. Every piece of Adrian's spirit intermingled with the rainstorm that fell in sheets over Green Bay, Wisconsin, and landed her on the balcony of the apartment where she and her husband, Jake, used to live.

This wasn't the first time Adrian had come to him since she had died, but it still didn't make it any easier. She pressed the palm of her hand up against the glass of the French doors while the rain plastered her long dark hair to her face. Jake stood on the other side, his hand matched up to hers, and stared apathetically up into the ominous sky.

A year and a half had passed since Adrian had died. Jake and Cassie, Adrian's best friend, had been officially dating for about a year now. They had started apartment hunting three months ago, and this weekend they were moving in together.

This was Jake's last night in this apartment—the home he and Adrian had made together.

Adrian shook her head. "Still can't shake that Riley stance, can you?"

Jake turned away as he withdrew his clenched fist from the pocket of his jeans.

Adrian collapsed onto the balcony floor, struck down by the thunder that rocked the night. She felt like the wind had been knocked out of her when she saw what was in her husband's hand.

"Still feels like a sucker punch right to the gut, doesn't it?" said a male voice.

Adrian stared wide-eyed and open-mouthed into the face of Jake's deceased father, Kevin.

"What's the matter?" Kevin asked her. "You look like you've seen a ghost."

Adrian gave him a dirty look, which didn't affect Kevin at all.

"I haven't seen you in a while, is all," she replied.

"I wasn't about to miss this," Kevin said. Adrian wrinkled her eyebrows in confusion. "My son's got a big decision to make about that ring he's got in his hand."

That ring was the one Kevin had given Jake's mother, Laura, when they had gotten married. Laura had continued to wear that ring around her neck after Kevin had died, right up until the day she had been remarried two years ago. She had then passed it down to Jake.

"Yeah," Adrian spoke softly, "I know."

She hated to admit it, but it wasn't just the proposal that upset her. That ring held history, meaning, and—no—there was no way Jake could've given it to her when they had gotten engaged even if he had wanted to. It was just the idea of Cassie possibly having it now....

"C'mon," Kevin said, interrupting Adrian's thoughts as he helped her to her feet. "Let's go inside."

The rain subsided as they crossed the threshold. Adrian froze; her husband sat at the kitchen table inches away from her. She moved tentatively toward him, then stopped when he threw the ring onto the table. Jake leapt up and marched to the refrigerator. He didn't see the imprint the ring had left on the palm of his hand until after he reached inside for a bottle of beer.

Marriage, he thought as he took a long swig. *Now why in the hell would I want to go through that again?*

"Excuse me?" Adrian snapped, while a loud clap of thunder accompanied her words.

"Retract your claws there, Catwoman," Kevin leaned back against the kitchen counter and swung one foot over the other, "and tell me what the most important thing to remember here is."

Adrian sighed and rolled her eyes like a sullen teenager. "Don't jump to conclusions."

"Ah, so you do remember. Then why are you still doing it?"

Adrian was about to retaliate, but the flashes of lightning distracted her. One illuminated her husband's exquisitely chiseled bare chest. A slow smile of satisfaction spread across her lips as she allowed herself this one small indulgence, which lasted only until Jake's thoughts picked up where they had left off.

Don't get me wrong; being married to Adrian was...

"Was what?" Adrian asked.

...amazing, but...

The suspense killed Adrian. "But what?"

And then, the apartment plunged into darkness.

Yeah, exactly. And she was gone, just like that.

Adrian let out a huge sigh of relief that left her hollow inside. She listened to Jake fumble around the apartment in search of matches, a candle, anything that could shed some light.

Adrian didn't need light to find Jake. All she had to do was reach for him and he was there in her arms.

It was too tempting to resist. Adrian's lips brushed Jake's at the exact same moment the power came back on. Jake stood in the living room and felt shivers trickle down his spine. He jumped but blamed it on the volume of the television. He searched for the remote, then froze once he saw what was actually on.

Fuck. A Cubs game.

"My favorite team." Adrian smiled fondly.

Jake took a moment before he rolled his shoulders back and kept looking. He didn't find the remote, but he did see the engagement ring on the table.

Jake stared hard at it and sighed.

Nope, he thought as he turned sharply away. *Not now; not yet.*

"What?" Adrian shouted. "Why? Just because you saw my favorite baseball team on TV?"

She stopped when she felt Kevin's eyes on her.

"What?" she snapped at him.

"So, let me get this straight," Kevin replied calmly. "You're upset now because your husband doesn't want to ask your best friend to marry him?"

"Yes...no...it's just that I..." Adrian stammered.

She eventually gave up and got right in her husband's face.

"Just tell me. Do you love her?"

Jake didn't speak. His face revealed nothing, but his thoughts—to Adrian—were perfectly clear. She shut her eyes as she felt a sudden stab of pain slice through her heart.

"Then there's your answer," she told him.

*

Jake sat in the driver's seat of his truck a few days later and stared blankly out the windshield. His hands left a thin trail of sweat behind them as they ran up and down the steering wheel before coming to an abrupt halt.

This is ridiculous, he thought.

"I think it's kind of cute myself." Adrian giggled from the passenger seat. "Kind of like you're going on a first date or something."

I've been sitting in this damn driveway long enough, Jake thought as he flung his door open. Let's just do this already!

He strode purposefully to the front door and knocked without hesitation. His mind didn't become riddled with doubt until just before the front door opened.

"Jake," the older man spoke gruffly.

He was in his late forties, with dark hair and a scruffy beard. He and Jake were about the same height and build, but the older man seemed to take up every inch of space in the entranceway.

"Benjamin."

The older man's eyes narrowed into thin slits. Jake cleared his throat.

"Uh...um...Mr. Adler," Jake mumbled as he glanced down at his feet.

"Whoa," Adrian said while she leaned against the door frame. "This is a first: the great Jake Riley intimidated. And by Cassie's father no less. Hmm...I never thought I'd live to see the day."

Kevin raised his eyebrows at her in disbelief.

"Well, you know what I mean," Adrian said, trying to explain herself.

"If you're looking for Cassie," Mr. Adler told Jake, "she's not here."

"Actually," Jake said as he locked eyes with Cassie's father, "I'd like to talk to you, if you have the time."

Mr. Adler looked mildly surprised as he stepped aside. "Okay, let's talk."

He's just another guy, Jake thought as he walked cautiously into the foyer with Adrian and Kevin close behind him. *Yeah, he's Cass's dad and he deserves respect, but that doesn't make him any better than you. Don't make this any bigger than it needs to be.*

"Have a seat," Benjamin told Jake while he motioned toward the living room.

Adrian could see her husband morphing into his Riley stance with every step he took.

"And there it is," she said, her voice laced with disappointment.

"You of all people," Kevin reminded her, "should know it never stays gone long."

"Yeah," Adrian replied as she watched Jake sit back on the sectional as if he owned the place, "but I still keep hoping anyway."

"Can I get you a beer?" Benjamin asked Jake on his way into the kitchen.

"No, thanks. I'm good," Jake answered.

Adrian's eyebrows shot up in surprise. "What? No beer?"

Need to keep all my senses straight for this one, Jake thought.

Jake's attention was suddenly caught up in the pre-season football game playing on the large flat screen TV that hung above the fireplace. He watched for a minute until it was interrupted by a commercial break. That's when his eyes wandered around the room and fell first upon the gun cabinet in the corner, then the massive twelve-point buck mounted on the tongue-and-groove paneled wall.

Jake's legs twitched uncontrollably.

"Stop it!"

Adrian's jaw dropped, not because Kevin got angry, but because his anger was directed at her.

"Stop what? I'm not doing anything! I can't control what Jake's looking at, can I? He's reacting all on his own. Free will, remember?"

Kevin was about to respond when Cassie's dad returned to the living room. Jake put his hand subtly on his knee to steady his leg.

"So," Benjamin said as he sat down in his recliner, "what did you want to talk to me about?"

"I want to marry Cassie," Jake blurted out, "and I'd like your blessing."

Adrian groaned as she buried her face in her hand. Mr. Adler nearly spilled his beer, but he recovered quickly enough to grab the remote and shut the TV off without his eyes ever leaving Jake's.

Jake leaned forward and pressed both of his hands down on his knees while his father's voice roared through his mind:

"Do not back down!"

"Kevin!" Adrian berated him once she realized this wasn't a memory but something he was telling his son right now.

Kevin kept on, oblivious to Adrian's objections.

"Do not give in to him. Stand your ground. You're a Riley man; he's got nothing on you...."

"No."

The word came so softly out of Mr. Adler's mouth that Jake barely heard it.

"Excuse me?" Jake asked.

There was no mistaking it this time. "I said no."

A stunned silence fell upon the room; even Adrian and Kevin didn't know what to do.

Jake couldn't keep his eyes from widening, but his voice remained calm while he asked why.

"I have my reasons," Cassie's dad said while he set his beer bottle down on an end table.

Adrian's eyes blazed as she watched Benjamin sit back in his recliner like a king on his throne.

"He's smirking at Jake," she hissed.

"Easy," Kevin warned her as if he were a trainer trying to control a wild animal. "Easy."

Reasons, Jake thought. *Plural. Great. Just great.*

"And I have a right to know just what those reasons are," Jake replied as he rose to his full height.

"Uh-oh," Adrian said.

"All right." Benjamin sighed. "I'll tell you the truth. I just have a bad feeling about you."

A bad feeling, Jake thought as he nodded his head.

That's all Jake heard, but Adrian and Kevin got the full story straight from Benjamin's thoughts.

There's just something about you I don't trust. You may have charmed your way into my daughter's heart with your whole brooding bad boy routine, but you've done nothing to prove yourself to me.

A light breeze blew through the trees in the front yard while Adrian tried to control her temper.

"Yeah, well," Adrian said. "I never thought much of you either, you self-righteous, holier-than-thou, son-of-a—"

"Adrian!" Kevin stopped her.

She threw her hands up in exasperation. "Did you not just hear him?"

"Yes, I did," Kevin answered, "but the trick is to not listen."

"Yeah, okay, whatever," Adrian replied.

Any man who can forget his dead wife so easily and then sink his claws into my little girl, well that's no man at all in my book.

"What?" Kevin snapped when he heard Mr. Adler's latest revelation.

The wind picked up to full force and blew a cluster of leaves off the trees.

"A little trickier than you thought, huh?" Adrian asked Kevin.

The look Kevin gave her was enough to send her into a humbling silence.

But I'll tolerate you, Benjamin continued, *for as long as it takes my little girl to wake up and see you for who you truly are. But marriage? Oh...there is no way in hell I will tolerate that!*

"Well," Jake spoke to Cassie's father, "I'll be perfectly honest with you too. I really don't care if I have your blessing or not. I'm still asking your daughter to marry me."

Cassie almost tripped over her own feet after she walked through the front door and heard this, but she braced herself against the wall in the hallway before anyone saw her. She stood stock-still, as if the slightest movement—even breathing—might destroy the moment like waking up too quickly from an amazing dream.

"I'm not worried," she heard her father say to Jake. "Cassie's a smart woman; she'll make the right decision."

Cassie swallowed hard, her hand over her heart to keep it from exploding out of her chest. There were two ways she could handle this: stay pressed up against the wall and pretend she hadn't heard any of it, or come out guns blazing.

Adrian held her breath. It seemed to take Cassie forever to make up her mind.

"Yes," Cassie said as she stepped confidently into the living room, catching both men by surprise. The hint of a smile played upon her lips when her eyes met Jake's. "I will."

"Yes!" Adrian shouted as she pumped her fist.

Adrian's enthusiasm faded fast when she saw someone else come through the door.

"Uh-oh, here comes trouble," Adrian grumbled.

Julia Adler strolled into her home with her takeout bag swinging on her arm, but she stopped dead in her Sketchers when she saw the look on her daughter's face.

"What's going on?" she asked as she peered around the corner to see what had caught Cassie's attention.

"Jake wants to marry me." Cassie sounded as if she were floating on air, her eyes locked onto Jake's, "and I said yes."

Julia's bag of food fell to the floor with a thud. Cassie's bubble burst as soon as her mother spoke.

"Please tell me you're kidding."

Cassie whirled around to face her. "No, Mom, I'm not."

"This is all happening way too fast. You need to sit down and really think this through before you make any serious decisions." Julia turned to her husband. "Benjamin, tell her."

"No," Cassie said before her father could speak. "There's nothing you or Dad could say that would make me change my mind. I know how I feel. I know what I want, and that's to marry Jake."

"Well, I just wish I could say I was happy for you," her mother replied.

Adrian gasped. The words stung Cassie as if she had been slapped across the face. Tears sprang to her eyes, but she willed them back in. Her voice started off shaky but grew stronger with every word.

"I wish you could too. Thanks for lunch."

Jake bit his tongue as he watched Cassie turn on her heel and head for the front door.

Respect, my ass, Jake thought as he shot Cassie's dad a disgusted look before he chased after her.

"Bitch," Adrian sneered as she brushed past Julia.

Julia rubbed her arms as a chilling sensation suddenly shot through her body. Adrian couldn't help but notice, as Julia rushed outside, how quickly her demeanor changed.

Julia stood on the sidewalk and casually flipped her fingers through her hair. A tight-lipped smile forced itself upon her face while she gave her daughter a feeble goodbye wave.

"Well, of course," Adrian scoffed from her spot on the top step, "you've got to put on a good show for the neighbors, don't you, Julia?"

Cassie didn't even glance back at her mother. She did freeze, though, once she realized she didn't have a car to take off in.

Shit! She picked me up for lunch!

That's when she felt Jake's hand on the small of her back. He guided her to his truck, opened the passenger door, and helped her inside.

He then proceeded to rev the engine before he peeled out of the driveway, leaving a thick, black cloud of smoke hanging over the pristine cul-de-sac.

Neither of them said a word until they had left the suburbs.

"Where are we going?" Cassie asked Jake.

"Well, I thought we could both use a drink right about now," Jake replied, his eyes focused on the road ahead of him.

*

The joy in Maggie's eyes when she saw the two of them enter The Borderline faded faster than a summer fling by the time Cassie and Jake had approached the bar.

"Lunch go that well, did it?" Maggie asked Cassie.

"Lunch was great," Cassie answered while she pulled up a stool. "It was Jake's proposal that shot everything to hell."

Maggie's eyes bugged out of her head. "Wait; he did what now?"

"Yep," Adrian said, her lips curled up into a mischievous smile while she leaned her elbows back onto the bar, "if there's one thing my husband's gotten really good at, it's memorable marriage proposals."

Jake pressed his lips together in a sheepish grin and nodded to Maggie in response.

"So..." Maggie pressed on, "why are we not celebrating then?"

"Because Cass's parents are a couple of judgmental hypocrites," Adrian mumbled.

Kevin crossed his arms over his chest and gave Adrian a dirty look.

"What? It's the truth. And besides," Adrian shrugged, "I've never really liked either one of them, especially her mother."

"My parents don't approve." Cassie's voice fell flat as she responded to Maggie's question.

"Well, surprise, surprise." Maggie snickered as she pulled the tap forward to pour herself a mug of beer.

She looked up after she had finished to find the same mopey expression on Cassie's face.

Maggie tilted her head to the side. "I'm sorry, darling," she began as she grasped Cassie's hand. "I know this isn't the big Hollywood reconciliation you were hoping for, but you got to remember their track record."

Adrian's chin rested in her hand. "You do speak the truth, Miss Maggie." Then she turned to her friend.

"I mean, c'mon, Cass," Adrian said. "They practically disowned you when you dropped out of medical school to become an EMT.

They didn't even bother to speak to you until they heard about the accident that killed me. Hell, your mother didn't even come up with these lunch date ideas with you until after videos from my art show went viral."

Adrian scoffed. "God forbid she be portrayed as Mommie Dearest. I mean, what would the women in her church group think?"

Kevin cleared his throat. Adrian tipped her head back to look at him.

"Too much?" she asked him.

"Maybe just a little," he replied.

"Oh, believe me, I do," Cassie told Maggie while she stared pensively down into her bottle of beer. "But that still didn't stop me from hoping."

"Well," Jake said, "maybe this will make you feel a little better."

Cassie watched while he fumbled to pull something from the front pocket of his jeans.

"That's a ring," she stammered after he set it gently on the bar between them.

"Wow." Jake chuckled. "Can't put anything past you."

Cassie fell silent while her mind raced.

Holy shit, that's a real engagement ring! This is really happening; right here, right now.

"Cass?" Maggie leaned in close after she noticed Cassie's complexion grow paler than usual.

Maggie drew back once Cassie reached for the ring. She held it delicately between her fingers and studied it from every angle as if she had never seen one before.

Maggie and Jake exchanged nervous glances; neither one of them knew what to do next.

"This…this is your mom's ring." Cassie spoke softly to Jake, but her eyes never left that ring. "The one your dad gave to her when they got married; the one she never took off until the day she got remarried, and then she gave it to you."

Adrian felt the weight of those words fall heavily onto her best friend's heart.

"Oh, shit," Adrian said to Kevin. "This is hitting her way too hard, way too fast. She's in over-thinking mode. We need to do something to calm her down."

"I think Jake has it covered," Kevin replied as he put a comforting hand on Adrian's arm.

"That's right," Jake said to Cassie while he plucked the ring from her fingers.

Their eyes locked as he took her left hand in his right.

"And now it's yours, if you want it."

Jake's fingers held steadily onto the ring. He maintained the perfect Riley stance that hid his inner anxiety well, but he couldn't hide anything from Adrian and Kevin.

Please, he thought, *please don't tell me you were just caught up in the moment at your parents' house.*

All the knots in Cassie's stomach suddenly unraveled; the tightening in her chest eased; every single doubt vanished the second she recognized the certainty in Jake's breathtaking blue eyes.

"Yes." She smiled eagerly while she thrust her hand forward. "I will."

"Hallelujah!"

Maggie slapped the counter with the palm of her hand so hard she made everyone in the bar jump.

"We got an engagement here!" she yelled in explanation. The entire place erupted with cheers and applause.

"Well," Jake joked, "at least we got the bar's approval."

"Thank God." Cassie laughed before she pulled her fiancé's lips onto hers.

Chapter Two

ADRIAN SAT ACROSS THE AISLE from Kevin, her mouth agape while her eyes attempted to take in all the phenomenal architecture that surrounded her.

Four massive pillars stood on either side of her, each archway bathed in a soft, soothing light. Adrian looked up in awe at the gold patterns that crisscrossed the high, rounded ceiling; then her eyes descended upon the hand-painted scene of The Crucifixion that dominated the wall behind the altar.

"This cathedral is gorgeous," she told Kevin, "but it's not where Cassie really wants to get married."

"Really?" Kevin asked while he turned toward her. "And how do you know that?"

"Because we've been best friends since high school."

"Which means…what…that the two of you have talked about this subject before?"

"Yes," Adrian answered with a frustrated roll of her eyes at Kevin's cluelessness, "and not once in all of those times did Cassie ever mention anything to me about having her dream wedding in a cathedral."

"Well, maybe she changed her mind."

"Nope, not possible," Adrian said adamantly. "It's too big, too bold, and so not her. But I've got a pretty…" she paused, remembered where she was, then swallowed the word she intended to use and tried again.

"…good idea who would love to have it here."

"Cassie's mother," Kevin replied.

"Exactly," Adrian agreed, her voice noticeably hushed.

She sat back in the pew with her arms folded over her chest.

"I just don't get it," she said.

"What's that?" Kevin asked.

"Why Cass is trying so…hard to get her parents' approval."

Adrian felt Kevin's eyes boring into her skull.

"What?" she asked after she finally turned to face him.

"You mean to tell me you never needed your parents' approval?"

"I don't know." Adrian shrugged. "My parents were never the 'rah, rah, rah'," she extended her arms out as if she were a cheerleader shaking her pom-poms, "you can do anything you want Adrian, type, but I still always knew I had their approval."

"Unlike Mommie Dearest," she added under her breath.

"Adrian," Kevin warned her.

"I'm sorry, but I've just never liked that woman."

"Is that because she thought you were a bad influence on her daughter?"

Adrian's jaw dropped.

"Don't forget: I know all and see all," Kevin said.

Adrian slowly shut her mouth. "No, it's not that. It's just…" she paused at a loss for words. "It's just the way she treats Cass, you know. Like she thinks Cass doesn't know how to live her own life, and that just kills me. I mean, how could any parent treat their child like that?"

Adrian winced. She regretted saying the words the second they left her mouth.

"I'm sorry, Kevin. I didn't mean...."

Kevin's eyes were focused on the polished, mosaic floor tiles. He lifted them up slowly to meet Adrian's.

"It's all right. You said exactly what you meant to say."

"Look," he continued, "I knew you hated me for the longest time. I wasn't even sure this whole thing would work, me being your mentor."

"But it did," Adrian replied. "It took me a while, but I finally realized you only did everything you did out of love for your son."

Kevin didn't say a word, but Adrian had no trouble reading his face.

"Ah...I see what you're doing," she said.

"What?" Kevin asked, feigning innocence.

"You want me to believe Cassie's mom is only acting like this because she loves Cassie."

Kevin didn't get a chance to respond. The sound of the side door opening and closing caused them both to turn their heads.

Adrian leaned forward in her pew at the sight of Julia Adler strolling amicably through the front of the cathedral with the priest.

"What the...?" Adrian stammered.

"Thank you again, Father Andrew," Julia's voice sounded so sickening sweet to Adrian that it made her want to throw up, "for taking the time to listen to me."

Adrian turned to Kevin in confusion.

"She wouldn't have suffered an attack of conscience that caused her to confess all the horrible things she'd done to Cassie, would she?" Adrian whispered.

Kevin raised a brow and narrowed his eyes at her.

"Or not," Adrian answered.

"I always have time for one of my parishioners," Father Andrew told Julia. "But really, I should be the one thanking you for having the courage to come to me with this."

The hairs on the back of Adrian's neck stood up when she heard this.

What the hell is she up to? Adrian thought.

"Well, Father," Julia said while she wrung her hands, "it's like I told you earlier; this wasn't an easy decision for me to make, but in the end, I just knew it was the right thing to do."

"Of course," Father said with a somber nod of his bald head.

"As much as I wanted to speak to you on my daughter's behalf…" She paused to let out an overdramatic sigh.

"Oh please," Adrian mumbled.

"…I just can't lie for her either."

"Nor would I want you to." Father Andrew scratched his gray beard thoughtfully. "We can't have your daughter building a new life on a lie either."

"Lie? What lie?" Adrian wondered until Julia's thoughts suddenly became crystal clear to her.

"Adrian." Kevin spoke cautiously as if he were trying to subdue a mother bear from attacking a potential predator.

But Adrian wasn't listening. She shot up from her seat, her knuckles white from gripping the pew too hard. Her eyes—normally a soft, gentle, brown—now blazed with anger.

"You bitch!" Adrian hissed as she lunged at Cassie's mother.

"Adrian. Stop!"

Kevin intercepted her before she had the chance to do any real physical damage to Julia.

An explosive sound rocked the church, followed by a cold gust of air. Julia nearly jumped out of her skin, but Father Andrew remained calm.

"What was that?" Julia asked.

"That," Father Andrew chuckled, "is our air conditioning system reminding us once again how desperately we need a new one."

"Oh, good. I thought maybe the world was coming to an end there for a moment," Julia said, laughing.

"Oh, no. Nothing quite that serious," the priest replied.

Meanwhile, Kevin and Adrian lay sprawled out before the altar. He kept a firm hold on her until he saw the natural color return to her eyes.

"You can let go of me," she insisted. "I'm fine now."

"Oh, no," Kevin said.

He waited until Julia and Father Andrew went back to his office before he released her.

"Now I think we're safe."

Adrian glared at him while she got back to her feet.

"Well, can you blame me?" she asked him.

"No, not really, but you still have to control—"

Adrian didn't let him finish. "How can I possibly control myself when she's purposely sabotaging Cassie by telling the priest they've been living in sin?" She accentuated the last phrase with air quotes.

"I know," Kevin said softly.

Adrian shook her head, her eyes focused on the doorway that Julia had just exited through.

"For the love of Cassie, my ass."

*

Cassie sat in the passenger seat, her fist propped up against her temple, as a sly smile spread across her face. She watched Jake, out of the corner of her eye, maneuver his truck through the downtown Green Bay traffic.

His jaw was set, his lips frozen in a permanent scowl. He shifted awkwardly in his seat and craned his head around another seemingly slower vehicle in front of them. Cassie's eyes darted back to her window when he groaned under his breath. Another opportunity to pass had eluded him. She lowered her fist to her mouth and giggled.

"You know I can see you over there, right?" Jake asked, his eyes never once leaving the road.

"I can't help it," Cassie said while she unclenched her fist.

"What's so funny?"

"You," Cassie said, turning toward him. "I know it's more than just the traffic that's bugging you."

Jake scoffed. "These people are driving like turtles. Don't they realize they are allowed to go sixty-five on the freeway now?"

His shoulder twitched ever so slightly, which was just enough to give him away.

Adrian and Kevin were squeezed together between the truck's front and back seats.

"Did you see that?" Adrian asked Kevin.

"Yes, I did, and thank you for the added bonus of elbowing me in the ribs," Kevin replied.

"I'm sorry. I got excited."

"No kidding."

"Not just because of what Jake did, but because Cassie caught it too! See?"

Kevin gave her a dirty look as Adrian was about to elbow him again. She managed to re-route her arm back to her side just in time.

"She's reading him better now," Adrian finished calmly.

"Mm-hmm," Cassie said to Jake while she bit her bottom lip.

Jake expected her to say more, but he got nothing.

"What?" he asked after he still felt her eyes on him.

"Nothing," she replied with a casual shrug of her shoulders.

"You know I'm not a big church person."

"I know."

"And as far as I knew, you weren't either. I mean, really, when was the last time you even went to church?"

"I may not go to church, but that doesn't mean I don't have faith."

"Exactly. So why all the pomp and circumstance then?"

Cassie stared at Jake in confusion.

"This gigantic cathedral," he said. "Four hundred of your parents' closest friends. I mean, c'mon; it's not like we're the royal family or anything."

"Uh-oh." Adrian said the words right before Jake thought them.

Now it was Cassie's turn to clam up. She snubbed him with a flip of her chin before she turned abruptly to her window. Jake knew right away he was in trouble.

Oh, shit! Here we go. Why didn't I just keep my big mouth shut?

"Free will," Adrian replied with a sideways glance at Kevin.

Now I've got to think of a way to save this...fast.

"Hmm," Adrian said as she sat back and folded her arms, "this ought to be good."

Jake sighed. *Time to suck it up and take one for the team.*

"But I'll do it," he told Cassie as he reached for her hand, "if that's what you really want."

"Not bad." Adrian nodded her approval.

They were off the freeway now and stopped at a red light. Jake bit his lip while he waited for her response.

C'mon, Cass; don't leave me hanging.

His eyes widened as she leaned forward, but his hopes were dashed when all she did was reposition herself.

Damn! That should've worked. And it was the truth besides.

Jake was about to swallow his pride even further when he noticed Cassie's gaze had shifted from her window to the windshield, and her mouth hung slightly open.

"Cass, what is it?" he asked.

"That's my mom's car," she said.

They were maybe a block from St. Xavier's Cathedral. Sure enough, a metallic red Ford Equinox was just pulling out of the church parking lot.

"Are you sure?"

"I saw her 'Choose Life' front plate.

"Yep, that's her all right."

"I wonder what she was doing down here?"

"Maybe she had to do something for the little kids' classes she teaches," Jake suggested.

Cassie gave him a look. "You mean catechism classes?"

"Yeah," Jake shrugged, "same difference."

Cassie shook her head at him. "I doubt it."

"Hmm. Well, I'm sure it was nothing."

"Oh," Adrian said, "it's something."

As much as Jake tried to reassure Cassie, and as much as she wanted to downplay it, neither one of them could deny their gut reaction that something just wasn't right.

Their suspicions were confirmed once they met with Father Andrew.

"Unfortunately," the priest told them, "I cannot, under good conscience, marry the two of you."

Cassie almost fell out of her chair. "What? Why?"

"Because it has come to my attention that you're living together, and that's something I just can't condone."

"You're kidding, right?"

Cassie shot Jake a dirty look, but that still didn't stop him. "You do realize this is the twenty-first century?"

Cassie put her hand over her face and sank lower in her chair.

"Well," Father Andrew rose from his chair, "that may be, but this is still my church."

"That's all right, Father," Cassie said before the conversation could get any worse. "We understand."

"We do?" Jake asked incredulously.

"Yes, we *do*," she told Jake.

"It is your decision," Cassie said to the priest, "and we have to accept that. Thank you, Father, for your time."

Cassie was halfway out the office door; Jake just stood there shocked.

"C'mon, Jake," she said. "Let's go."

Jake shook his head in bewilderment before he followed her out the door.

"What the hell was that?" Jake asked once they had reached the parking lot. "I mean, can you believe him? Where does he get off...?"

Jake's rant would've continued if Cassie hadn't raised a weary hand.

"Jake...please...stop."

He did, and that's when he really saw Cassie.

She stood with her shoulders hunched over, her face drawn. The light in her eyes had faded, and her bubbly smile simmered down to a look of utter hopelessness.

Jake felt like he had just been sucker-punched in the stomach.

Jesus, he thought, *that priest sucked the life out of my girl.*

Adrian stiffened slightly when she heard those words.

"C'mon," Jake said to Cassie as he opened his arms out to her. "Let's go home."

She fell into them and, for a moment, Jake wondered if he'd have to carry her into the truck.

"Wow," Adrian said as she and Kevin trailed behind Jake and Cassie, "she really wanted this more than I thought."

"I think there's more to it than that," Kevin replied.

*

Jake stared longingly at the spiral staircase that led to their bedroom loft. As much as he wanted to, he couldn't retreat to their roomy king-sized bed because it wasn't where Cassie wanted to be.

She preferred to be downstairs, stretched out on the couch alongside him. Jake kept his arms wrapped protectively around her and held her as close to him as he possibly could.

He never voiced one objection; not when she pulled the throw blanket down over them, even though it was seventy-two degrees outside; not when she took control of the remote and found a chic-flic marathon on that consisted of *Pretty Woman* and *Sweet Home Alabama*, and not even when his phone was blowing up and it was just inches away from him on the coffee table.

Ah...it's probably just Mom calling anyway, he thought. *She can wait.*

"See!" Adrian exclaimed. She sat on a chair next to the window and uncurled her legs out from underneath her. "That's what that piranha of a mother should've been doing for Cassie."

Kevin sat opposite Adrian and watched her with his chin in his hand.

"You can't tell me her actions were for Cassie's own good. Uh-uh. No way. What she did to her own daughter was malicious and pure evil."

"Are you finished?"

"I think so." Adrian touched her fingertips together while she took several deep breaths. "Yep, I'm good for now."

"Good," Kevin said as he stood up. "Because we need to go."

"Go? Go where?"

"You'll see," he replied while he motioned for her to follow.

Adrian rose up reluctantly from her chair, then paused to take a last look at Jake and Cassie on the couch.

She smiled fondly at her best friend.

"Don't worry, Cass," Adrian said. "I'll always be looking out for you."

She squeezed Cassie's shoulder. Cassie stirred. Jake instinctively soothed his girlfriend with soft shushing and rubbing her shoulders.

Jake and Adrian's hands collided. They both jumped as if they had been struck by a bolt of lightning.

Whoa, Jake thought, *I must've dozed off there for a second too.*

He placed a gentle kiss on the top of Cassie's head just as Adrian kissed him softly on his temple.

All three of them shivered. Jake pulled the blanket tighter around him and Cassie while his eyes began to droop.

Adrian let her hand linger on them for a moment before she joined Kevin by the front door.

*

The next thing Adrian knew, she was standing beside a square island in a large, open kitchen. She glanced up in bewilderment at all the copper pots and pans that hung above her. It wasn't until she looked to her left, into the living room, and saw the deer heads mounted on the wall that she knew exactly where she was.

Adrian tilted her head and rolled her eyes at Kevin.

"Why are we here? And don't say—"

"You'll see," Kevin smirked.

Adrian growled in frustration.

Just then, the door from the garage opened and Julia stepped into the kitchen.

"Ben?" she called out. "Benjamin," she said louder this time.

"Yeah," he answered while he tipped his head back from his recliner seat.

"I'm home."

Julia set her purse down on the island and started rummaging through it until she produced something from within the inside zippered pocket.

"A rosary?" Adrian sneered. "Really?"

Kevin looked at her. "Boy, for someone who went to Catholic school, you sure are cynical."

"Yeah, well," Adrian shrugged, "people have a way of doing that to you sometimes."

Fake people, Adrian added to herself as she stared daggers at Julia.

"You keep forgetting I can read your mind," Kevin told her.

"Hard habit to break," Adrian replied. "Sorry."

The rosary was hand-crafted, its beads a crystal-clear pale blue, the cross a well-worn silver with a few knicks and scratches.

Julia cupped the rosary in her hands and held it close to her heart. She shut her eyes. Adrian scoffed.

"So..."

Benjamin snuck up beside his wife. The sound of her husband's voice so close startled Julia so much she shrieked. The rosary dropped onto the island. Julia recovered quickly enough to snatch it up and toss it back into her purse before Benjamin noticed.

Adrian turned to Kevin with wrinkled brows.

"What was that all about?" she asked.

Kevin shrugged. Adrian bit her tongue.

"Sorry," Benjamin said as he wrapped his arm around Julia and kissed her on the cheek. "I didn't mean to scare you."

"It's fine," Julia replied while she patted his cheek with the palm of her hand.

"So, how'd it go? Did you tell him?"

"We talked, yes. And I told him everything."

"And?"

She sighed. "He agreed. They should not be married in a Catholic church, and they won't be at St. Xavier's."

"Adrian," Kevin instinctively warned her.

"You have no remorse," Adrian snarled at Cassie's mother. "None. At all. You care more about being right than you do about your own daughter."

The pots and pans swayed and clanked loudly together above them. The breeze from the kitchen window chilled Julia to the bone. She broke free from her husband's embrace to close the window.

I did the right thing, Julia thought before she turned around to face Benjamin.

"We did the right thing. Right?"

"Yes," Benjamin nodded. "We did."

Chapter Three

"WHOA.... THIS WOMAN SOUNDS LIKE a total whack job," Charlie said.

He was just about to break up the balls on the pool table when Jake updated him on everything that had happened with Cassie's mother.

They were at The Borderline. Charlie and Jake were shooting pool. Cassie was sitting at the bar talking to Maggie.

"I don't know if I'd say 'whack job'," Jake replied. "Devout Catholic might be a little more accurate."

"Oh Jesus, a devout Catholic, huh?"

"What, you're not a fan?"

"I'm just saying," Charlie shrugged, "religion, especially the Catholic kind, makes about as much sense to me as monogamy."

"Yeah, well, it makes about as much sense to me as women do in general."

Jake raised his bottle of beer to his lips while he looked over at his fiancée.

*

"So what's your plan now?" Maggie asked as she pulled her barstool up closer to Cassie.

"My plan?" Cassie's eyes blinked rapidly.

"Yeah. What's your next step? What are you thinking?"

"Oh. Well, I haven't really thought about it."

"Just please promise me you're still going to marry Jake."

Maggie was only kidding, but she saw Cassie's eyes drift slowly down to her twiddling fingers.

"Cass!" Maggie and Adrian shouted in unison.

"What?" Cassie asked as she glanced over her shoulder to see if Jake had heard Maggie.

"Don't you 'what' me," Maggie replied. "What the hell are you thinking?"

Cassie groaned while she buried her face in her hands. "I don't know."

"Yes, you do," Maggie said as she gently pulled away Cassie's hands.

"But...."

"No 'buts'."

"Where are we supposed to get married now?"

Maggie leaned in close and smiled. "Anywhere the fuck you want, sweetheart."

"Just not in a Catholic church."

"Oh my God." Maggie threw her hands up in the air. "Why are you so hung up on this church thing?"

"You really want to know?"

"Yes!" Adrian yelled.

"Yes, please," Maggie replied in a much more subdued tone, "enlighten me."

"Because my parents won't show up if I get married anywhere else." Maggie drew back and let Cassie's words sink in. "I know they've done a lot of shitty things to me, but they're still my parents, and I never imagined them not being at my wedding. I can't see anyone but my dad walking me down the aisle and giving me away to Jake. I just can't."

"Aw, Cass," Adrian said when she heard the hurt in her best friend's voice.

"I get that," Maggie replied as she placed her hand over Cassie's.

"So you tell me: What do I do now?"

"Well, you could allow me the honor of giving you away," a deep, raspy, male voice spoke up from behind Cassie, "wherever you decide to get married."

Maggie's eyes welled with tears. Cassie whirled around to see Maggie's boyfriend, Tony, standing there.

"I know I'm not your dad, but I think I'd make a pretty decent stand-in," he added.

Cassie didn't know what to say, and even if she had, Maggie never gave her the chance to respond.

"I just got an idea! Tony, do you mind watching the bar for a minute?"

"No problem, babe. Go ahead."

"C'mon," she said to Cassie.

"Where?" Cassie asked.

"Just c'mon. Please?"

"Yeah," Kevin said to Adrian. "C'mon."

And just like that, Kevin and Adrian disappeared.

*

"Quit stalling," Jake teased Charlie, "and take your shot already."

"Don't rush me, man," Charlie replied while he prowled around the pool table.

"Rush you? Tony's going to come over here any minute and announce that it's last call."

"Bullshit."

Charlie leaned over the table to finally take his shot when people charging up the stairs distracted him.

"What the...?" Charlie asked.

Jake glanced toward the stairs and was shocked to see Maggie dragging Cassie up them.

"What the...?"

Jake abandoned his pool stick—the game forgotten—and chased after the two women.

*

"So," Maggie said to Cassie once they reached their destination, "what do you think?"

"I think," Cassie replied, "we're on a roof."

It used to be the place where all the smokers congregated up until a few months ago when Maggie had decided to keep up with the times and transform it into a rooftop bar.

Glass tables and neon green and gold barstools and metal chairs lined the edge of the roof that overlooked the Fox River. A large circular firepit, with a sectional couch wrapped around it, had been built into the center of the roof. A brightly colored tiki bar stood on the opposite side of the roof, complete with lighted tiki torches and a gigantic stuffed parrot swaying in the evening breeze.

"Yes," Maggie agreed with Cassie, "but can you picture it?"

"Picture what?"

"Your wedding. We could have it right up here."

Cassie squinted at Maggie as if her brain cells were too buzzed to comprehend what her friend was telling her.

"The ceremony," Maggie tried again, but she still got nothing but a dazed and confused reaction. "Here, let's try this."

Maggie came up behind Cassie, put her hands on her shoulders, and positioned her toward a better view of the skyline.

"Now, take a look at that and tell me this isn't the perfect place for a wedding."

Cassie looked up at the hazy sky. The sun—a large, warm, orange-colored sphere—melted into the clouds, tinting them pink.

"Can't get any closer to God than this," Maggie said.

"I agree."

Both women whipped their heads around to see Jake standing by the open stairwell door.

"But," he added, "that's just my opinion."

Kevin and Adrian sat on the edge of the roof facing everyone. Adrian looked over her shoulder at the sky, slack-jawed.

"Did you?" she asked as her eyes darted between him and the sun.

"Me? No, I had nothing to do with that. Our job was just to get Cassie up here in time to see it."

"So, we want her to get married up here?"

"We want her to know all of her options so she can make the best decision for herself."

"Wow, how diplomatic of you."

"Thank you."

"Now tell me how you really feel."

"It doesn't matter how I really feel."

"It does to me."

"Yeah," said Kevin, laughing, "because I won't let you read my mind, and that's driving you crazy."

"Well, there is that too," Adrian mumbled. "But seriously, aren't you curious about how I feel?"

"Oh, there's no mystery to you, Sister Cynical," Kevin teased her. "You've made your feelings perfectly clear."

"I'll have you know Jake and I got married in a Catholic church."

"I do know that."

"Of course you do," Adrian said. "Anyway, I knew Father Martin all my life. He loved Jake and me, plus he was a lot more easy-going than Father Andrew."

"See?"

"See what?"

"There is a little bit of religiousness hiding inside that great wall of cynicism."

"That is all my grandma's doing. The one thing she insisted upon was that her only grandchild—me—got a good, proper, Christian education."

Adrian looked at Cassie. "If only everyone had family that cared about them that much."

"She does," Kevin replied.

"Oh really? Who?"

That's when Cassie's cell phone rang.

She pulled it out of the back pocket of her jeans and grinned the second she saw his brown eyes, that so much resembled her own, staring back at her.

"Benji!" Cassie shouted.

"Benjamin James Adler, Jr." Adrian couldn't help but blush while she spoke his name. "Cass's oldest brother. She's got two of them you know."

"Ben and Nick," Kevin replied. "Yes, I know. There's a pretty big age difference between them too, like fourteen and ten years older than her if I'm remembering correctly."

"You are. Cassie's always been closest to Ben, though. I suppose," Adrian added while she turned to Kevin, "you also know why Cassie calls him 'Benji'?"

"When she was little," Kevin replied, "she couldn't say 'Benjamin.' It always came out as 'Benji.' He hates it, but she refuses to call him by his given name."

"And," Adrian raised her index finger for emphasis, "he has a name for her too."

"Hey, Soap Star!" Ben shot back at his little sister with his killer, megawatt smile.

Cassie groaned. *Everyone else in my family*, she thought, *got a name with meaning. Ben after dad; Nicky after mom's dad. Me? They had no idea what to call me, until the lady my mom was sharing a hospital room with turned on* One Life to Live. *And there was Cassie Callison. My namesake, or 'Soap Star' as Benji loves to call me to this day.*

"What's up, Dr. Benji?" Cassie asked.

"And of course," Adrian explained, "they both have prestigious medical careers. Ben's the chief of surgery at Woodson Memorial in Madison, and Nicky has his own family practice down in Appleton. Tough acts to follow, if you ask me."

"Well," Ben answered Cassie, "I hear congratulations are in order!"

"Really? Who'd you hear that from?"

Cassie turned her death stare onto each person on the roof with her.

Maggie's eyes widened while she shook her head vigorously from side-to-side. Charlie didn't seem to have a clue, which only left....

"Hey, Ben," Jake said as he strolled up alongside Cassie.

"Hey, congrats again, man," Ben told Jake. "Thanks for keeping me in the loop."

"No problem."

Adrian saw Cassie's grip tighten on her cell phone. "Oh," she whispered to Kevin, "she is pissed at him."

"Where are you guys anyway?" Ben asked.

"We're checking out a venue for the wedding actually," Jake answered while he skillfully wrestled the phone out of Cassie's hand. "What do you think?"

Cassie bit down so hard on her lip she tasted blood. *What the hell is he doing?* she thought as she watched Jake give her brother a tour of the rooftop with her phone.

"Very cool," Ben said when Jake returned the phone back to Cassie. "I bet Mom and Dad's heads exploded when you told them."

"Well…"

"Oh Jesus, Cass, not again!"

"It's a long story, Benji."

"It usually is when it comes to them."

Ben's pager suddenly went off.

"I got to get going," he said as he ran a hand through his dark blonde hair. "We'll talk more about this later. Just promise to save me a seat at the wedding, okay?"

Cassie's smile lost some of its joy. *I know you mean well, Benji, she thought, but you have a wife, two very active kids, and a career that leaves zero time for yourself. So forgive me if I don't hold my breath on this one.*

"We will." Cassie tried to keep her voice upbeat. "Love you."

"Love you too, Soap Star."

Jake had his arm around Cassie, but as soon as Ben hung up, she flung it off her faster than Miranda Priestley discarding one of last year's coats.

"Whoa!" Adrian said while she leaned forward. "We should have popcorn for this."

"What the hell were you thinking," Cassie fumed, "dragging my brother into this?"

Charlie and Maggie exchanged nervous glances before exiting the rooftop as quickly and discreetly as possible.

"Dragging your brother into what?" Jake asked incredulously. "All I did was tell him we were engaged, since you hadn't gotten around to it yet!"

"Well, forgive me for not hiring a skywriter to announce it, but I've been a little preoccupied with…."

"Go on," Jake said. "Please finish your thought."

Cassie's face went blank. She seemed to be staring off into space, but Adrian felt like her best friend's eyes saw right into her soul.

"Cass," Jake asked nervously, "are you all right?"

"Yeah," Adrian added, equally anxious. "What is going on?"

"Now's your chance," Kevin told Adrian.

"My chance? To do what?"

"Cassie's connecting with you."

Adrian, Cassie thought, *never would've thought twice about this. She would've jumped right in, guns blazing, yelling "Fuck them; let's do this!"*

"Show her what you want her to see," Kevin continued. "Give her the best option right now."

"Okay." Adrian sounded less than confident. "I can do that."

"This isn't about me," Adrian said to Cassie as she approached her. "This is about you, and what you want. The question is: Is this what you want?"

The horn from The Nitschke Bridge sounded—a signal that the bridge would be drawing up soon to let a boat pass through. It was also what caused both women to focus their full attention on the breathtaking skyline.

Just as the navy blue rose up from the horizon to overtake the cotton candy pink sky, so too did the darkness inside Cassie's mind fight to extinguish the light.

"This is absolutely gorgeous," Adrian told her.

Yeah, it is, Cassie thought, *but you can't guarantee it'll be like this on your wedding day. I mean, what if it rains? Have you even thought about that? What are you going to do then?*

Adrian watched the darkness cloud Cassie's mind.

"Hey," Adrian countered, "what's wrong with rain? Besides, I'm sure Maggie has a tarp or something to cover everything if need be."

That pushed back the darkness, but not for long.

What about your family? thought Cassie. *Is the view so good you can forget that your family won't be there?*

"Your family will be there," Adrian seethed, her face right up in the darkness, "just like we always have."

"Adrian!" Kevin yelled. He tried to pull her back, but there was no budging her.

But what about Mom and Dad? Can you really get married without them there? Are you really going to be okay with that?

Cassie tipped her head back, covered her face with her hands, and let out an anguished groan.

Adrian stood frozen, her eyes still trained on her best friend. "I don't know what to do," she said panicked.

"Kevin, please, tell me what to do for her."

"Nothing," Kevin replied.

"What?" Adrian whipped around to face him.

Kevin motioned with his chin to his son.

Jake came up behind Cassie and held her tight. She shut her eyes, instantly calmed by the feel of his arms around her. Adrian watched in awe while the darkness swirled up into a funnel cloud and withdrew underneath the horizon.

"Cass," Jake spoke softly in her ear, "it's all right. You don't have to decide anything right now."

Cassie turned in Jake's arms to face him, and that's when she saw it. All of it.

Jake in a dark suit and tie standing before her, holding her just as he was now. The rooftop bathed in strings of multicolored lights. Maggie and Tony hovering in the background like proud parents; a few rows of white folding chairs filled with all the people who cared about them.

Adrian felt the peace flow through her friend's mind and heart.

"You're going to do it, aren't you?" Adrian asked, barely able to contain her enthusiasm.

"I don't need more time. I want to marry you. Here," Cassie told Jake.

Adrian screamed triumphantly just as the horn signaled that the bridge was going back down.

"I am so glad you made the right decision!" Adrian exclaimed.

Chapter Four

"Jesus," Jake moaned while he wiped the sweat off the back of his neck with the palm of his hand, "it's not supposed to be this damn hot in the middle of October."

"It's called Indian Summer, man," Charlie said as they headed out of the city garage to their trucks, "and you better get used to it because it's supposed to last all weekend."

"Great," Jake replied sarcastically.

"C'mon," Charlie grinned as he clamped his hand down on his best friend's shoulder. "I know just the thing to get you out of that pissy mood you're in."

"Oh, really? What's that?"

"Beer. And I'm buying."

"You're buying?" Jake arched his eyebrows in disbelief. "Willingly?"

"Yeah, now c'mon before I change my mind."

"Okay, okay. On one condition."

"What?" Charlie sighed while he stopped dead in his tracks.

"We can't go to The Borderline."

"Why not?"

"Because…every time Maggie sees me now, she ambushes me with more wedding shit, but we're not getting married until the middle of August!"

Charlie couldn't help but laugh.

"You know, bro, you could've avoided all this misery by just…"

"…staying single." Jake finished Charlie's sentence for him with much less bravado. "Yeah, yeah, yeah. I hate to tell you this—again—but that's not going to happen. The Master is retired."

"Not yet you're not."

"Don't worry. I'll still try to teach you everything I know, but honestly," Jake leaned in close to Charlie as if about to divulge a well-kept secret, "you can't teach a God-given gift."

"Shut the fuck up," Charlie said good-naturedly while he back-handed Jake in the chest. "Just for that, I'm going to get you so drunk Cassie's going to call off the wedding."

"Yeah, right. Good luck with that."

Nothing's going to make my girl change her mind now, Jake thought.

*

Jake returned home two hours later, slightly buzzed and eager to see Cassie.

He opened the front door and smiled when he saw her sitting on the couch watching television.

There's my girl.

Adrian gritted her teeth; Kevin couldn't help but notice.

"Still hard for you to hear, huh?" he asked her.

"What?" Adrian shrugged. "I was his sweet thing; she's his girl now."

"Uh-huh."

"Don't give me one of your judgmental 'uh-huhs'," Adrian said as she looked down at Kevin from where she sat above him on the spiral staircase. "It took you nearly a decade to be okay with Clint and Laura."

"Calm down, Miss Defensive. I'm not being judgmental. I just know exactly where you're coming from, and it's okay. As long as you don't hold him back like I did to Laura."

"Yeah, well, nothing's holding him back now."

Adrian watched Jake make a beeline for Cassie. He snuck up behind her, lay his hands on her shoulders, and brushed the nape of her neck with his lips.

Cassie jumped. Jake backed off. Whatever amorous feelings he had for her died the second she turned to him with a crazed look in her eyes.

Oh, shit, Jake thought. *What happened? It couldn't have been anything I did. I just walked in the door. Or was it? She's not pissed that I went out with Charlie, is she? I gave her a head's up. Normally it's not a big deal, so long as I tell her. But what else could it be?*

"C'mon, babe; be observant," Adrian said. "Look around her. What's she watching on the television?"

Shouts of excitement caused Jake to turn his attention to whatever was on the flat screen television.

It's that wedding dress show she can't get enough of, he realized. *Wedding. Fuck! What has her mother done to her now?*

"Just please, babe," Adrian warned him, "don't poke that hornets' nest right now."

I can't ask her that, though.

Adrian let out a huge sigh of relief.

She might go ballistic. Better to proceed with caution.

"Good boy." Adrian nodded her approval.

"Cass," Jake asked, "what's wrong?"

"What's wrong?" she said, shocked he even had to ask.

Oh, shit. Jake took a step back.

"Do not question her," Kevin instructed his son. "Just listen to her."

Don't say a word, Jake thought. *Just listen.*

"Some of the girls at the hospital decided to throw me a surprise bridal shower today," Cassie said.

"Well, that's good," Jake replied.

Adrian tilted her head back and groaned.

"What happened to not saying a word?" Adrian asked while Cassie's eyes grew wilder.

"That's...uh...not good?" Jake asked.

"No," Cassie replied, "not when they're doing it because they think I don't have anybody else who will."

Jake went to hug her; she waved him off.

"The worst part is they're right. They're absolutely right. I've been watching this damn show all night, and I haven't seen one bride walk in alone. Not one. They all have an entourage with them, and I can't help but think: Who the hell do I have? My best friend's gone and my mom doesn't want anything to do with me or my wedding, so who does that leave me with?"

Me, Jake thought. *You've got me.*

Cassie's voice rose higher while the words flew faster out of her mouth. Jake couldn't make sense out of anything she was saying, but it didn't matter.

All he wanted was to show her how loved she was.

He marched purposefully around the couch to her. His blue eyes ignited with such intensity that even Adrian's breath got taken away.

"Holy...hell...that look," Adrian said.

Kevin glanced up at her. "You all right? You need a glass of water, or a cold shower maybe?"

"I'm fine," she said as she sat up straighter and tried to regain her composure.

"Uh-huh," Kevin replied.

Cassie was still rambling on when Jake pressed the palms of his hands against her cheeks and kissed her full on the lips.

Cassie's arms shot up to resist him, but then they fell feebly back down a moment later as her body gave into him. Jake slid his arm around her waist to keep her from falling, but it was no use. Cassie shrieked as they both tumbled onto the carpeted floor.

"Are you okay?" Jake asked.

"Yes," Cassie giggled. "I'm fine."

"Good."

Something in Jake's voice caught Cassie's attention. Her laughter subsided as he rose up over her and she fell victim to his insatiable eyes.

"Then I can continue."

"With what?" she asked.

Jake lowered himself down close to Cassie's ear and whispered, "My plan to make you forget everything."

"Oh, please do."

Jake smiled wickedly when she tipped her head back.

He proceeded to stroke the length of her neck with his fingertips ever so slowly before finally grasping her chin and bringing her mouth to his.

While their tongues intertwined, his hand moved deftly underneath her sweatpants to begin its sensual assault on her.

Cassie's eyes popped open. Her fingernails dug into his shoulders while she bit down hard on his neck.

"Okay." Adrian abruptly stood up. "I don't think we need to be here for the rest of this, do we?"

"No," Kevin agreed. "We can take off for a while."

They began to descend the stairs when Adrian saw Jake reach behind Cassie and yank her short blonde hair. His intention was to lock eyes with her, but something distracted her.

Cassie gasped, but to Jake it sounded more fearful than pleasurable.

"Cass," he asked, "what is it?"

"I swear I just saw shadows moving over by the staircase."

Adrian froze while she and Kevin exchanged nervous glances.

"Oh, baby, you're stressed out. It's probably just the glare from the TV or something."

Jake sat up and felt around for the remote control.

"There," he said once he had found it and shut the television off. "There's no one here but you and me, and you know what I would like to do?"

"What?" Cassie grinned.

"Help my girl relax."

"Oh, really?" she asked playfully. "And just how do you intend to do that?"

"Oh, don't you worry about that. All you need to do is lie back down and just enjoy the process."

"Well, I'm going to enjoy the process of getting out of here as quickly as possible," Adrian said as she turned to Kevin. "You with me?"

"I'm right behind you."

She sailed toward the window and, with one last glance at her husband, disappeared through it.

"So now where to?" Kevin asked her as they stood outside on the sidewalk.

"I don't know; I hadn't really thought about it."

Adrian suddenly tilted her head back to the sky and breathed in deeply.

"What are you doing?" Kevin asked.

"I smell rain in the air. You know what that means?" she answered, practically giddy.

"Oh, no. I am not going there with you."

"Oh, c'mon, Kevin. Why not?"

"That's your thing; not mine."

"You don't know what you're missing."

"I did it once. I will not do it again."

"Well, what are you going to do then?"

"I'll find someplace to go."

"Uh-huh."

"Hey, don't give me one of your judgmental 'uh-huhs'," Kevin teased her.

"Me? Judge you? Never," Adrian fired back with a sly smile.

"Meet you back here at daybreak?"

"Yes, sir." She saluted him while she backpedaled away into the night.

*

Adrian sat on top of the highest point of The Fury, the old-fashioned roller coaster at Kingston Beach in Green Bay. Her feet dangled freely over the edge. She didn't even hang onto the railing while she leaned forward, her eyes to the sky in eager anticipation of the next thunder and lightning strike.

The hours went by quickly. The storm eventually passed. Adrian sat back and sighed as if the final encore of a spectacular concert had just finished playing.

She stared off into the distance and saw just a hint of light peeking out over the horizon.

Daybreak.

It was time to return to Jake.

She stood up, stepped calmly over the roller coaster's edge as if she were walking off a curb, and dropped back into Jack and Cassie's living room beside Kevin.

"How was your night?" he asked her.

"Good. Yours?"

"Good." His face and voice revealed nothing.

"You're not going to give me anything, are you?" Adrian asked.

"Nope," Kevin answered with a faint smile.

Fine, she thought, *if that's the way you want to play this.*

"I do," Kevin said out loud.

His smile widened just as there was movement from the floor.

Jake and Cassie had fallen asleep in each other's arms. Jake rolled away from her to stretch out. He grimaced when he felt a knot of pain in his back. He couldn't figure out why, but then it hit him.

Oh yeah, we did spend the entire night here on the floor.

Last night.

Jake's lips curved up into a gratifying smile as he thought about his night with Cassie.

"Please," Adrian begged him, "don't go into detail."

Jake sat up and lingered over Cassie's shoulder.

"Mmm," he purred while his stubbled chin glided up and down her arm. *How I would love to have an encore performance with you right now.*

But he resisted. Cassie looked too calm and peaceful to disturb just yet.

So Jake forced himself to get up, and that's when he saw the throw blanket on the back of the couch. He reached over to grab it to cover Cassie when he accidentally bumped into her laptop, which was still sitting open.

Jake's eyes were drawn to the screen as the laptop burst to life. He lay the blanket lightly over Cassie, then waited to make sure she was still sound asleep before he decided to snoop on her.

He found room for himself on the edge of the couch, among all the bridal magazines and her open wedding list notebook, and took a closer look.

The website she had last been on was all about wedding invitations. There were tons of them. Each one had different colors, fonts, and designs. A blank box at the bottom of the screen also gave the option to design your own invitations.

Kevin stepped forward without saying a word to Adrian.

"What are you doing?" she asked him.

"Stop looking at the screen," he told his son, "and look around you on the couch."

"What is it?" Adrian asked. "What do you need him to see?"

Jake kept scrolling through the pages.

"It's right there; right in front of you."

"What is?" Adrian asked again.

Kevin still didn't respond.

"Kevin," Adrian shoved him in the arm, "tell me!"

Jake sat back on the couch and rubbed his eyes. When he opened them, he caught a glimpse of a crumpled-up sheet of paper wedged into the corner.

"Finally," Kevin said.

Jake grabbed it, smoothed it out, and then ran his fingers through his hair in frustration while he read it.

It looked like Cassie had attempted to come up with her own wording for their invitations, but nothing had worked.

The first one read, "Mr. & Mrs. Benjamin Adler request the honor of your presence at the marriage of their only daughter." Her parents' names were crossed heavily out in pencil.

She had tried again: "Jake Riley and Cassie Adler along with their families." Then she had scribbled, "Family? WHAT FAMILY OF MINE? NONE."

Then finally she had written, "Cassie Adler and her brothers," only to stop and write, "(well, maybe Benji if he can actually make it)."

Jesus, Jake thought as he covered his mouth with his hand, *no wonder she was so freaked out when I got home.*

"Hey," Cassie said sweetly from the floor, nearly scaring the life out of Jake, "what are you doing up there?"

"Nothing," Jake replied while he snatched his phone off the arm of the couch. "I was just looking for my phone."

Cassie stood beside him wrapped in the throw blanket and nothing else.

"Uh-uh," she said while she shook her head from side to side.

"What?" Jake asked as he stood up to face her. "No phone?"

"No phone."

"But," he held up his phone to show her, "my mom just texted me. She wants to know if we can have lunch with her today."

"Tell her yes," Cassie said, her voice low and seductive. "Then meet me upstairs."

Jake nearly dropped his phone while he watched Cassie ascend the stairs and let the blanket slide slowly down her body.

Ah...if only I could figure out a way to keep you this relaxed and happy, he thought.

"Yeah," Adrian said to Jake. "Unfortunately, you can't sleep with her every time she freaks out about the wedding. I mean, you could, but it's not going to help anything. You're going to need backup."

*

"You dreamt about him last night, didn't you?" Jake asked his mother.

They were at Mama Jo's Pizzeria for lunch. Jake and Laura stood across from each other at the bar while Cassie went to grab a booth.

"Who?" Laura asked as she pretended to dust the counter.

"C'mon, Mom," Jake covered her hand with his. "This is me you're talking to. The only time you ever call me so early in the morning is if there's an emergency, or you dreamt about dad."

"So, you want to tell me what this thing is you've got going on here?" Laura asked while she motioned to her son's newly forming beard.

Jake pressed his lips tightly together and gave his mother the evil eye.

"Okay, okay," Laura gave in. "You win. I did dream about your father last night."

"I knew it!" Adrian shouted.

Kevin merely shrugged his shoulders.

"But," Laura continued, "I haven't seen you in a while either. I wanted to make sure you were okay."

"I'm fine." Jake paused to take a swig of his beer. "Now Cassie on the other hand."

"Why? What's wrong with Cassie?"

"She's just really stressed out with all the wedding stuff."

"Oh." Laura sounded relieved. "Well, that's normal."

Her son's face said otherwise.

"Or not," she replied. "What's going on?"

Do I tell her everything or don't I? Jake thought. *Cass might kill me, but I can't keep watching her do this to herself.*

Jake let out a deep breath before he explained everything to his mom.

"Say no more," Laura said as she moved swiftly around the bar.

"Mom," Jake replied nervously, "where are you going?"

"You just stay here and finish your beer. I'm going to go have a chat with Cassie."

"Mom!"

"Don't worry. I know how to be subtle."

Jake groaned while he buried his face in his hands. *What the hell have I done?*

"So," Laura began as she slid into the booth opposite Cassie, "I would like to offer you my services."

Cassie's mouth dropped open while she stared at Laura in bewilderment.

"For what?" Cassie asked cautiously.

"Wedding planning."

"Oh." Cassie's face instantly relaxed. "I really appreciate the offer, Mrs. Riley...I mean Mrs. Walker...."

"Stop. Please, Cassie, for the millionth time, call me Laura. Calling me Mrs. anybody just makes me feel old."

"Okay, sorry." Cassie laughed. "Laura, thank you for the offer, but I think I've got it under control."

Laura arched a skeptical eye at her.

"Cassie...honey...I've been there before—twice in fact—so I know this is something you cannot do alone."

"Who said anything about me doing it alone?" Cassie returned the same skeptical eyebrow to Laura.

Touché, Laura thought.

"What did Jake tell you?"

"Nothing I wouldn't have recognized on my own eventually."

"Recognized?" Cassie squinted at Laura in confusion.

"Mm-hmm," Laura replied before she took a drink of her soda. "See, my father never thought Kevin was good enough for me. He kept trying to convince me of that, too, every chance he got, from the day we announced our engagement right up until I found out I was pregnant with Jake three months before our wedding day."

"What?" Cassie couldn't believe her ears.

"Really?" a shocked Adrian asked Kevin.

"Really," Kevin said calmly. "We never hid it from Jake either. In fact," he chuckled, "we always told him he was hiding behind Laura's bouquet of flowers."

"Jake never told me that."

"And that surprises you why?" Kevin asked.

"Good point," Adrian said.

"I kid you not," Laura replied to Cassie. "My father was so angry he didn't even want to walk me down the aisle."

"Shut up!" Cassie covered her mouth once she realized how loudly she had reacted.

"Hand to God," Laura said while she raised her right hand.

Kevin nodded before Adrian had a chance to fix her inquisitive eyes on him.

"Kevin and I were ready to elope, until my mom caught wind of it. She read my dad the riot act and he did eventually give in, but I knew he still wasn't happy about it."

"Yeah, well unfortunately, my parents are on the same side of this argument."

"My point is," Laura said, "you should be enjoying every single moment of this, and you can't do that if you're not surrounded by people who are genuinely happy for you and Jake. Which is why it would be my honor to take over for your parents until they come to their senses."

"And if they don't?" Cassie looked Laura straight in the eye.

"Then they don't." Laura shrugged. "And that will be their loss."

"My sentiments exactly," Adrian chimed in.

Cassie sat back in the booth and let Laura's words sink in.

Their loss, she thought, *again.*

"You can't keep putting your happiness on hold while you wait for them to wise up," Adrian told Cassie.

Just then Jake approached their booth.

"So, how's everything going over here?" he asked as he slid in beside Cassie.

"Well," Cassie answered, "I was just about to take your mom up on her offer to help with planning the wedding."

*

"What happened to the small, intimate wedding with just a few close friends?" Adrian asked.

They were standing in Jake and Cassie's kitchen. Jake wasn't there, but Cassie, Laura, and Maggie were.

The wedding was only two months away now. Each woman sat at the table with a drink in hand and a mountain of invitations to address.

"There may be a lot of invitations, but that doesn't mean they'll all come," Kevin said.

"Yes, I know that," said Adrian, "but still. I don't think Jake and I had this many for our wedding."

"They've been doing a pretty good job trimming down the list," Kevin observed as he peeked over the women's shoulders at the names that had been crossed out.

That all came to a screeching halt when Maggie rattled off Cassie's parents' names. Maggie and Laura exchanged anxious glances before looking to Cassie for an answer.

"Send it," Cassie said softly.

"What?" Adrian asked.

"Are you sure?" Maggie asked Cassie gently.

"She can't be serious," Adrian said before she turned to Kevin. "She doesn't really want to do this, does she?"

"Yes," Cassie answered Maggie, "I want to send them one."

"Isn't there anything we can do?" Adrian asked Kevin.

"Sounds like her mind's made up to me," Kevin replied.

"So that's it then?" Adrian stared at her friend in disbelief. "I just don't get it. Why are you even bothering? I mean, I can't remember the last time either one of them even tried to get in touch with you!"

There's still time, Cassie thought. *If I send them an invitation, they could still change their minds and come.*

"Damn it, Cass, how long are you going to let them keep doing this to you?"

Adrian slammed her hand down on the table. Several invitations slid off the edge and spilled onto the floor.

Cassie scoffed while she got on her hands and knees to gather them up.

That's probably Adrian rolling over in her grave right about now, Cassie thought.

Adrian knelt underneath the table beside her best friend. "Yes, if I were lying in a grave, I definitely would be rolling over in it!"

But I'm not you, Adrian. Cassie thought this to herself, but Adrian swore she was saying it directly to her.

"No, you are not," Adrian agreed. "You are a way better person than I ever could be."

And they're still my parents.

"But they're treating you like—"

"Adrian," Kevin warned her, "that's enough."

"All right, all right. I'll back off."

"Thank you," Kevin said.

Cassie went to get up and banged her head on the table. Kevin stared accusingly at Adrian.

"What?" she asked him. "You think I had something to do with that?"

Kevin didn't say a word.

"Although, knocking a little sense into her wouldn't have been a bad idea," Adrian mumbled.

"Adrian!"

"What? I'm sorry; I couldn't help it!"

"Cassie, are you all right?" Laura asked.

"Yes," Cassie grumbled while she got back into her chair. "Now, where were we?"

An hour or so later, all the invitations were addressed, sealed, and ready to be mailed. Maggie offered to drop them off at the post office for Cassie in the morning.

So, all that was left was to wait and see who would RSVP.

*

"Hello!" Julia called out as she walked through the front door.

Benjamin's car was in the driveway, so she knew he was home. She wasn't expecting an answer, but a little help would've been nice.

Julia set the grocery bags down on the bench and kicked off her shoes before she went off in search of her husband.

It didn't take long. All she had to do was follow the sound of John Mellencamp music coming from the garage.

Julia opened the door to find Benjamin under the hood of his old
'69 Dodge Charger.

She leaned against the door frame and watched him work until
she realized he was being way more aggressive to the Charger than
usual.

Benjamin didn't even hear her walk over to the boombox and shut
it off. He barely even acknowledged her when she spoke to him.

"Was it that bad of a day?"

"The mail is on the kitchen counter," he snapped without looking
up at her.

"What?" Julia asked, taken completely off guard.

"The mail." The look Benjamin gave her while he wiped his greasy
hands on a rag scared her to death. "It's on the kitchen counter."

"Okay," Julia replied slowly. *What could be so horrible in the
mail?*

She walked tentatively into the kitchen and froze when she saw it.
It sat on top of a stack of bills and supermarket flyers. A large, thick,
cream-colored envelope addressed to them. The words written out in
perfect calligraphy on a pre-fixed label:

Mr. & Mrs. Benjamin Adler.

It could only be one thing.

"Dear Lord, no," Julia said.

She opened the flap and held her breath until she saw her
daughter's wedding invitation.

"Damn it!"

She flung the invitation on the table and threw her head back in
defeat.

"She's still going through with it."

"Invitations don't lie," Adrian said as she leaned over to take a
peek from her spot on the counter. "And this one's pretty good, I do
have to say. Cassie did an awesome job without you."

Kevin glared at her while Benjamin came in from the garage.

"You want to take a swing at the Charger?" he asked his wife. "It might make you feel better."

"Nothing will make me feel better," Julia replied.

"Okay," Adrian told her, "I think you're being just a tad overdramatic right now."

"How could she do this to us?"

Adrian did a double take.

"Do what to you?" she asked.

Her eyes turned blood red as she jumped off the counter and stood toe-to-toe with Cassie's mother.

Julia suddenly felt warm and light-headed. Her knees went weak. Benjamin rushed to her side.

"Jules!"

"I'm fine. I'm fine."

"No, you're not." Benjamin held out a chair for her. "Sit," he insisted.

Julia didn't argue.

"I just got worked up, that's all."

"Yeah," Kevin's voice was full of sarcasm as he spoke to Adrian, "she just got worked up. It had nothing to do with someone's hot head."

Adrian crossed her arms emphatically.

"And I bet you didn't eat lunch again either, did you?" Benjamin asked as he brought her a glass of water.

"How could I when I had to chase five-year-olds outside for recess?"

Benjamin tilted his head at his wife in disbelief while she drank the water.

"Better?" he asked after she finished.

Julia gave him a half-hearted shrug, her eyes drawn to the invitation. Her heart sank even further after she picked it up and actually read it.

"She's really doing this. Our daughter is getting married. On the rooftop of a bar."

"I know," Benjamin said solemnly.

"It's not supposed to happen like this. She's supposed to get married in a church—our church—the one she grew up in."

She turned to face her husband. "You are supposed to walk her down the aisle and give her away. How did this go so wrong?"

Adrian almost felt sorry for Cassie's mom when she heard her voice catch in her throat.

"What are we going to do?" Julia continued. "What are we going to say? I mean, people are going to ask, especially members of our parish. How do we explain why she's not getting married in the church, and why we won't be there? What will people think?"

"What?" Adrian asked incredulously, her anger renewed. "She can't be serious. That can't be the biggest thing you're concerned about right now: What will everyone else think of you? Really? What about your daughter? Your only daughter?"

"Those who know us," Benjamin said as he reached for his wife's hand, "know we did the best we could for Cassie."

"Yeah, sure," Adrian said, "if doing your best for your daughter means practically disowning her for following her heart and becoming an EMT instead of the doctor you wanted her to be. And now you're about to do it to her all over again because she's going to marry a man who doesn't live up to your high standards!"

"And everyone else's opinion," Benjamin finished, "we'll just have to deal with as they come."

Julia let out a deep sigh. "How did we get here? I mean, we never had to deal with anything like this with the boys."

"Maybe it's a female thing," Benjamin teased while he gave her a lopsided grin.

Julia returned his grin with a feeble smile. "Or maybe..." she began.

"Oh, no. Don't even." Kevin could practically see the veins popping out of Adrian's neck as she spoke. "It's bad enough you're thinking it. You don't need to say it out loud."

"...it's who she chose to be friends with."

"You mean Adrian?" Benjamin asked.

"Of course I mean Adrian."

"And there it is," said Adrian. "You're blaming me for all of this? What about you?"

Kevin thrust his arm out to hold Adrian back just as the smoke detector wailed in the garage.

"Damn stupid thing," Benjamin grumbled as he got up to silence it. "I just put new batteries in that thing the other day."

Kevin's eyes were on Adrian, who was breathing hard and nearly had smoke coming out of her ears.

"Adrian," he said calmly.

"What?" she snapped.

"Go."

The intensity of his voice grabbed her attention.

"Where, after Cassie's dad?" she asked.

"No. Just go. Leave. Now."

"What? Why?"

"Because you're not doing anybody any good right now."

"How can I when no one is willing to listen to me?"

"Adrian, please, don't make me say it again. You can come back after you've cooled off."

"Fine. Whatever." Adrian glared at Cassie's mother. "I'm not here for her anyway."

*

The kitchen was shrouded in darkness when Adrian returned, but Kevin immediately sensed her presence.

"Welcome back," he told her.

"What are you still doing here?" she asked him.

No sooner had the words left her mouth than the kitchen suddenly became bathed in light.

Julia came in wearing a thin, gray bathrobe over her matching pajamas. She rubbed the back of her head, her hair pulled up in a high ponytail, while she decided what to grab from the refrigerator.

Julia's slippers scraped against the floor as she took the bottle of water and made her way over to the island. She sat down wearily, her shoulders hunched over, and studied the invitation again.

She put the palm of her hand against her forehead. No matter how hard she tried, she couldn't fall asleep. All Julia kept thinking about was her daughter's wedding.

Cassie, I dreamt about this day from the moment you were born, Julia thought. *I imagined it so many times in my head. I couldn't wait for it, but I didn't want it to come too soon. And now here we are.*

She ran her fingers lightly over the words on the invitation:

Cassandra Anne Adler,
daughter of Benjamin and Julia Adler,
requests the honor of your presence
as she marries
Jacob William Riley,
son of Laura Walker and the late Kevin Riley

Julia sighed. She set the invitation back down and retrieved the rosary from the pocket of her bathrobe. Kevin stared at Adrian as if he expected some smart-ass response from her, but it never came. He pressed his lips together and gave a small nod of approval while he turned back to Julia.

I can't, Julia thought. *I just can't watch you make the biggest mistake of your life.*

And with that, she grabbed a pen and with a slightly shaking hand marked the "will not be able to attend" box.

Julia sealed her RSVP into the return envelope and slipped the rosary back into her pocket. She got up, shuffled over to the fridge, and took one last swig of water before she put it back inside.

Her hand lingered on the handle of the closed refrigerator door.

Don't look back, she told herself.

She tipped her chin up and kept her eyes focused in front of her. Adrian and Kevin stood in the kitchen in companionable silence. The only sound came from the soft click of the light switch when Julia shut it off on her way back upstairs to the bedroom.

"I have a question," Adrian spoke up shortly thereafter.

"Yes," Kevin said patiently.

"Where's the darkness?"

"We're standing in it."

"No, not that. I mean the darkness darkness. The big, ugly, bad stuff that hovers over people when they have to choose good from evil, right from wrong. Why wasn't there any around Cassie's mother?"

"Because," Kevin answered, "she believes what she's doing is right."

"So that makes it okay?"

"No, but it doesn't make it evil either."

Chapter Five

CASSIE STOOD ON THE SIDEWALK outside The Borderline, lifted her face up to the sun, and smiled.

Ah, she thought, *so this is what it feels like to not stress.*

She had spent most of the day at the bar brainstorming wedding ideas with Maggie, and it had been an absolute blast.

Maggie's enthusiasm was contagious. Her hands and mouth both moved a mile a minute as she shared her decorating vision with Cassie. Cassie couldn't help getting caught up in her whirlwind. Plus, she hadn't felt that relaxed in a long time.

"It's about time you started enjoying this," Adrian told her.

The positive vibes continued to flow after Cassie got into her car. She put on her sunglasses, rolled down the window, and jammed out to Miranda Lambert's "Famous in a Small Town" over and over again, all the way home.

Cassie breezed through the front door of their apartment, then felt a twinge of dread when she saw the look on Jake's face.

"What?" she asked fearfully.

"I got the mail," Jake said.

"And?"

Jake didn't say another word; he just got up from the couch and handed her the unopened envelope.

Cassie didn't take it from him right away, but she couldn't take her eyes off it either.

"Cass," his voice was soft but concerned.

"I'm all right," she replied while her eyes darted up to meet his. "Let's just get this over with."

Cassie ripped the envelope open with her thumb and slowly pulled out the card. Jake tried to gauge her reaction, but her face gave nothing away.

"Well?" he asked, the suspense killing him.

"Well," Cassie answered as she flipped the card around nonchalantly for him to see, "it's a no."

Oh, shit, Jake thought. *This isn't going to be good.*

He reached out to her, but she backpedaled into the kitchen.

"Are you hungry?" Cassie asked. "Because I'm starving." She peered into the fridge. "What do you think? Should we make something, or just go pick up some takeout?"

I think you're in shock or denial, or both, Jake thought.

"Shock," Adrian replied to Jake's diagnosis.

"I think dinner can wait," Jake answered Cassie as he made his way over to her and shut the refrigerator door softly with the palm of his hand.

"Jake." Cassie tilted her head to the side and folded her arms in front of her. "I'm fine. Really."

"Mm-hmm. Sure," he replied while he pressed his forehead up against hers. "So why don't I believe you then?"

"I'm not lying; I swear."

Kevin turned to Adrian. "You're being awfully quiet over there."

"Hmm?" Adrian responded a little too innocently.

"We knew it was coming, and this," Cassie said as she held up the card, "was just a formality."

"Yeah, but still."

"But still I managed to have the best time today planning our wedding with Maggie. And I'll be damned," She paused to tear the card in half and toss it in the garbage, "if I'm going to let my parents ruin that for me."

"Whoa," Jake replied, his eyes suddenly infused with desire. "I'm kind of liking this new attitude of yours."

"Oh, really?" Cassie asked with a mischievous grin. "Well, I guess I owe it all to that dream I had the other night."

"Dream?" Kevin's interest was piqued.

Adrian avoided looking at him.

"What?" she shrugged. "People have dreams all the time."

Kevin just kept glaring at Adrian until she couldn't take it anymore.

"Okay, so I may have gone to see Cassie that night you told me to leave her parents' house."

"Seeing her is one thing," Kevin replied through gritted teeth. "Creating a dream for her is another."

"Wait," Jake said to Cassie. "That wasn't the night you woke up all freaked out about that nightmare you had, was it?"

"Yeah," Cassie replied as she stared at her feet. "It was. That was one of the worst nightmares I've ever had. My parents had me locked up in some tower somewhere, and the room I was in was filling up with these gigantic Bibles. It was like I was drowning in them. I was screaming for help, but nobody heard me. I ended up scaling the wall and reached the ceiling, but the Bibles just kept getting higher and higher. They were up to my neck, and I felt like I couldn't breathe. It was so real. I was literally gasping for air."

Jake pulled her close to him. She lay her head on his chest while he rubbed her back.

"And then I woke up," Cassie sniffled, "and I felt your arms around me just like they are now, and that's when I knew."

"Knew what?" Jake asked gently.

She looked into his eyes. "That I can't let my parents take my life from me anymore."

"See?" Adrian said to Kevin. "Everything turned out just fine."

"You still shouldn't have done that," Kevin replied. "Not on your own."

"Why not?"

"You know why."

"But nothing happened," Adrian said defensively.

"This time."

"Well, if you were so concerned, why didn't you come with me then?"

"I couldn't. I had to stay behind."

"Why?"

"Because," Kevin sighed, "He wanted to see how you would do on your own."

"He who?"

Kevin gave her a sideways glance.

"Oh, you mean...Him?" Adrian pointed upward and spoke the last word softly as if she were a child cursing.

"Yep, that's the one."

Adrian took a moment to process all of this before she responded. "So, how'd I do?"

"Well, if it were up to me, I would've given you a C+."

"A C+?"

"Hey, it's a passing grade."

"Just barely," Adrian grumbled. "So, what does He think?"

"Don't know."

"What do you mean, 'don't know'?"

"What? It's not like He sits down with me and discusses you like at a parent/teacher conference."

"So what do you do then?"

"Nothing."

"Nothing?" Adrian asked incredulously.

"Believe it or not, He doesn't share his opinions with me, unless it's about me. And He'll do the same with you too."

"How? When?"

"You sound like a three-year-old asking way too many questions."

"I can't help it. I need to know."

"No, you don't."

Adrian couldn't hide her disappointment.

"Look," Kevin said. "He's not here now is He?"

"No."

"Then don't worry about it. If He needs to talk to you, believe me, you'll know."

Chapter Six

THE SUN FADED SLOWLY BEHIND the clouds to usher in Cassie's last night as a free, single woman.

Well, technically, she still had about a week to go, but Maggie didn't want to ruin Cassie's wedding day by throwing her bachelorette party the night before.

Cassie had no idea what to expect from Maggie. All Maggie told her was to be at The Borderline at 7 p.m. sharp, looking hot.

So she slipped into a long-sleeved, black lace top and her favorite pair of hip-hugging blue jeans and left Jake with his mouth hanging open on her way out of their apartment.

It was only six o'clock, but Cassie needed to make a few stops first.

She parked her car and threw her jacket on before she stepped outside. The warm summer nights were coming to an end, and Cassie knew she might be out here for a while.

She opened the back door, took out the large, brown paper bag, and carried it delicately in her arms, careful not to break anything.

The wet blades of grass tickled Cassie's toes. She was tempted to take off her strappy black sandals, but she was almost there and didn't want to waste any more time.

Cassie set the bag down when she got there and took a quick look around just to make sure no one was in earshot.

"Well, here I am," she said on the heels of a deep breath, "as promised."

"I wasn't sure you were still going to come," Adrian replied. She appeared from out of nowhere in the cemetery and stood across from her best friend.

"Not exactly how we planned this, is it?" Cassie asked Adrian's headstone.

The original plan—way back when they were still lounging in their lifeguard chairs fantasizing about which hot guy at the pool they were going to marry—was that each one would have complete control of the other's bachelorette party; no questions asked.

"I so wanted to do this night for you," Adrian lamented. "I mean, really do it up right; go all out; truly blow your mind."

Cassie's lips curved up into a bittersweet smile.

"I remember you telling me your goal was to make *The Hangover* look like a kindergarten class field trip."

"And I would've done it too," Adrian said with an evil grin, "no doubt."

"But...we're here instead." Cassie paused to swallow the lump that had suddenly formed in her throat. "So, I had to improvise."

Adrian wrinkled her brows while she watched Cassie pull a blanket out of the bag.

"I just hope," Cassie said as she laid the blanket out on the ground before her, "this doesn't land me in jail or worse. Although I'm sure you would've considered that a bonus."

"Well, yeah," Adrian agreed, "if it would've involved hot, half-naked male strippers we refused to let go of. Not because you're sitting on a blanket in a cemetery."

Adrian's voice trailed off when she saw Cassie set the bottle of Patrón reverently onto the blanket.

"Damn, Cass." Adrian instantly dropped to her knees to take a closer look. "That's the good stuff."

"I know it's a far cry from the Montezuma and Taco Bell we used to do in college," Cassie said as she poured the tequila into two shot glasses, "but I figured you'd only want me to have the best tonight."

"You figured correctly," Adrian replied.

"So, without any further ado," Cassie took one last nervous glance around the cemetery before she rose to her feet, "I'd like to make a toast to the end of my single existence. And to thank you, Aide, for being there with me through most of it. You were my bad influence, my partner in crime, my best friend. And there's nobody else I would've wanted to share my single life with than you."

"Amen to that, sister," Adrian said.

Cassie threw back her shot, winced while it slid down the back of her throat, and then wiped her mouth with the back of her hand.

"Good stuff, huh?" Adrian laughed.

"Worth every penny," Cassie said, her voice slightly hoarse. "But don't just take my word for it."

She took the other full shot glass and set it down in front of Adrian's headstone.

Cassie took a step back but couldn't leave. Her eyes were transfixed on her best friend's name and the dates written on the black granite.

"Stop it," Adrian told her. "Go. Have fun. For me."

Cassie blinked and snapped out of her trance.

"Okay…well…I guess I better get going," she said as she awkwardly collected her things. "Bye, Aide."

"Bye, Cass."

Adrian drank her shot to drown the sadness building up inside of her while she watched her best friend walk away.

*

The roar of the motorcycle engine as it careened through the gates disrupted the cemetery's peaceful atmosphere.

It was mid-morning, and there didn't appear to be anyone around to complain. Not that it would've mattered to Jake if anyone did.

He continued on his way down a route he knew practically by heart, then pulled off alongside the path into his usual parking spot.

Jake swung his leg over the seat and knocked the kickstand down with the tip of his boot before he slowly unstrapped his helmet. He left it hanging on the handlebar and kept his sunglasses on as he made his way to her.

"Hey there, sweet thing."

"Hey," Adrian replied.

She stood mere inches away from her husband. The urge to touch him was so strong, but she resisted.

"Not yet," Adrian told herself.

"I'm sorry I didn't bring you any flowers this time," Jake said while he took off his sunglasses, "but this was a spur-of-the-moment visit…. I had to ride," he explained.

Whenever Jake needed to clear his head, he took his dad's motorcycle out of storage and went for a nice long ride.

"And my bike just brought me here to you."

Adrian averted her eyes from her husband and onto Kevin, who was leaning up against his motorcycle.

"On the morning of your wedding day," she muttered.

Jake sighed. "It's not that I don't want to marry Cass; I do, but I had to show you something first."

Adrian turned around to face Jake and found him on his knees with his right hand spread out over his left. Her eyes widened in shock when she saw the wedding ring she had given him on his third finger.

"No way. You didn't?"

"It's the only thing I could do with it that felt right," Jake said.

Adrian crouched down beside him to get a better look.

"And Cassie?" she asked while her eyes reluctantly met his.

"Cass is cool with it too." He paused as he rolled his shoulders back. "But, like I said before, I just wanted to show you as long as I was already here."

"Bullshit." Adrian smirked. "You came here to get my approval. And if Cass is cool with it," she added as she took Jake's right hand in hers, "then so am I."

A gust of wind suddenly swept through the cemetery. Jake glanced up at the blue sky and noticed a few stray gray clouds, but nothing menacing.

Adrian placed a single, soft kiss on Jake's ring finger. He felt a random raindrop plop down on his right hand, then saw another one land in the empty shot glass someone had left next to his wife's headstone.

Jake leapt to his feet, his body in full-on Riley stance mode.

"Those better be the only raindrops falling today. My girl's got enough going on without having to contend with a thunderstorm."

Chapter Seven

"**Y**OU BETTER NOT BE FUCKING with me right now, Charlie."

Dead silence followed on the other end of the line. For once, Charlie was speechless.

Even Adrian halted her ascent up the spiral staircase that led to Jake and Cassie's bedroom loft when she heard that word come out of her best friend's mouth.

"Whoa," Adrian said. "Cassie dropping an F-bomb is like Mother Teresa posing for *Playboy*; it just don't happen."

Adrian turned to Kevin, who was leaning back against the railing. "What set her off?"

"She can't find Jake," he replied. "He's not back from the cemetery yet."

"Oh," Adrian said as she sank onto the chest at the end of the bed. "Yep, that would do it."

She looked over her shoulder at Cassie, who sat bolt upright in bed, in complete panic mode.

Where are you, Jake? Cassie thought. *Why can't I get ahold of you? Why won't you call me back? Please*, she pleaded as she shut her eyes and desperately tried to keep her worst thoughts at bay, *don't be baling on me now.*

"He's not," Adrian reassured her while she reached for her hand.

"Charlie," Cassie eventually spoke into the phone, "answer me."

She sounded intimidating, but Adrian knew that deep down Cassie was terrified to hear his response.

"I swear, Cass; I wouldn't fuck with you—not today. Jake was gone before I got up this morning. He left a note…."

Charlie stopped, obviously distracted by something. Cassie's heart leapt into her throat. She couldn't hold it together much longer.

"Charlie!"

"Hang…hang on a second, Cass."

"Hang on a second? You're kidding, right? Charlie, what the hell is going on over there?"

"That's what I'd like to know too," Adrian said. "And I intend to find out."

She stood up purposefully, then after a moment turned reluctantly to Kevin.

"I…um…I can get to Charlie's apartment immediately, can't I?"

"Yes," Kevin answered while he tried to contain his smirk. "All you have to do is concentrate on where you want to go, and you just go there."

"Okay, good," Adrian replied with her head held high. "I'll be back then."

She marched out of Cassie's bedroom and right into Charlie's apartment.

Charlie had his phone to his chest so Cassie couldn't hear him. Jake stood in the doorway, clueless why his best friend was whisper-yelling at him.

"What's going on?" he mouthed to Charlie.

"What's going on?" Charlie's eyes nearly bulged out of their sockets. "Your girl is going ballistic 'cause she can't get a hold of you!"

Jake cringed. "Oh, shit."

"Yeah, 'oh shit'." Charlie nodded emphatically. "Now talk to her."

He tossed his phone to Jake, who could already hear Cassie's frantic voice on the other end of the line.

"Hello? Charlie? Hello? Is anyone there?"

Jake took a deep breath before he put the phone to his ear and talked to her.

"Hey, Cass."

"Jake? Oh, Jake, thank God." The relief in Cassie's voice instantly switched to outrage. "Where the hell were you? Why didn't you answer me? You had me scared to death. I thought...I thought you...."

"Okay," Adrian said. "I think it's time to switch sides again."

She returned to Cassie's bedroom and sat down beside her on the bed. Adrian rubbed Cassie's back with one hand while she tried to still her best friend's trembling fingers with the other.

"Baby," Jake spoke soothingly, "it's all right. I just went for a ride; that's all. I left my phone here. I wasn't expecting you to call."

"I didn't plan on it." Cassie sniffed. "I just woke up and wanted to hear your voice."

Jake couldn't help but grin when he heard that. "I'm sorry I scared you."

"You should be," she replied.

"Can you ever forgive me?"

"I'll think about it."

"I love you."

Cassie laughed when she heard Charlie pretend to gag in the background.

"I love you too. And Jake?"

"Yeah?"

"The next time I call you, you better damn well pick up the phone."

"Yes, ma'am."

"I'll see you in a few hours."

"Looking forward to it."

"See," Adrian told Cassie. Adrian's hand stopped mid-motion so she could wrap her arm around Cassie. "Jake's not a runner. It's not in his Riley man DNA."

Cassie's lips curved up into a giddy smile as an overwhelming sense of peace suddenly enveloped her.

"You're getting married today!" Adrian happily exclaimed while she squeezed Cassie's shoulder. "My best friend, to my husband, but still. Today is the day."

Just then, Cassie's phone buzzed like a broken alarm clock that wouldn't shut off. She wasn't expecting it and jumped, knocking Adrian off the bed.

"Adrian," Kevin asked, "are you all right?"

"I'm good," she replied from the floor, part of the comforter gripped in one hand while the other was raised to show she was okay.

"What the...?" Cassie asked in bewilderment.

Sitting cross-legged on the bed, she tucked a loose strand of her blonde hair behind her ear before she checked all the text messages flooding in.

From Maggie, earlier that morning when Cassie was still trying to track Jake down: *Good morning! Blue skies = perfect day for a Borderline wedding!!*

Cassie craned her neck, but she couldn't see over the railing to the downstairs window.

I'm going to have to take your word on that one, Mags, Cassie thought.

Then, a few minutes later, Maggie again when she hadn't heard anything back from her: *I have the perfect remedy for wedding day jitters. If you need me to bring it, just say the word.*

Not necessary, Cassie wrote back. *Cool as a cucumber. Now.* She thought this last part to herself.

She scrolled down to the next message from her brother: *Hey, Soap Star! Can't wait to get rid of—I mean, give you away today. LOL.*

Oh. BTW: Sara wants to know what time you want her and the girls to come over to get ready.

Cassie responded: *Ha Ha. Very funny,* to the first part. Then to the second part: *IDK. About an hour or so?*

The last message came from Jake's mom. Laura wrote: *Congratulations, sweetheart! You're going to be a beautiful bride, and a welcome addition to our family!*

Cassie touched her fingertips to the corners of her eyes before she continued to scroll through her text messages. She even checked her Facebook page, but she found nothing from either one of her parents.

She set her phone aside, drew her knees up to her chin, and couldn't help but wonder what they were doing right now.

*

Julia came downstairs and stopped short when she saw her husband hunched over the kitchen table.

"Ben?" she asked with a nervous tilt of her head. "Everything all right?"

"Yeah," he said solemnly while he sat back in his chair. "Just thinking."

"About what?" she asked as she came closer to him.

"Today."

Julia froze, her eyes drawn to the open photo album on the table. *Cassie's baby book,* she thought.

"Oh," Julia responded coolly.

Benjamin turned to his wife. "You do remember what today is, don't you?"

"Saturday."

He gave her a look.

"Well it is, isn't it?" she replied.

"Yes, but it's also our daughter's wedding day."

Julia shrugged while she poured herself a cup of coffee.

"Just another Saturday to me."

Benjamin shook his head in disbelief.

"What?"

Julia took a sip of her coffee and tried to read her husband's face over the cup's rim.

"What?" she asked again after the cup came slowly back down, her tone accusatory. "You're not seriously considering...."

"I don't know how you can't."

"Benjamin!"

"Julia!"

"I thought we agreed?"

"We did, but..."

"...but what?" Julia snapped. "What changed?"

"Nothing. Cassie's still our daughter—our only daughter."

"Who's still marrying a man you wouldn't even give your blessing to, and now you want to be there to see her marry him?"

"I want to be there for her. Don't you?"

"Not to watch her make the biggest mistake of her life, on the rooftop of a bar, no less! My God, Ben." Julia marched across the room to shut the window. "It won't even be considered a real marriage."

He stared blankly at her.

"Not in the eyes of the Catholic Church," she explained.

"Well, whose fault is that?" he muttered.

"Excuse me?" Julia hissed. "And just what is that supposed to mean?"

"It means, you purposely prevented her from getting married in a Catholic church when you told Father Andrew they were living together."

"Because it's a mortal sin! And don't you dare try to blame this all on me! We talked about this; we discussed it, and we both agreed we were doing the right thing by telling him."

"I thought we were," Benjamin replied remorsefully.

"But now you don't?"

He didn't say a word. He couldn't even look her in the eye, which was answer enough for Julia.

"Fine," she huffed as she snatched her car keys off the hook on the wall. "Do whatever the hell you want to today."

Benjamin didn't move.

Why bother to chase after her? he thought. *It'll only piss her off more if we make a scene in front of the entire neighborhood.*

"Good Christian man, my ass," Julia mumbled loud enough for him to hear.

Benjamin tipped his head back and raised his eyes to the ceiling after his wife slammed the front door shut behind her.

"Whoa," Adrian said as she peeked through the living room curtain and watched Julia drive away. "What brought that battle royale on?" she asked Kevin.

"I think it might've been me," he replied.

"What now?"

"I may have played the dad card on him last night. You know, from one guilt-ridden father to another."

"Oh. Well, it looks like it worked, but," Adrian couldn't resist saying, "you really shouldn't have done that on your own."

Kevin glared at her.

"Sorry," Adrian said while her eyes dropped immediately to the floor.

"It's fine. Besides, we've got bigger things to think about right now."

Adrian lifted her eyes to see Cassie's dad immersed in the photo album. Each picture awakened a long-hibernating memory, and each memory made Benjamin's heart ache even worse, as if someone were squeezing the life out of it.

Benjamin rubbed the palm of his hand over the back of his neck.

No matter what she's done, he thought while he flipped through the pages again, from the day they brought her home from the hospital to her first birthday party, *or who she chooses to be with, she'll always be my little girl.*

Adrian pressed her fingertips together at the bridge of her nose, unprepared for how Benjamin's true feelings would affect her.

"How could you not think that, too?" Benjamin asked as he looked over his shoulder at the closed front door.

"Yeah," Kevin said while he turned to Adrian, "how could Julia not think that, too?"

Adrian stared at Kevin in confusion, until his intentions suddenly became perfectly clear to her.

"Oh, no!" she protested. "I am not following her!"

"Consider it gathering intel," Kevin replied.

"What if I refuse?"

"Not an option."

"Why not?" Adrian asked, crossing her arms defiantly.

"Because it's an assignment given to you by a much higher authority than me."

"Oh." Her face fell while her arms dropped to her sides.

"So you better get going before you miss some vital information," Kevin said with a devious grin.

Now it was Adrian's turn to glare.

"And just what will you be doing while I'm gathering intel?"

"More one-on-one dad time," he replied as he looked at Benjamin.

"And Adrian," Kevin added.

"Yeah?"

"Try to keep an open mind, please."

Adrian sighed. "I will do my best," she promised while she made her way reluctantly to the front door.

Her jaw dropped when she stepped outside and saw Julia's Equinox still parked in the driveway.

"What the...?" Adrian asked while she approached the vehicle. "What did she do, decide to go for a walk instead?"

"Nope," she answered her own question after she placed her hands on the passenger window and peered inside.

There Julia was, sitting behind the wheel and staring blankly ahead of her, until something caused her eyes to dart eagerly to the front door.

She swore she caught a glimpse of her husband, but the door remained closed.

Disappointment hung heavily over Julia's face while she forced her hand to turn the key in the ignition.

I guess I'm not worth chasing after...again.

Adrian wrinkled her eyebrows at Julia.

"What are you talking about...*again*?"

Julia's mind suddenly flashed back to a moment in her early twenties with her own mother.

They were in Julia's childhood bedroom. She was home from college and hadn't been acting like herself—something her mom had picked up on right away.

"Look," her mom had told Julia. "I know something's going on with you, but since you won't talk to me about it, maybe this will help."

"A rosary?" Julia stared at it as if it were the tackiest thing her mother could have given her.

Her mother shrugged. "It's always worked for me. Otherwise, my door is always open."

"So, that's where you got that from!" Adrian said.

Adrian wanted to know more, but Julia shook her head fiercely to clear her mind of the memory just as one of her neighbors shouted a cheerful good morning to her.

Julia plastered on a pleasant smile and waved before she backed out of the driveway and left Adrian standing there dumbfounded.

"So," Kevin asked as he suddenly appeared beside her, "what did you find out?"

"That there's a lot more to learn about...." Adrian swallowed the biting adjectives she wanted to use to describe Cassie's mom when she saw the warning look Kevin gave her, "...Julia."

"Oh, you will. All in good time."

"Wait. What?" Adrian asked while she watched Cassie's mom drive out of sight. "You mean, that's it?"

"For today. Yes."

Adrian scoffed. "That wasn't much of an assignment."

"It's ongoing," Kevin replied without missing a beat. "Besides, you don't want to miss the wedding, do you?"

Chapter Eight

"HELLO?" BEN JR. CALLED OUT.

He simultaneously knocked on his sister's front door while opening it with extreme caution, his eyes partially closed just in case he walked in on something he wasn't supposed to see yet.

But Ben Jr. saw nothing. No one was downstairs, and the apartment seemed unusually quiet.

"Hey, where is everyone? What, did you guys decide to leave without me?"

Just then, he heard very familiar giggling coming from the upstairs. He pretended not to hear it.

"Oh my gosh!" he continued. "I think they really did leave without me. Well, I guess I better go catch up with them at the wedding."

Ben Jr. took a few steps toward the door before he heard his two little girls shout out: "Wait, Daddy. Wait. Don't go. We're right up here."

He raised his eyes to the top of the spiral staircase where five-year-old Kayla and three-year-old Caroline stood, twirling from side-to-side in their white, sleeveless flower girl dresses.

"Oh, my goodness," Ben Jr. began as he stepped back to admire his girls, "you two are just the prettiest young ladies I have ever seen."

His daughters giggled as only little girls can when they receive a compliment.

"If you think we look good, Daddy," Kayla proudly proclaimed, "just wait till you see Auntie Cass."

Ben Jr. covered his mouth to contain his laughter at his daughter's flare for words.

"Well, I can't wait," he replied once he recovered. "Where is she?"

"Right here, Benji."

He turned toward the sound of his little sister's voice and was blown away by what he saw.

Cassie stood on the threshold of her bedroom, glowing brighter than a candle flame.

She wore a cap-sleeved, off-the-shoulder, white lace gown. Her sun-kissed blonde hair fell softly onto her shoulders and was accentuated by a sparkling silver headband.

"Isn't she beautiful, Daddy?" Caroline asked.

"She sure is," Ben Jr. agreed, "and your Auntie Cass doesn't look too bad either."

Cassie's sister-in-law, Sara, had been fanning Cassie's long, lace veil out for maximum effect. Her head perked up at her husband's comment.

"Not too bad?" Cassie teased her big brother. "That's all I get?"

"Well," Ben Jr. said as he climbed the rest of the stairs to join them, "you, Soap Star, are my baby sister, but Sara," he paused, his eyes locked lovingly onto Sara in her sleeveless, knee-length, vibrant blue dress, "is my wife, and she will always be the most gorgeous woman in the room to me."

His words were immediately followed by a loud chorus of cooing from Cassie and her nieces.

Sara's cheeks flushed crimson while she ran her fingers self-consciously through her long, dark hair.

"All right, that's enough now." Sara grinned before she spoke to her daughters. "We don't want to make your Uncle Jake wait any longer than he has to for Auntie Cass."

Uncle Jake. Now it was Cassie's turn to blush.

"Okay, let's get this show on the road then," Ben Jr. said with a clap of his hands. "Girls, you go get in the car with your mother, and Auntie Cass and I will follow right behind you."

He extended his arm out to his sister. "Madame, your chariot awaits."

Cassie expected them to be driving to The Borderline in Ben's Mercedes BMW, so she was shocked to find a limousine waiting for them.

"Surprise!" Ben Jr., Sara, and the girls shouted in unison.

Cassie was at a loss for words.

"Part of our present to you and Jake," Ben Jr. explained to her.

"Benji."

"Oh, no. There will be none of that," he said as soon as he saw tears welling up in her eyes. "Because if you start crying, it'll ruin your makeup, and Sara will have to bring you back inside to fix your face, and then we'll never get you to your wedding."

"Okay." Cassie laughed as she dabbed at her eyes. "No crying. I promise."

"Good. Now let's try to get you inside this limo as gracefully as possible."

It didn't take as long as Ben Jr. thought to get Cassie situated. He shut her door and was about to run around to the other side of the limousine when something caught his eye.

"Is that…?" he asked himself while he gave a sideways look at the old, tan, Ford pickup truck parked across the street, just a few blocks up from Cassie's apartment building. "Nah, it can't be."

"It sure as hell looks like Cassie's dad's," Adrian said. "Go on," she urged Ben Jr. "Go see if it really is him."

Ben Jr. was tempted, but his sister's voice brought him back to his senses.

"Benji, c'mon!" Cassie yelled through the open window. "You know how Sara is; she'll send a search party out for us if we don't catch up with her."

"All right, all right," Ben Jr. replied while he pried his eyes away from the truck. "I'm coming."

Adrian threw her head back and groaned from her vantage point on the sidewalk.

"Sucks, doesn't it," Kevin asked her, "when people use their free will instead of doing what we want them to?"

"Yeah, yeah, yeah," Adrian grumbled while she got into the limousine.

All the speculation about the truck got pushed aside on the ride to The Borderline.

Cassie remained in awe of the limousine and her big brother for going all out for her. Ben Jr. sat back and took his younger sister's enthusiasm in with humble pride.

Like our dad should be doing, he thought.

Ben Jr. derailed that train of thought with a glass of champagne.

"Hey," Cassie scolded him, "that's for after the ceremony."

"Aw, c'mon; it's not a Federal crime to have one drink before the wedding, is it?" Ben Jr. asked while he waved the bottle of champagne under Cassie's nose.

"All right, fine. Pour me a glass."

"Good girl," Ben Jr. said with a triumphant grin.

They reached their destination much faster than Cassie had expected.

"We're here already?" she asked, nearly choking on her champagne.

"Yeah we are, Soap Star," said Ben Jr., laughing, "and you can't exit the vehicle until you finish your drink."

Cassie's eyes bulged out of her head. "Seriously?"

"Seriously. I finished mine." Ben Jr. tipped his empty glass upside down.

Just then, the door opened and Sara poked her head inside.

"Everything okay in here?" she asked.

"Yeah," Ben Jr. answered. "Just waiting for Cass to finish her drink."

Sara did a double take. "Her what?"

"Mommy," Kayla chimed in, "how come Auntie Cass can have something to drink, but you told us we have to wait until after the wedding?"

"Yeah, how come?" Caroline joined in.

Sara shot her husband a look that said, "See what you started."

"Well," said Sara, grappling for an answer, "it's Auntie Cass's day and she can do whatever she wants today."

"Thank you, Sara," Cassie said as she raised her glass to her and chugged down the rest of her champagne.

Sara shook her head good-naturedly at her soon-to-be sister-in-law.

"Okay, girls," Sara told her daughters, "let's step back and make some room for Auntie Cass to get out."

By this time, a small crowd had gathered on the sidewalk around them. Most people tried to act nonchalant, but it wasn't every day that a stretch limousine pulled up to the front door of The Borderline.

Cassie had leaned forward to accept her brother's outstretched arm when she suddenly froze. Her eyes practically doubled in size, and for a horrifying moment, Ben Jr. truly believed she was going to faint.

"Cass," he asked anxiously, "are you all right?"

"Now I know Cassie's a lightweight," Adrian said to Kevin, "but there's no way that one glass of champagne affected her that quickly."

Kevin didn't respond to her. He just stood stoically staring off into the same direction Cass was, which left Adrian with an uneasy feeling in the pit of her stomach.

"Kevin," she asked, "what's going on?"

Still nothing from Kevin.

Okay, Adrian thought, *let's think this through. What, or who, could possibly rattle Cass that badly?*

Adrian's head snapped back like a military cadet being ordered to attention as soon as the answer came to her.

"No," she dragged the word from her mouth as her eyes darted onto Kevin.

"No," Kevin replied matter-of-factly, "but you're close."

"Cass," Ben Jr. tried again, "talk to me. Please."

Dad? Cassie thought hopefully.

Cassie blinked, and whatever she thought she saw had vanished.

"I'm fine, Benji. I'm fine. Just my mind playing tricks on me I guess."

Ben Jr. wasn't convinced. He heard the disappointment in his sister's voice, but he played along with her anyway.

"Okay, if you say so."

He continued to search the crowd, having that same uneasy feeling Adrian had now transferred through to him.

Ben Jr. caught sight of Tony smoking a cigarette outside the bar and immediately motioned him over.

"Would you mind escorting these lovely ladies inside for me please?" he asked Tony.

"It would be my pleasure," Tony replied.

"Where you going, Daddy?" Kayla asked.

Ben Jr. stooped down so he was eye-level with his daughter.

"I'm going to make sure Uncle Jake isn't outside trying to sneak a peek at Auntie Cass."

Adrian wasn't buying it, and her suspicions were confirmed moments later when she tapped into his thoughts.

That sounds believable enough, Ben Jr. justified his little white lie to himself. *And I am trying to find out who's trying to sneak a peek at Cassie.*

"Okay," Kayla replied with complete seriousness, "but don't take too long."

"I won't. I promise."

Ben Jr. stood up and waited until Tony had ushered all the girls inside the bar before he made his way down the sidewalk.

It didn't take long. The crowd dispersed quickly once Cassie and the limousine were gone.

Show's over, Ben Jr. thought.

Then he saw black exhaust fumes swirling out of the nearest alley.

Or not.

He ducked into the alley where he found the beat-up tan pickup truck parked.

"You know, Dad," Ben Jr. said after he approached the driver's side door, "you'd make a terrible spy."

"Jesus, Benji!" Benjamin clutched his chest.

"What the hell are you doing here, Dad?"

"I wanted to see Cassie today."

"So go inside and see her! Stay for her wedding. Give her away for Christ's sake, instead of laying low in a back alley like some obsessive stalker."

"It's not that simple, Benji."

"I just don't get it," Ben Jr. replied with a shake of his head.

"What?" Benjamin asked.

"How you and Mom had an easier time accepting Sara and me, and she's black."

His father gave him a look.

"Well, it's the truth."

Benjamin sighed. "I just have a feeling about this guy."

"A feeling?"

"Yes. A bad feeling."

"So, Mom has her religious objections," Ben Jr. said with a slight roll of his eyes, "and you have a feeling—a bad feeling. And that's enough to justify everything you've both done to Cass?"

His dad shifted uncomfortably in his seat.

"Well," Ben Jr. said as he tapped the palm of his hand on the open windowsill, "I hope Mom and her religious righteousness, and you and your feeling have a good day."

"You tell him, Benji," Adrian cheered him on. "Now walk away and don't give him another thought today."

Ben Jr. did storm out of the alley, but his father still dominated his thoughts.

"That's okay," said Adrian, willing herself to stay positive. "We still have some time to work on him before he gets to Cass."

She started to chase after him, then stopped once she realized Kevin wasn't with her.

Adrian doubled back to find Kevin leaning against the brick wall staring bleakly into the cab of the pickup truck.

Chills ran down her spine; she had never seen Kevin like this before. She raised her trembling hand to her lips while she tried to wrap her brain around what was happening.

"Kevin?" Adrian didn't recognize the sound of her own voice, so timid and unsure.

"I thought I had you," Kevin said to Cassie's father, whose own eyes were lured to the empty entrance to the alley. "I really thought I had you convinced."

Adrian bit her lip, her confidence mounting.

"C'mon, Kevin," she said, offering him her outstretched hand. "We can't waste any more time on him. Besides, I have a plan."

*

"Oh, no," Maggie said as soon as she saw Ben Jr. march up to the bar like a man possessed. "You are not coming in here all fired up like that!"

She had come outside to take a quick smoke break with Tony, but now she stood—in her short, fire-engine red dress with its plunging neckline and blood-red stiletto heels—and blocked the front door of The Borderline.

"There will be no bad vibes in this building today, do you hear me?" she continued while she rose up to her full height of 5' 5".

"But," Ben Jr. protested.

"I don't care what, or who, brought it on, but you better get rid of it fast!"

Ben Jr. looked to Tony for support, but all he did was shrug his shoulders.

"You better listen to the woman," Tony said, "unless you want to be standing out here during the ceremony."

Ben Jr. sighed while he shoved his fingers through his hair.

"Look," Maggie's eyes softened as she spoke to Ben Jr. "I've got to get back upstairs and convince Cassie those storm clouds she just saw will blow over before the wedding starts. That should give you enough time to do whatever you need to do—kick a wall, punch Tony—to get whatever this is out of your system."

Ben Jr. wrinkled his eyebrows at her. Maggie tilted her head to the side and looked back at him as if to say she wasn't born yesterday.

"Smart woman Maggie is," Adrian said.

"And you," Maggie said as she pointed her finger at Tony, "better make damn sure he doesn't come upstairs until he's ready."

"Yes, ma'am." Tony's lips curved up into a smile as he bent down to kiss her.

Maggie smiled back at him before she turned on her heel and disappeared back inside the bar.

Kevin suddenly felt Adrian's eyes on him.

"What?" he asked her.

"You heard Maggie," Adrian answered. "You can't go up there until whatever you've got going on is out of your system."

"It is," Kevin replied adamantly.

"Good."

Ben Jr. seemed to have calmed down too. He and Tony made their way inside a few moments later, neither one aware of the tan pickup truck that passed by the bar and out of sight.

*

"You sure you still want to do this?" Charlie asked Jake. "'Cause there's still time for me to come up with a getaway plan for you if you want me to."

Jake looked up from buttoning his cuff links to laugh at his best friend.

"So, that's a 'no' then?" Charlie teased him.

"That's a 'no'," Jake replied.

"All right then." Charlie pretended to be disappointed. "Let's get you to that altar."

The dark, menacing clouds did pass through to reveal a peaceful, blue sky. A light breeze floated through the air on the rooftop and gently blew the colored paper lanterns back and forth above Jake. He was fascinated by them until Cassie made her entrance.

Oh. My. God, Jake thought, unable to take his eyes off her. *How the hell did I get so damn lucky? Not just once, but twice in a lifetime.*

Adrian wiped a tear from the corner of her eye when she heard that.

Do not get emotional; do not get emotional, Jake kept telling himself while he arched his back and clasped his hands together in front of him.

Cassie still saw the overwhelming love he felt for her in his eyes, despite his best efforts to control it.

She squeezed her brother's arm tighter as it all sank in.

This is really happening. He is standing there...waiting for me... to walk down the aisle to him...to spend the rest of his life with me.

"You ready?" Ben Jr. whispered to her.

Cassie nodded, too choked up to speak.

The next thing Cassie knew, the familiar strains of "The Wedding March" wafted through the loudspeakers; they were about to step forward when Cassie saw shock register on the faces of the entire wedding party.

Oh. My. God, Jake thought.

Cassie felt his presence before she heard her nieces shout out:

"Grandpa! Grandpa!"

Grandpa? Cassie thought. *What? No!*

She saw a hand tap her brother on the shoulder, heard a voice ask him, "May I?", but it wasn't until she turned around and laid her own eyes on him that she believed it.

"Dad!"

Tears spilled down Cassie's cheeks while Ben Jr. stepped back to let their father take his place.

Benjamin reached out to wipe his daughter's tears away, but her veil prevented it. So he wrapped her in his arms instead.

"Stop that," he whispered into her ear, "before you get me going too."

"I can't help it." Cassie's words were muffled, her head buried in the crook of her father's neck. "I'm just so happy you're here."

Benjamin shut his eyes. His little girl's reaction made direct contact with his heart.

"I am too," he replied as he eased her away from him so he could look her in the eye. *Against all my better judgment,* Kevin heard him think, *but I'm here. For you.*

Kevin remained slack-jawed while father and daughter proceeded down the aisle together. Adrian grinned, as if she had known the outcome all along.

"How are you not as shocked as I am about this?" Kevin asked her.

"Well," Adrian replied with a sly smile, "I believe it's called having faith."

"Speaking of faith," Kevin jerked his head toward Cassie's father. "How do you think he's going to handle Pastor Tracy?"

Benjamin had been so caught up in the moment with his daughter that he didn't see her until she was right in front of him.

A female—what?—pastor? Minister? he thought. *Definitely not a Catholic priest.*

"Not this again." Adrian threw her head back and sighed. "She tried to find a Catholic priest—she really did—but none of them would perform an outdoor ceremony. All Cassie wants is to be married by a legitimate member of the church. Any church. No justice of the peace or quick internet ministry will work for her. She told Jake that in so many words. Be glad for that. Swallow your pride, just one more time, and please don't make more out of this than it is. Please," Adrian begged Benjamin.

Cassie looked to her father, her eyes full of apprehension.

Please, Dad, just let this be.

Benjamin's mouth shut as quickly as it had opened.

"Thank you." Relief gushed out of both Adrian and Cassie.

Pastor Tracy smiled at the group that stood before her.

"Who gives this woman away in holy matrimony today?" she asked.

The silence seemed to last an eternity.

Woman? Benjamin turned to look at Cassie. In that moment, all he could see was his only daughter, his baby girl.

Images of her—from infant, to toddler, to teen, to now—all flashed before him and meshed together into one in the framework of her beautiful face.

Then he zeroed in on his soon-to-be son-in-law.

Benjamin stared at Jake, as sober as a gladiator about to do battle. His eyes became more threatening than any storm clouds Cassie had seen all day.

"Holy shit." Each word came slowly from Adrian's mouth.

Even Pastor Tracy's smile grew uncertain.

But Jake never wavered. He maintained eye contact with his future father-in-law and met his fierce glare with a look of determination, not defiance.

Then he gave the most imperceptible of nods, one Kevin noticed right away.

"Did you see that?" he asked Adrian.

"See what?" Adrian replied.

"Jake nodded," Kevin said. "He's telling Cassie's dad that he got his message."

"Oh." Adrian sounded genuinely interested.

She paid close attention to Jake's eyes as they shifted onto Cassie. His complete devotion for Cassie plainly lived inside of them.

"And now," Adrian took a stab at it, "Jake is telling Cassie's dad she...is his everything. He...truly loves her and would never do anything to hurt her."

"Pretty much...yeah," Kevin replied while he put a comforting arm around Adrian.

And that was all Benjamin needed to know.

"I do," he finally answered the pastor's question.

"And that," Kevin said to Adrian while Benjamin relinquished his daughter to Jake, "is how it's done."

"Wow." Adrian smirked. "Men really can communicate. Who knew?"

Chapter Nine

THE REST OF THE CEREMONY was uneventful. Jake and Cassie had chosen not to write their own vows, which came as a surprise to no one. The traditional vows they spoke to each other were just as heartfelt and left just as many people reaching for Kleenex.

Then they exchanged rings. Pastor Tracy pronounced them husband and wife, and Jake and Cassie shared their first kiss as a married couple.

It was Benjamin's intention to sneak away after the ceremony, but Cassie had other ideas. She wasn't about to let this opportunity go to waste.

"Dad," she said when she caught him at the top of the stairs, "please don't go yet."

He smiled fondly at his daughter. "This is your time to celebrate with your husband. You don't need me for that."

"No, but there is something I do need you for."

The chairs hadn't been cleared away from the ceremony yet, but Cassie's brothers made good time of it once they saw her leading their father back to the center of the floor.

"Don't let him leave," Cassie whispered to Ben Jr. before she rushed over to a stunned Maggie.

"Tell the DJ to play something slow...now," Cassie told her. "Please," she added sweetly while she touched Maggie's shoulder and awakened her from her trance.

"Oh...yeah...slow song. No problem. I'm on it."

Cassie returned to her father, her arms out to him as the music began to play.

To be honest, Cassie didn't even hear the song she and her dad danced to. All that mattered was she was dancing with him on her wedding day.

It ended way too soon. Cassie still had her head on her dad's shoulder when the music died. It took a moment for them to separate from each other, and nobody pushed them.

"I love you, Dad."

"I love you too, sweetheart." He kissed her on the cheek. "Now go...enjoy the rest of your night."

"I will," she promised, even though her feet didn't move.

Cassie looked as if she wanted to say more but wasn't sure if she should.

"Oh, just say it!" Adrian urged her.

"Dad?" Cassie asked tentatively.

"Yeah?"

"Make sure Mom knows what she missed."

He stared compassionately at his child.

"I will."

*

Cassie was standing alone on the rooftop later that evening, looking up into the darkening sky, when she felt her husband's arm wrap around her.

"How are you doing, Mrs. Riley?" Jake asked.

Cassie felt butterflies at the sound of her new name. Adrian sat on the edge of the rooftop with her chin in her hands.

"I remember that feeling," she said fondly.

"Well," Cassie tipped her head back and grinned up at Jake, "I'd be doing much better if I could be alone with my husband."

"Patience," he whispered while he leaned in slowly to kiss her.

Then, just as their lips touched, explosions erupted throughout the sky.

Cassie jumped, her eyes drawn up to the rapid succession of fireworks that rained down over them.

"What the...?" she asked, momentarily rendered speechless. "What's all this for? It's not the Fourth of July."

She turned to Jake, who watched her reaction with irrepressible amusement.

"What?" Cassie asked him.

"All these fireworks," Jake said, "they're for you. Well, us, actually."

Cassie's jaw dropped lower each time her eyes shifted back and forth between the fireworks show and Jake.

"I know," Adrian told her. "I'm just as shocked by his romantic gesture as you are, and I knew it was coming."

"Wait. What?" Cassie stammered. "You...did this? How?"

"Well, I do have some connections with the city, seeing as how I work there and all," Jake replied with a mischievous smile.

He had barely gotten the words out before Cassie pulled him to her, desperate for their tongues to entwine.

"Wow," Jake said eventually. "If this is your reaction to fireworks, I can't wait to get you into bed."

"So what are we waiting for then? Show's over," Cassie replied as she glanced up at the quiet sky.

"Oh, no." His voice in her ear nearly made her melt. "It's just getting started."

*

They left the rooftop amid a shower of bubbles, and once they reached the stairs, Jake insisted on carrying Cassie the rest of the way to their waiting limousine.

Cassie eyed the vehicle with glee.

"What?" Jake asked her.

"Have you ever gotten laid in a limo before?" she asked.

His eyes lit up like a winning slot machine.

Thank you, Jesus! Jake thought.

"Have I ever told you how much I love you?" Jake replied.

"Not nearly enough," she said, laughing.

The driver tried to maintain a professional attitude while he held the back door open for them.

"Drive slow," Jake instructed him with a wink. "And pay no attention to whatever you may hear back here."

"That's what my earbuds are for, sir," the driver replied. "Enjoy your ride," he added with a tip of his hat.

Adrian remained rooted to the curb. She watched the limousine pull away, but in her mind's eye, all she saw was the back of Jake's truck with a string of beer cans and condom packages trailing behind it.

Only Charlie, Adrian thought.

"Adrian." Kevin suddenly interrupted her thoughts. "We need to be in that limo."

"You're kidding, right?"

"I wish I were, but..."

"Yeah, I know," Adrian replied, "you're just doing your job."

She materialized inside the limousine just in time to find Jake stretched out on top of Cassie, his lips forming a trail of kisses that led down to the crevice of her cleavage.

Adrian sat as far away from them as she possibly could and shut her eyes.

"Let me know when it's over," she told Kevin.

"Jake!" Cassie called out. "Baby."

Adrian cringed. The words still didn't sound right to her coming from her best friend's mouth.

"Yeah?" Jake asked breathlessly.

"Don't be gentle."

Adrian's eyes flew open. Jake raised his head sharply. His eyes were on his wife, but for a moment, he was lying on a blanket in the bed of his truck with Adrian beside him in her wedding gown.

"Now aren't you glad we ditched the rest of our wedding party?" Adrian asked him.

"I just wish it hadn't taken us so long to lose all of them," Jake said.

"I guess Charlie's smarter than we thought, huh?"

"Not really, because if he knew what I'm going to do to you, he wouldn't have kept following us down all those backcountry roads."

"Hmm. Well, I'll let you do whatever you want to me out here in this hayfield, so long as you don't be gentle."

"Oh, shit!" Adrian said.

Cassie saw something in her husband's eyes that he couldn't hide from her. It was fleeting but lasted long enough for her to understand.

He's thinking about Adrian, Cassie thought. *Great, now what do I do?*

"Forget about me," Adrian told Jake.

She was on the edge of her seat when she spoke to Cassie.

"Do whatever you have to do to help him forget about me."

"Or," Cassie said, giving Jake her most devious smile, "you could let me do the honors."

Adrian was thrown by her friend's behavior.

"Whoa, Cass. Who knew?"

Adrian watched her moment with Jake break apart and disintegrate from his mind like a broken frame of movie film.

"Yep," she said as Jake's desire for Cassie reignited inside of him, "that should do it."

"Our work here is done," Kevin agreed.

*

The front desk clerk at the Lorelei Hotel did her best not to gawk at Jake's ripped open dress shirt, Cassie's disheveled hair, or their flustered cheeks while she handed them their room keys.

"Enjoy your stay," she told them with a knowing smile.

"Oh, we intend to," Jake replied before he swept Cassie off her feet. "And please make sure we're not disturbed."

"I'll make a note of it," the desk clerk called after them as Jake carried Cassie to the elevators.

"How many more times are you going to do this?" Cassie asked as they stepped inside.

"Until it gets old," Jake replied.

"I think I'll take the stairs," Adrian said as the elevator doors closed behind Jake and Cassie.

"And I think I'll join you," Kevin replied.

Jake pushed the hold button with his elbow before he repositioned Cassie in his arms.

She was facing him now. Her legs instinctively wrapped themselves around his waist as best they could before she pulled him closer.

Jake shut his eyes in ecstasy. His hands grabbed layers of lace before he pressed Cassie back up against the corner of the elevator wall.

She tipped her head back and moaned while he devoured her neck with his mouth. His hands actively searched for an entrance beneath her dress to her garter, but he was having no luck.

"Baby." Jake could barely contain himself. "Oh, my girl, we need to get you out of this dress."

"Well, then," Cassie said while she leveled her eyes on him, "you better start this elevator back up and get us into our room fast because I'm not walking out of here naked."

Adrian jumped moments later when she heard the front door of the hotel room slam open.

She left the balcony and stepped inside the spacious room. Its forest green walls and dark mahogany furnishings felt so inviting that she wanted to curl right up in the middle of the huge four-poster bed, until she saw Jake set his bride down on her feet, his lips never leaving hers.

"Oh, dear God," Adrian said with a roll of her eyes, "they're still going at it?"

"Well, this is their honeymoon," Kevin said from his seat by the rolltop desk.

"Now," Jake told Cassie after he kicked the door shut with the back of his foot, "let's get you naked."

"Okay." Adrian leapt away from the bedpost she had been leaning against. "I'll be out on the balcony until I'm needed."

*

Adrian laid back in her chair and counted stars in the calm, black sky until she heard the balcony door open.

"Well, I'll be damned," Cassie said as she stepped outside, her eyes on her best friend, "you can appreciate a beautiful night."

"I've been praying for thunderstorms the entire time I've been waiting for you to get out here. Took you long enough, by the way," was Adrian's response.

"Yeah, well, I've been kind of busy tonight."

Cassie blushed before she remembered who she was talking to.

"Oh, sorry."

"Don't be," Adrian said as she sat up in her chair. "He's yours now."

"Yeah," Cassie smiled self-consciously while she held up the hand with her wedding ring on it, "it's all legal-like now and everything."

"Stop that. You don't have to hold anything back around me. I'm happy for you both. I really am. Just promise me one thing."

"Anything."

"Just keep fighting for each other..."

The rest of Adrian's words were drowned out by a rumbling in the sky that grew so loud it shook the hotel to its core. The air suddenly turned bone-chilling cold, and the sky dark as midnight.

Terror washed over Cassie's face as two large funnel clouds on opposite sides of the horizon rapidly approached them.

Cassie tried to run, but she couldn't move. She gripped onto her chair for dear life while Adrian stood with her back to the funnel clouds as if it were just another late summer afternoon.

Cassie screamed to warn her best friend, but Adrian paid her no mind. She remained serenely calm, even after the clouds bore down upon her and yanked her up inside the eye of the storm.

Cassie screamed again. She felt it reverberate throughout her entire body, but all she heard was an ear-piercing siren that jolted her awake.

She shot up in bed. Her heart raced while her brain tried to process what had just happened.

Kevin turned to Adrian and realized she was doing the exact same thing.

"You okay?" he asked.

Adrian glared at him. "You know," she said after she finally caught her breath, "you didn't have to pull me back up so hard."

Kevin smirked. "Well, I had to make it believable."

"Do you think it worked? Did she get the message I was trying to send her?"

"Only time will tell."

Adrian was about to make some smart-ass comeback when Kevin shushed her.

The fog had finally lifted from Cassie's mind. She searched frantically for her cell phone, which she now knew was the source of the siren in her dream.

"Damn notifications," she muttered under her breath.

Cassie intended to silence the phone and toss it back onto the nightstand, but then she saw who had written the Facebook message.

Kathleen Adler.

"Her brother, Nicky's—oh, excuse me, I mean Nicholas' as he has preferred to be called ever since he started dating her—wife," Adrian explained to Kevin as if he didn't already know.

"Not a fan, are you?" Kevin asked.

"Of *Kathleen*?" Adrian mocked. "Not Kathy, not Katie. Kathleen. A point she made crystal clear to Cassie's family when Nicky first introduced her to them, or at least that's how I heard it from Cassie."

"So no," Adrian concluded, "I am not a fan of that pretentious, New York City snob."

She stopped ranting when she saw Cassie sink back down onto her side of the bed, her eyes locked onto her phone's screen and Kathleen's most recent comment:

Bedrest not so bad when you get spoiled. Thanks for a wonderful day Julia Adler! #bestsecondmomever!

Adrian's eyes burned red with rage.

"Oh, you little…"

"Adrian," Kevin instinctively flung his arm out to hold her back, "calm down."

"I know," she replied through clenched teeth. "I know she's due to have Nicky's first child any day now and she's had a really rough pregnancy, but that's still no excuse for her to slam Cass like that."

Best second mom, Cassie thought. *Yeah, well, I needed her to be my mom yesterday, but she just couldn't bring herself to do it, so she spent the entire day with you instead, Kathleen. A woman she barely tolerates and only because you married her son. Nice.*

"Especially," Adrian added, "when it hurts my best friend so badly."

Adrian felt Cassie's pain slice through her own heart. She dropped to her knees in front of Cassie, her hand splayed out on her friend's leg just as Cassie doubled over the edge of the bed with her phone pressed close to her heart.

Adrian raised her head slowly to Cassie's closed eyes when she felt their hands touch.

Just then, Jake reached out to his wife.

"Baby, is everything okay?" he asked.

His touch startled Cassie. The phone tumbled out of her hands and onto the floor while Adrian lost her balance and fell backward.

"Ye-ah," Cassie stammered. "I think all that champagne I had last night is doing a number on my stomach this morning is all."

She was up and off to the bathroom before Jake even had a chance to respond.

"Don't believe her," Adrian told Jake while she stood back up. "You know her better than that."

Something's wrong, Jake thought while he stared at the closed bathroom door. *But what?*

"Lean over the bed; find her phone and you'll know!" Adrian said in exasperation.

"Wait," Kevin said.

"What?" Adrian asked.

"Isn't looking at her phone an invasion of her privacy?"

Adrian stared at him in disbelief. "Not when he's looking at her public social media account. And it's for her own good."

Adrian felt Kevin's skeptical gaze on her.

"What?"

"Not a thing."

It didn't take long to persuade Jake. He kept his eyes on the bathroom door as he inched over to Cassie's side of the bed. Then he peeked over the edge and there it was.

Now, let's find out what got you so upset, Jake thought.

"I don't like this," Kevin said.

Adrian waved him off.

Jake snatched up Cassie's phone and started scrolling through some of the comments.

So glad you're there to take such good care of my baby, Kathleen's mother had written.

It was my pleasure! Julia had written back.

"Yeah, right," Jake mumbled.

Where's Nicholas? someone Jake didn't know asked, referring to a photo Kathleen had posted of her and Julia.

Oh, Kathleen replied back, *he had a prior commitment he couldn't get away from.*

A prior commitment? Jake's blood boiled. *It was Nicholas's sister's wedding for Christ's sake, not a business meeting!*

"What are you doing?" Cassie asked while she stood in the open bathroom doorway.

"Uh-oh," Adrian said when she saw the look on Cassie's face.

"I told you I didn't like this," Kevin replied.

"Jake?" Cassie waited for an explanation from him.

"I found your phone," he said as he waved it meekly at her.

"And you just had to read what was on it, didn't you?"

Jake sighed helplessly. "I needed to know what was wrong, but you wouldn't tell me anything."

"Well, now you know," she said, looking glum.

"You know what I think?" Jake asked as he made his way over to her.

"What?" she pouted.

"I think they both deserve each other. I mean, really, what better punishment is there for your mother than to spend an entire day waiting on Kathleen hand and foot?"

Cassie shrugged half-heartedly. "Didn't you read my mom's response? It was her pleasure."

"Yeah, sure, because no one ever exaggerates or embellishes anything on social media."

Jake waited while the faintest hint of a smile began to form on his wife's lips.

And that's when he knew he had gotten through to her.

"You know I'm right," he teased her.

"Yes," she reluctantly admitted, "you're right."

"Good. Now that that's settled, come back to bed with me because it's really lonely in there without you."

Chapter Ten

B ENJAMIN ROLLED OVER TO GET a face full of couch.

He sat up, ran his hands over his face, and then saw through his bleary eyes the mounted deer head staring down at him.

"Don't look at me like that," he said to it while his feet hit the floor. "If anything, you should be giving Julia that look, not me."

Julia.

He sighed while his eyes shifted reluctantly toward the stairs.

I really don't want to go up there, he thought, *but I can't go to church in my boxers either.*

Benjamin put his hands on his knees and was about to force himself up off the couch when he heard his cell phone buzzing.

He glanced at it, lying among all the loose change, his watch, and his wallet that he had tossed onto the coffee table before he fell asleep last night.

Don't do it, Benjamin warned himself. *It's probably nothing. You're just looking for a distraction; anything to keep you from going upstairs and dealing with Jules.*

He took his eyes off the phone, stood up, and made it a few steps away from the couch before his parental instincts kicked in.

But what if it's not?

All he could think about was the night of Adrian's accident.

"Me?" Adrian questioned. "Why would he be thinking about me?"

We heard—either on the radio or the TV, I can't remember how— about this horrible freeway accident, and we didn't know.

We didn't know if Cassie was working, if she had been called to that scene, if she were involved in the accident herself. We just didn't know. We knew absolutely nothing, and that scared the shit out of me.

So Jules called her, over and over again, but it just kept going to her voicemail. That time, before we heard anything back from her, in her own words, in her own voice, telling us she was okay, I swear that was the longest stretch of time I have ever lived through.

So, yeah, I have to pick up that phone just in case.

What Benjamin saw on his phone motivated him to take the stairs two at a time up to their bedroom.

He threw open the door to find his wife sitting in her armchair in the corner absorbed in her Joyce Meyer book.

Julia saved the page with a bookmark and calmly removed her reading glasses before she spoke to her husband.

"You didn't need to sleep on the couch last night."

"You didn't need to spend the entire day with Kathleen, but you did," he replied with restrained anger.

Julia's eyes narrowed.

"And where exactly is it you think I needed to be instead of with our bedridden daughter-in-law?" she snarled back.

"At your daughter's wedding!" Benjamin, Adrian, and even Kevin all yelled in unison.

Adrian did a double take after she heard Kevin's reaction, but she didn't have a chance to call him on it. Not in the middle of this war.

Julia pressed her lips so tightly together they all but disappeared, but that didn't stop Benjamin.

"Our daughter, Jules. Have you forgotten what it felt like when we thought we had almost lost her for good not that long ago?"

"No," Julia said indignantly as she rose from her chair, "I have not."

"Yet you have no problem doing it on purpose now?"

"Whoa!" Adrian couldn't help but wince, even though she wholeheartedly agreed with him. "There's a direct shot right to the heart."

Julia's lips parted while she struggled to swallow that bitter truth.

Benjamin grabbed his clothes out of the closet and started to head straight for the door when he remembered something.

"Oh, yeah," he said half-glancing at his wife over his shoulder, "I promised Cassie I'd make sure you knew what you missed out on last night, in case you didn't already know."

Then he continued on his way downstairs, leaving Julia alone.

She clenched her fists and lifted her chin up to keep the tears glistening in her eyes from falling down her cheeks, but they did anyway.

Why are you crying now?

That thought, coming from Julia's mind, threw Adrian. She looked to Kevin, whose own steel trap of a mind was sealed off to her.

*

Julia came downstairs twenty minutes later in her sandals, khakis, and a light short-sleeved blouse. Her eyes showed no signs of tears or redness.

"I'm ready whenever you are," she told her husband as she slung her purse over her shoulder.

"Well, of course," Adrian said while she and Kevin followed them out to Benjamin's truck. "The show must go on."

The radio roared to life when Benjamin turned the ignition on. Adam Ant's "Goody Two Shoes" was playing, much to Julia's chagrin. She immediately reached over and switched the station while Kevin gave Adrian the evil eye.

"What?" Adrian asked. "I have no control over what radio station they have on."

"Uh-huh," Kevin said. "Sure."

Julia sat back in her seat and got lost in Ben E. King's "Stand By Me."

Adrian shot Kevin a dirty look.

"Out of our control, remember." He smirked.

Julia perked up once they pulled into the cathedral parking lot.

"Time for them to get into character," Adrian said.

Anyone who saw them would have never suspected anything was wrong. Benjamin held Julia's door open for her; they walked hand in hand into the church and sat close to each other in the pew just like always. They even kissed each other on the cheek during the sign of peace, much to Adrian's annoyance.

"Ugh," she groaned. "They're just so fake."

"Like you've never done the exact same thing when you were pissed off at Jake but still had to go somewhere in public with him?" Kevin asked.

"Well…" Adrian stammered, "that was different."

"How?"

"Julia's doing it to maintain her image. I did it so I wouldn't be arrested for trying to murder your son."

Kevin laughed.

"And," Adrian added, "I never hid anything from my real friends, like Cass."

The church service had ended, and most of the congregation had spilled outside into their own little circles to socialize, Benjamin and Julia included.

"Oh, this ought to be good," Adrian said while she folded her arms over her chest.

Julia was chatting away to Father Andrew while Benjamin stood idly beside her when one of Julia's friends approached them.

"I hate to interrupt you," she said.

"Oh no, Elizabeth, you're fine," Father Andrew replied. "We were just finishing up."

"Oh good." Elizabeth smiled. "I just wanted to come over and ask you how Kathleen is doing."

Benjamin shifted uncomfortably from one foot to the other. Julia felt her cheeks growing increasingly hotter.

"Um, she's taking it one day at a time until the baby comes," Julia replied.

"Well," Elizabeth gushed, "I just can't say enough about you staying with her all day yesterday considering..." her voice trailed off when she saw the look on Julia's face.

"Considering what?" Julia asked.

Elizabeth chose her words carefully. "That it was Cassie's wedding day too."

An awkward silence hung over the small group. Father Andrew cut a sharp look of confusion Julia's way.

"I...uh...saw something about it on Facebook," Elizabeth hurriedly explained, mistakenly thinking that would help.

Julia struggled to come up with an answer until Benjamin intervened.

"I made sure to be there for Cassie."

And with that he turned swiftly away from the group.

"Benjamin," Julia called after him, but he ignored her. "Ben!"

He swung around, pulled his hand out of his pocket, and shook his cell phone at her before he kept walking.

Julia turned back to Father Andrew and Elizabeth with her best fake sincere smile.

"Important phone call he had to take."

They nodded politely, then went their separate ways not long after.

Julia couldn't get inside the truck fast enough.

"What the hell is wrong with you?" she hissed at her husband.

"And the gloves are back off, Ladies and Gentlemen," Adrian announced.

"Kathleen is in labor." Benjamin spoke matter-of-factly while he thrust his phone at her so she could read the text Nicky had just sent them.

"Oh," Julia replied in a much more subdued tone.

"So strap yourself in because we're going to have a new grandchild to meet soon."

*

Cassie lay stretched out alongside her husband—the blankets scattered across the floor—her body warmed by his touch. Jake held her in his massive arms, his breath soft on the back of her neck.

Adrian hugged herself while her body remembered how it felt to be cocooned with Jake.

"I really hate to wake them," she said.

"Oh, but we must," Kevin told her.

Jake suddenly twisted and turned his head until he found a more comfortable position. It seemed to fit perfectly within the curve of Cassie's neck. He pulled her closer to him and inhaled her sweet scent. His scruffy chin skated over her shoulder until it reached the edge. Then Jake's lips touched Cassie's skin, a test to make sure she was real and not just a dream he had conjured in his mind.

Cassie groaned with pleasure, her eyes still shut to reality. Jake leaned in to kiss her and felt her smile before he saw it as he reached around her to check the time on his phone.

"Uh-oh," Jake said.

"Uh-oh what?" Cassie asked dreamily before she glanced back at her husband.

"What?" she asked sternly as she sat up beside him.

"It's…uh…it's your brother. He's been trying to get a hold of us. Well, you actually, for a while now."

"Benji?"

"No," Jake answered while he watched in fascination as his wife shot out of bed and scrambled to turn her phone back on. "Nicky."

Cassie let out a high-pitched squeal after her phone came back from the dead.

"It's a boy," she said.

The light in her eyes grew with each piece of information she shared with Jake.

"Seven pounds, twenty ounces. Nineteen inches long. Dominick Benjamin Adler. She actually let Nicky name him after our grandpa: my dad's dad."

"What?" Cassie asked when she caught Jake looking at her.

"You," he replied with a lop-sided grin.

"Me?" She arched an eyebrow at him. "What about me?"

"Well," Jake began as he climbed out of bed, his grin widening the closer he got to Cassie, "if you're this excited about having a nephew, I can't wait to see how you're going to react when we have our first kid."

Jake's arms were looped around her waist. Cassie tipped her head back so she could look up into his eyes. She was all smiles, while Adrian's body went as rigid as a sheet of plywood.

"First kid, huh?" Cassie teased him.

"Oh, yeah. We're going to have a ton of kids. My plan is to keep you barefoot and pregnant."

Jake leaned in to nibble on an extremely sensitive part of Cassie's neck.

"You're okay with that...right?" he whispered into her ear.

"You keep doing that," she said breathlessly, "and I'll give birth to an entire baseball team if you want."

Adrian didn't make a sound; she didn't need to. Kevin could just tell. He reached for her hand and gave it a gentle squeeze. She squeezed back while she raised her chin up and forced herself to listen to the rest of their conversation.

"But," Cassie whispered provocatively into Jake's ear, "there's something else I'd really love to do with you right now."

Jake pulled away, intrigued. "What's that?"

Cassie's eyes gleamed as she spoke. "Go meet my new nephew."

Kevin felt all the tension leave Adrian's body, only to be replaced with a new worry that Jake felt too.

"Right now?" Jake asked.

"Yeah. Why not? It's only a half hour or so away from here."

Cassie paused when she saw the look of concern cross her husband's face.

"We have the room for a couple of more nights." She did her best to entice him. "I promise I'll make it up to you when we get back."

"Oh, that's a given."

"So what's the problem then?"

"Tread carefully now, son," Kevin warned.

"Have you thought about how many people will be there to visit them today?" Jake added silently, *Including a certain someone I know you are not yet ready to face.*

"I can handle a crowd." *And my mother*, Cassie thought, *if she just so happens to be there.*

"I know, but maybe it would be better if we wait until they come home and get settled in first."

"Oh, no! Once Kathleen gets that baby home, she'll decide who gets to see him. It'll be all her friends and family. I'll have a better chance of jumping to the front of the Packers' season ticket waiting list than getting to hold that little boy."

"She does make a good point," Adrian agreed.

"All right," Jake gave in, "you win. Let's go." I just hope you're not getting in over your head here."

"Me too, babe; me too," Adrian said.

*

The uneasy feeling in the pit of Jake's stomach only got worse the closer they got to the hospital.

"This isn't going to be good, is it?" Adrian asked Kevin, who responded by giving nothing away.

"Of course not." Adrian groaned while she threw her hands up in the air.

"Calm down, Adrian. Let's just wait and see what happens, please."

"They're not still here, are they? Cassie's parents?" Her words were met with silence. "We'll have to keep Cassie away from them if they are."

"No, we won't," Kevin said.

"What?" Adrian's jaw dropped.

"She needs to deal with her mother. We need to bring them together."

"But—"

Kevin threw Adrian a cautionary look that halted her resistance.

"Fine. I won't ruin your plan."

"My plan? I don't have a plan."

Adrian stammered, unable to form words until it finally dawned on her.

"Oh, no!"

"Oh, yes." Kevin smirked. "Good luck."

"Really?" Adrian couldn't believe Kevin had disappeared on her. "So you're just going to leave me now?"

"I'm always with you in spirit," he replied.

"Haha," she said.

Just then, Jake's truck came roaring around the corner of the parking ramp in search of an empty space.

Jesus, Jake thought, *by the time we find a spot, this kid will be in college!*

Although, he did use the opportunity to discreetly scan each row they drove through for any sign of either Benjamin or Julia's vehicles. So far they were safe, which was a relief, but he still couldn't shake that nagging feeling.

"Yep," Adrian couldn't resist, "that's me. The nagging wife."

Jake turned to ask Cassie something, then stopped when he saw her ashen face.

"Cass, are you all right?" he asked.

"Yeah," she said, but her voice betrayed her. "My stomach just needs to recover from all those hairpin turns you made driving up here."

"Oh, c'mon; they weren't that bad."

"Oh, yeah, they were." Her face contorted as if she were about to throw up. "I just need a minute. Please."

"I'm in no hurry." *In fact,* Jake thought, *the longer you take, the better our chances are of not running into somebody.*

"My sentiments exactly," Adrian said.

"Adrian." Kevin's voice loomed over her.

"I know. I know. What do you want me to do? She needs a minute."

"I know. After that."

"Yes, sir. I'm on it, sir."

"Feeling better?" Jake asked Cassie.

"Yeah, I think I'll make it," she answered with a smile.

"Good."

"Now," Adrian told Jake, "back to your original question for her."

"So," Jake began, "you think maybe you should call Nicky and let him know we're here?"

"Why?" Cassie asked as she opened her door. "I already texted him we're on our way. He knows. It's all good."

"All good," Jake repeated under his breath while he stepped reluctantly out of the truck. "Yeah. Sure it is."

"C'mon, slow poke," Cassie called out to him over her shoulder. She was already halfway to the hospital door.

"Coming."

"Great," Adrian said, her eyes to the sky. "Now what am I supposed to do?"

"Go find out where her parents are," Kevin said.

"Easy for you to say. You're not the one who has to run around looking for them."

"Neither do you."

"Oh, really? And just how do you figure that?"

"Not by figuring, but by focusing."

"Focusing? On what?"

"Not what; who."

"Cassie's parents?" Adrian asked.

"Cassie's parents," Kevin confirmed. "All you have to do is focus on them and you'll find out exactly where they are."

"And then I'll just be teleported to them, like whenever Scotty beamed someone up on *Star Trek*, right?" she asked.

"No," Kevin answered with a look of disdain, "not like *Star Trek*."

"But it's the same concept, isn't it?"

"How about you just try it and see for yourself?" he suggested, his patience wearing thin. "Before Cassie finds them first, without your help."

"Okay, I'll focus on them."

Adrian shut her eyes and tried to drown out all the noise around her.

"Pour all your energy into them," Kevin told her. "Don't let anything else in."

"No offense," Adrian said as one eye popped open, "but this would be a lot easier if you quit talking to me."

"None taken."

Kevin didn't say another word. It was as if he snapped his fingers and made the entire world fall silent. For a moment, Adrian feared she had lost her hearing, it got so quiet. She closed her eyes anyway and saw exactly what she needed to see.

It came at her like a silent movie montage. She saw everything—from the second they had left the church, had a brief argument in the truck, then rerouted onto the freeway straight to the hospital where they had sat for what felt like an eternity in the waiting room before Nicky came in to tell them the good news, which had led Benjamin and Julia to where they were right now.

Adrian was drawn to them like metal to a magnet. She felt as if she were moving in fast forward. Everything rushed alongside her in a colored blur and then just stopped.

Her ears erupted with sound, and life continued on in the hospital cafeteria where Adrian stood, dazed and slightly unsteady.

Adrian reached out for the nearest table, to find Cassie's parents sitting there.

"Whoa," she said.

"Quite the rush, isn't it?"

She whirled around to see Kevin beside her again.

"That's one way to put it...yeah," Adrian said.

"You just need," Benjamin was saying, "to sit back, relax, and just...chill."

Julia couldn't suppress the smile she felt.

"Chill?" she asked her husband. "Did you pick that up from one of the newbies at the paper mill?"

"No, but it did make you smile." *And I do still love to see you smile,* Benjamin thought.

"Good," Adrian said. "You two stay here; work your problems out; have a nice, leisurely lunch so Cassie can visit with her new nephew and you guys won't even know she was here."

"Adrian," Kevin scolded her.

"What?"

"Your job is not to keep them apart."

"But it's been working so well so far."

Kevin narrowed his eyes.

"Wow," Adrian said, "if looks could…." She caught herself. "Well, you know."

"Yes, I do."

If it weren't for the light in Kevin's eyes, Adrian would've sworn she had pissed him off.

"Now, do your job…please."

"All right," she replied, "but if they still decide to stay away from each other, that's not on me."

Adrian sighed while Kevin waved her on.

Benjamin got a text not long after that. He read it, then raised his wide eyes to meet his wife's.

"Aren't you done yet?" he asked her.

"Excuse me?" Julia replied after she swallowed her first bite of her sandwich. "What happened to sit back, relax, and just chill?"

"They're bringing the baby into the room."

"Well, why didn't you say so?"

She wasn't hungry anymore, despite her growling stomach. All she could think about now was holding her new grandson.

"There," Adrian's voice fell flat while she watched Cassie's parents race to the cafeteria exit, "are you happy now?"

"Yes," Kevin said, "because you did what you needed to do."

"Then why do I feel like I just sabotaged my best friend?"

"You didn't," Kevin said while he put a comforting arm around her. "Trust me."

"I'm trying to," Adrian replied as her head fell softly onto Kevin's shoulder.

"All right, that's enough of that now," Kevin said while he nudged her head back upright. "Let's go see this baby."

Adrian hesitated on their way through the cafeteria doors.

"What's wrong?" Kevin asked.

"Nothing. I just thought we were going to...you know...."

He watched Adrian in amusement while she motioned with her hands like an airline attendant indicating where the aisle was located.

"No." He smirked. "I don't know."

Adrian shot him a vicious glare. "I thought," she said slowly, "we were going to...focus...our way there."

"Oh, no. We might miss something if we did that this time."

"Like what?"

Kevin motioned for her to keep up with him, which she eagerly did.

They weaved their way through the halls until they reached a bank of elevators. Adrian held her breath when she caught sight of Cassie's parents entering one elevator just as Jake came to a screeching halt in the middle of the lobby.

"Where are you going?" Cassie shouted at him.

"To find Kathleen's room." Jake looked back at his wife as if his answer should be obvious.

"Really? How?"

"Oh, c'mon; it can't be that hard to find."

Cassie stared incredulously at the numerous hallways and confusing signs surrounding them. *Even Einstein would need help finding his way through this maze,* she thought as she turned on her heel and backtracked.

"Now where are you going?" Jake asked.

"To the help desk," Cassie said with a smug smile.

Adrian sounded like a tire with a slow leak once she allowed herself to breathe again.

"Wait," she asked Kevin. "I thought you wanted them to run into each other?"

"Not now," he replied, his eyes intent upon Cassie as she talked to the young woman behind the desk. "Not out here."

"Why not?"

His response was to follow Cassie as she strolled past Jake and pushed the button for the same elevator that had just brought Benjamin and Julia upstairs.

The ride to the fifth floor was relatively quiet, but once the doors opened, they could hear the shrieks of joy coming from all the way down the hall.

"I think I know where their room is now," Cassie told Jake.

And she was off and running, bounding down the hall like an Olympic sprinter to the finish line.

Adrian tried to stop her, but Kevin put his arm out to hold Adrian back.

"Now," Adrian stated more than asked as she searched Kevin's eyes for confirmation.

"Now." He nodded.

Adrian stared down the long hall and braced herself for the moment Cassie rushed into the room.

Chapter Eleven

C ASSIE'S ENTHUSIASM TOOK A NOSE-DIVE the moment her mother turned toward the door with baby Dominick in her arms. Words failed her; all she could do was stand there with her mouth hanging wide open.

Cassie felt the heat from everyone's eyes upon her. It got to be too much for her. Her father reached out to her, but she pulled away and walked back out the door past Jake.

He stood confounded in the hall, along with Adrian and Kevin. They all watched Cassie go mindlessly on her way, with no real destination in mind until she finally stopped in front of the nursery.

She peered in at the room full of sweet, innocent newborns all swaddled in their own pink or blue blankets.

"If only," Cassie said wistfully as she pressed her forehead against the window, "we could all stay this way, with our parents promising to always love us, no matter what."

Just then, she felt a hand on her shoulder.

"Jake, please, not now." Cassie's voice trembled while her head never moved.

"It's not Jake."

Cassie whipped her head around to see her mother standing before her.

"And I do love you," Julia said, "no matter what."

"Could've fooled me," Cassie mumbled.

Julia tipped her head back in frustration. "Everything I've done was out of love for you."

"Really?" Cassie snickered. "How do you figure that?"

"Because," the words caught in Julia's throat, "I don't want you to throw your entire life away for some guy like I almost did."

Cassie rolled her eyes. "What are you talking about?"

"Believe it or not," Julia said, prying her eyes away from the babies in the nursery, "I did have a life of my own once."

"Now this I have to hear," Adrian said.

Julia motioned toward a bench along the wall. Cassie trudged toward it and took a seat beside her mother.

"You know I dated someone seriously before your dad."

"Yeah, some hockey player from Michigan Tech, right?"

"His name was Chris." Julia's face flushed a bittersweet red. "Chris Bradley."

Something in her mother's voice grabbed Cassie's attention.

Mother and daughter locked eyes. Cassie saw a spark that she believed should've been reserved for only her father, while Julia saw sheer disappointment in her daughter's eyes.

"Cass looks like a kid who has just been told there's no Santa Claus," Adrian said.

Julia desperately wanted to comfort her daughter, but she needed to tell her everything first.

"I met him during my freshman year of college at NMU," Julia said. "He was a friend of my roommate's boyfriend. We were together for about a year."

"And?" Cassie asked, sensing more to the story.

"And..." Julia flinched while she struggled to find the words, but they just wouldn't come. *C'mon,* she thought. *You can do this. You have to; she needs to know.*

"Know what!" Adrian demanded. "What's the big secret?"

"I really thought he was the one, Cass, but looking back now, I can see a lot of red flags I chose to ignore." *My choice. No one else's,* Julia reminded herself.

"Okay," Cassie said. "So what happened?"

Julia sighed. "When we were supposed to spend the weekend together up in Houghton during the Winter Carnival at Tech is what happened. He cancelled on me at the last minute. Said the game was too big; he had to prepare for it and it wouldn't be fair to me to come up there for nothing."

"Wait a minute," Cassie interrupted. "He didn't go to school with you at Northern?"

"No," Julia mumbled, her eyes downcast so she wouldn't have to see the look her daughter shot her.

"I know now," Julia raised her eyes slightly, "but back then I was in love." She paused before she admitted, "and naïve."

"Let me guess: He cheated on you, didn't he?"

"With some sorority girl from Tech. My friends and I decided to go up there anyway—why waste a good room?—and we caught them making out behind one of the ice sculptures."

There's more to this than just a bad breakup, Adrian thought. *I'd bet any money on it, but there's no use asking Kevin about it right now.*

"He just left me so broken I didn't know if I'd ever recover. I couldn't bear to see that happen to you too," Julia said.

Just then, Jake rounded the corner. He stopped short when he found them together.

"Don't worry, Mom," Cassie said as she stood up. "It won't."

I was that confident once too, Julia thought while she watched her daughter head straight for Jake.

"Hey," he said to Cassie, his voice low and compassionate, "you okay?"

Cassie looked deep into her husband's eyes as if searching for something.

"What?" Jake asked.

There is no Chris in you whatsoever, she thought.

"No, there is not," Adrian reiterated.

"Nothing," Cassie replied to Jake with conviction as she took his hand and led him back to Kathleen's room with Adrian hot on their heels.

Julia was still sitting on the bench, lost in her own thoughts. *That boy is worse than Chris ever was. Probably a chip off the old block.*

She shrank against the wall, her skin suddenly scalding hot, as if it were on fire.

Oh, my.... Julia raised her hand to her forehead and tried to focus on her breathing. *What in God's name is happening to me?*

"Kevin?"

Adrian looked over her shoulder and realized Kevin wasn't following her.

She abandoned Jake and Cassie and returned to the nursery to find Kevin still standing in the hallway, his eyes zeroed in on Julia.

"Kevin?"

Adrian felt the need to approach him slowly. She reached out to touch him, but the closer she got to him, the hotter it became. His mind was open to her now, too, and his thoughts were filled with vengeance. Adrian experienced a fear she had never felt around him before, even though his thoughts weren't directed at her.

Watch it, Kevin was silently telling Julia. *You don't know a damn thing about his mother or me!*

Adrian retreated, her hand over her mouth when she saw Kevin's body silhouetted in darkness. *Oh shit! What do I do? What do I do, what do I do? What the hell am I supposed to do now?*

Adrian's heart raced while the blood pounded in her ears. She closed her eyes, summoned up all her courage, and did the only thing she could think of.

She charged at Kevin and tackled him with all her might, which was no small feat, seeing that he was built like a defensive lineman.

They crashed into the wall and lay stunned on the floor just as a housekeeper saw Julia on the bench. She slammed her cleaning cart to an abrupt halt in the middle of the hallway to check on her.

"Ma'am, are you all right?" she asked as she rushed to Julia's side.

Julia sat forward and gratefully accepted the bottle of water the housekeeper offered her.

"I'm fine. Thank you," Julia said between gulps as whatever strange heat wave she had experienced now passed. "Must've just been a horrible hot flash or something."

"Thank God," Adrian said to Kevin. "I don't know what I would've done if you'd made her burst into flames."

She turned anxiously to Kevin when he didn't answer her.

Oh shit. Now what? Adrian thought when she saw him staring at the ceiling, an ominous look haunting his handsome face.

A long, swirling sphere of incredible, multicolored lights descended upon the room and engulfed Kevin. They were so bright they nearly blinded Adrian, and by the time she could see again, both Kevin and the lights were gone, leaving her as terrified as a little girl who had lost her parents.

Chapter Twelve

ADRIAN SLUMPED UP AGAINST THE glass window of the nursery, her thoughts a jumble of questions and confusion.

"I feel you," she murmured to the baby screaming its lungs out, unable to express what it truly needed.

Need, Adrian thought as she forced herself upright and wiped a tear from her cheek. *It's not about my needs. It's about theirs.*

That thought helped her regain enough strength to trudge down to Kathleen's room to check on Jake and Cassie.

Adrian stood dumbfounded in the doorway.

"What's the matter? Cat got your tongue?"

All Adrian could do was run and throw herself at Kevin, who was kicked back in the recliner, watching Cassie cuddle her newborn nephew.

"I thought," Adrian stammered. "I thought... I didn't know what happened to you."

"Whoa! Take it easy." Kevin tried to comfort her. "It's all right. I'm all right."

"So what happened to you?"

Kevin sighed. "I made a mistake and got called out for it."

"Called out? By who? Him?"

Kevin got up from his chair and motioned for Adrian to follow him out into the hallway.

"Do you remember when I told you when He wants to talk to you, you'll know?"

"That was it?" Adrian asked incredulously.

"That was it."

"But why? It was because of Julia, wasn't it? Was it something she said? Or something she thought?"

"Doesn't matter. I know better than to let anyone get to me like that."

"But...."

"No buts. There's no excuse for it. Besides, it's over and done with now. We need to turn the page and move on to the next chapter."

Turn the page, Adrian thought confidently, even though her heart ached at the sight of her husband staring affectionately at his new wife and the baby she cradled in her arms.

Move on to the next chapter.

Adrian's confidence wavered as she sensed her best friend's longing for a child of her own grow stronger.

We can do this, Adrian thought, giving herself a peptalk. *We have to.*

Chapter Thirteen

"**D**UDE, I'M TELLING YOU, THIS woman's ass is just made to be spanked."

They were in Charlie's apartment. Adrian sat at the kitchen island with her chin settled in the palm of her hand and an unimpressed look upon her face.

"Really?" she asked Kevin. "This is the next chapter?"

"Not all of it," Kevin replied. "I promise."

"Good, because I can't take much more of this."

"See, that's the trouble with being omniscient," he said, putting a consoling arm around her shoulder. "We get to see all and know all, whether we like it or not."

"So, does this fine-assed woman have a name?" Jake asked Charlie.

"Ugh, this is torture." Adrian moaned. "Like being forced to listen to Billy Bush talking to Trump."

"Deidre," Charlie answered Jake's question. "No wait. Danni; it's definitely Danni. Or is it Debbie?"

"Dude," Jake admonished his best friend as he set his bottle of beer back down on the counter, "did I not teach you anything?"

"You were trying to teach me something?" Charlie teased.

"Some people never learn," Jake said with an exaggerated sigh. "The first, and most important rule is never to forget or confuse a woman's name if you ever want to see her again."

"Well, I would think that would be obvious," Adrian mumbled.

"I got her digits," Charlie said while he scrolled through his phone. "At least I think they're in here somewhere. Some parts of the night are still a little fuzzy for me."

"But her ass he remembers," Adrian said. "Unbelievable."

Jake shook his head while he made a feeble attempt to hide his smirk.

"What?" Charlie asked him.

"Nothing, man. I'm just so glad I'm retired from all of this."

"Yeah, right." Charlie said. "That's why you high-tailed it over here…. Don't look at me like that. You know exactly what I'm talking about. Normally, I can't pry you away from Cass, but today you called me. So what gives? Did she need some me time, or did you piss her off somehow?"

Jake's face turned stoic as he lifted his beer bottle to his lips.

Good question, he thought. Cassie had been acting strange all morning. She seemed nervous and jittery, bouncing around their apartment like a sprung pinball. She had also asked him what his plans were for the day, and when he had said he really didn't have any, she had suggested—a little too enthusiastically—that he call Charlie and go hang out with him.

"Dude," Charlie called out to him, "you still with me?"

"Something's up," Jake said more to himself than to his friend.

"What?" Charlie asked.

"With Cassie," Jake raised his voice. "Something's up with her." *And I bet her parents have something to do with it.*

"But they don't, babe," Adrian told him. "I swear. It's not what you think. Just stay here. You'll find out what's going on soon enough."

Adrian turned to Kevin. "Tell him," she pleaded.

"We can talk to him until we're blue in the face," Kevin said, "but if he refuses to listen...."

"Hey, man, where are you going?" Charlie asked as Jake got up to leave.

"I'll be right back," Jake said vaguely. *As soon as I find out what Cass is up to.*

Adrian groaned, then muttered something unintelligible as she trudged behind Jake.

"What was that?" Kevin asked her.

"I said," Adrian stopped to face Kevin, "why do men always have to be such stubborn jackasses?"

"Men?" Kevin replied with a skeptical arch of his eyebrow. "Really?"

"Yes, really. Two, in particular, jump to mind."

"Yes, well, there are some women who are just as stubborn, if not worse. One, in particular, jumps to my mind."

"Women are not stubborn," Adrian insisted. "We're just persistent. There's a difference."

"There always is," Kevin muttered.

"What was that?" Adrian asked with a curious tilt of her head.

"Nothing." Kevin knew better. "Nothing at all."

*

"See?" Adrian said to Kevin a few minutes later. "Stubborn jackass."

They were riding along with Jake in his truck back to his and Cassie's apartment.

Adrian did everything she could think of—red lights, traffic jams, Sunday drivers—to give her husband enough time to relax and let rational thought take over, but Jake blocked her every attempt.

In fact, the longer it took him to get home, the more he was convinced Cassie had something going on with her parents she didn't want him to know about.

"That's it." Adrian threw her arms up in defeat when Jake pulled into his parking spot. "I give up! There's not enough time in the world for me to get through that thick skull of yours! So, go! Go ruin this for Cassie if you must."

Jake barged into their apartment to find it quiet and empty.

Shit, he thought. *She went somewhere with them. Probably to the church to confess to their priest.*

"What?" Adrian did a double-take before they continued their room-to-room search. "Seriously, that's the first place your mind went to? Are you even hearing yourself right now?"

All Jake heard was the sound of water running in the downstairs bathroom. He approached the partially open door as if he were about to apprehend an intruder.

"Jesus Christ!" Cassie exclaimed. Adrian's eyes doubled in size, her ears not accustomed to hearing her best friend swear.

Cassie sank down onto the edge of the bathtub after she opened the door and found her husband there ready to pounce.

"You just took about ten years off my life!"

"I'm sorry, Cass," Jake apologized profusely. "I thought you were gone."

"Nope, I'm here," she said, her voice tinged with irritation. "Barely. What are you doing back already anyway?"

The question caught him off guard.

What am I doing back here already? I can't tell her the truth. She'll....

"Think you've lost your mind?" Adrian finished Jake's thought.

So what then? What good excuse can I possibly give her?

Jake's eyes roamed around the bathroom, anywhere except upon his wife's expectant face.

"Jake?" she asked impatiently.

And that's when he saw it sitting innocently on the counter next to the sink. A plain white stick he had only seen one other time, in Adrian's hand when she appeared heartbroken in the doorway of their bathroom not so long ago.

It's all right, Jake remembered comforting her. *We've got plenty of time.*

His throat suddenly went bone dry, and he couldn't move. His eyes remained locked onto that tiny stick as if it were a monster that could destroy them both.

"Cass?" Jake eventually spoke her name, now waiting for her to explain.

She pressed the palms of her hands down on her knees and sighed deeply.

"Surprise," Cassie said with a hapless shrug and even less enthusiasm than Eeyore.

"Wow, way to ruin a moment, babe," Adrian said under her breath before taking a closer look at her husband.

"Jake, are you okay?" Adrian asked.

It seemed like an eternity for the tension that had built up inside Jake to dissolve, and then for him to try to comprehend what Cassie had just announced.

"Surprise? Oh…my God…surprise! Does this mean what I think it means? Are we…?" Jake stammered. "I mean, are you…?"

"Uh-huh." Cassie's smile could have lit up the entire downtown.

Jake didn't say another word. He dropped to his knees before her; his hands rested delicately on her stomach while he looked up at her with inquiring eyes.

"Uh-huh," Cassie said again, her voice filled with laughter.

A baby; our baby, Jake thought as he pulled Cassie close to him and kissed her full on the lips.

Adrian stood over them, her eyes closed and her head bowed, as she placed a hand on each one's shoulder.

Suddenly, the elation Jake and Cassie felt subsided. Their hearts grew heavy while their minds became haunted by the same ghost:

Adrian.

"Cass, please, don't."

Jake reached out to cup his wife's face in his hands at the first sign of any impending tears.

"I'm sorry," Cassie said, sniffling, "but I just can't help thinking about how badly she wanted this for herself and for the both of you."

Adrian's head tipped back while she tried to suppress her mounting sorrow.

Adrian and Cassie both thought of the afternoon Adrian had spent sobbing on Cassie's shoulder after the pregnancy test Adrian had taken had come back negative.

"I don't know why I'm so upset," Adrian had admitted to her best friend. "It's not like we were even trying or anything."

"I really did want it," Adrian said now as her arms wrapped instinctively around her own stomach, "before I even knew it myself. But, He had other plans for me and you guys."

"I know," Jake told Cassie as he wiped a stray tear from her cheek with his thumb.

Cassie felt silly asking, but she did anyway.

"Do you think she'd be happy for us?"

"Oh, hell yeah!" Jake and Adrian answered together.

His immediate response brought another smile to Cassie's lips.

"That's better," Jake said. *Love seeing my girl smile.*

"C'mon," he added as he pulled Cassie up from the edge of the bathtub.

"Where are we going?"

"To celebrate," Jake said with a sly smile as his eyes drifted down to her non-existent belly. "Don't be alarmed little one by anything you might see or hear soon. Do they have eyes and ears yet?"

Adrian stood in the bathroom after Jake and Cassie left and tried to fling the faint tint of green off her fingertips.

Chapter Fourteen

JAKE BARELY MADE IT THROUGH the front door. Every muscle in his body was sore to its core, and he was covered from head to toe with dirt.

Thank God it's Friday, he thought gratefully just before his cell phone went off.

Jake closed his eyes while his shoulders sagged.

Oh, c'mon, he groaned internally while he dug his phone out of his jacket pocket. *I just walked through the damn door.*

He pried one eye open, then the other to look at the screen, and was momentarily relieved to see it wasn't work calling him back in. The actual message didn't leave him very thrilled, though.

Hey, it's me. Just wanted to let you know I'm staying a little later at work tonight.

"Damn it, Cass. You promised to take it easy."

And then came another text from her, as if she knew exactly what he had said.

I know I promised, but it's just paperwork. I swear!

"Yeah right, paperwork," he said with the hint of a smile. "I know you way better than that, sweetheart."

This wasn't the first time he had gotten one of these texts from her. Actually, the first time she had called him, but that conversation had ended so badly that Cassie had switched to the safer plan of texting.

It became one of their biggest fights. Cassie had worked so hard to get and keep her job as an EMT, especially after Adrian had died, that she had no intention of slowing down until she absolutely had to.

Jake never wanted to start anything with his wife, but he also worried her passion for her job might put their baby at risk.

"I just don't want anything to happen to you or our baby," Jake said now to his phone as he sat down in their rapidly darkening kitchen. "Why is it so hard for you to understand that?"

But, he thought as he reached for the nearest light switch, *I also know this is one battle I'll never win.*

"Smart man," Adrian said.

"Stubborn woman," Kevin replied with a wink at Adrian.

"Mmm, more like a woman who knows what she wants," Adrian replied with a self-assured smile.

Jake also knew Cassie had a decent partner in Max. He looked out for her like she was his own daughter, which was why Jake wrote back to her:

Make sure Max doesn't let you lift any paperwork that's too heavy for you.

Jake ended the sentence with a winking emoji.

Will do, Cassie wrote back a few minutes later with a big grinning emoji. *I love you!*

Love you too! Let me know when you're done.

KK.

A wave of exhaustion suddenly washed over Jake as he checked the time on his phone.

"Oh, shit." He sighed while he ran his hands up and around his face.

He needed to shower; it was late. Cassie wouldn't be home for at least another hour, and that was being optimistic.

And he was starving and assumed his wife would be too. Too hungry and too tired to even attempt cooking anything.

"What to do?" he asked himself while he tapped his chin with his finger. "Only one thing really."

The number was in his contacts, but it was one of the few he knew by heart.

"Mama Jo's Pizzeria."

"Hey, Mom. How busy are you guys down there tonight?"

"Never too busy for you, sweetie. What do you need?"

*

There was a knock at the front door half an hour later.

"Mom, you didn't have to deliver the food yourself."

"Well, you didn't sound like you had the energy to stay on the phone, much less come pick up your order," Laura replied as she breezed past him. "So here I am."

"You know," Jake said as he shut the door behind her, "you could've just sent one of the delivery guys over here. That is what you're paying them to do."

Jake could feel his mother casting her infamous "Oh, really?" stare upon him before he even turned back around and saw it.

"And miss the perfect opportunity to talk to my ever-elusive son?" she replied. "I don't think so."

I should've known, Jake thought. "I've been busy," he replied.

"So have I, but I still managed to squeeze some time in now for my son."

Damn it, here she goes with the guilt shots.

"Priorities, Jacob."

"Speaking of priorities," Jake asked with a sly smile, "how's the pizzeria running without you right now, Mom?"

"It's all under control, smart ass."

Laura grinned back at him as she took a seat at the kitchen table, crossed her legs at the ankles, and flipped open one of the pizza boxes.

"Now, c'mon," she said. "Sit down and start eating before it gets cold."

The mouth-watering scent of his mother's homemade pizza seduced Jake from across the room and made his stomach growl louder than a lion. There was no way he could possibly resist it.

"So," Laura began, her hand resting on her chin while she watched Jake practically devour one large slice in a single bite, "Cassie working late again tonight?"

Jake froze in mid-chew.

"Mm-hmm," he said slowly, it suddenly becoming much more difficult for him to swallow his mouthful of food.

"And you're good with that, I hope?"

Jake looked up to see his mother's eyes leveled on him like the barrel of a shotgun.

"Gotta be."

"Good." Laura relaxed back in her chair, but not before she snagged a piece of pizza for herself. "Because I'd hate to hear that you two went at it again over this."

Jake crossed his arms and gave his mom his own "Oh, really" look as he watched her eat his pizza.

"The only thing I might go at it about tonight is you stealing my pizza," Jake replied while he reached over to take his mom's slice away from her.

"Hey, now," Laura said as she playfully swatted at her son's hand. "I made that pizza for you, so I think I'm entitled to a slice or two."

"Okay, you can have a slice…to take with you on your way back to work."

"Oh, no, I'm not going anywhere until I know the two of you are okay."

Jake fought the urge to roll his eyes.

"Mom," he chose his words carefully as he rose up out of his chair, "we're good."

"How far along is she again?"

"Almost three months," he replied through gritted teeth.

Adrian and Kevin stood side-by-side. She leaned back against the kitchen counter and tried to stifle her snickering.

"What?" Kevin asked.

"He's not going to make it," Adrian replied. "Uh-uh. No way, no how. She is pushing every single one of his buttons."

"But he's a Riley man and this is his mother."

"Doesn't matter." Adrian kept shaking her head. "She's going to break him."

"We'll see."

"She's still got a long way to go," Laura told her son. "Are you sure you're up for it?"

"And here she goes again," Adrian said.

"Up for what?" Jake asked, even though he knew he shouldn't have.

"See?" Adrian pointed out to Kevin as Jake got up. "He needs to keep his distance from her so he's going to the fridge."

"Or," Kevin countered, "maybe he's just thirsty and needs something to drink."

"Yeah, right," Adrian replied.

"She's only going to get more stubborn the longer she's pregnant," Laura said.

"See?" Kevin told Adrian. "Laura just called Cassie a stubborn female."

Adrian waved him off as if he were an annoying fly buzzing in her ear.

Do not engage; do not engage, Jake thought as he stuck his head in the fridge and reemerged with a bottle of beer.

"Did you want something to drink?" he asked his mother.

"And as if that weren't bad enough," she said as if she had never even heard him, "you're going to have her mother to contend with. In fact, I'm kind of surprised Mother Julia hasn't gone a couple of rounds with you two already about all of this."

"Mom."

Adrian's eyes widened when she saw Jake roll his shoulders back into his Riley stance. "Oh, shit," she said," we got to stop this now."

And that's when Jake's phone went off.

"Oh, look at that," Jake said after he read the text. "Cassie's on her way home. So sorry you have to eat and run."

"Who said anything about running anywhere? I'm the boss; I can take all the time I want," Laura replied with a devious smile.

Jake gave his mother a pointed look.

"Relax, Jacob. I'm just messing with you. I know how to take a hint."

"Really? Since when?"

"Ha. Ha. Very funny," Laura said as she slung her purse over her shoulder and made her way to her son. "Give Cassie and the little bambino my love."

Jake grinned from ear-to-ear. *Our little bambino.* "I will."

"Love you, sweetheart."

"Love you too, Mom."

"And remember to keep that hot head of yours under control," she called out on her way out the front door.

"Goodnight, Mom," he said, promptly shutting the door behind her.

*

"Jake?" Cassie shouted when she got home a few minutes later.

There was no answer and no sign of him anywhere.

Shit, Cassie thought. *Don't tell me he's pissed and upstairs asleep already. Or worse, out somewhere with Charlie.*

She sighed and forced herself away from the door and toward the kitchen to search for anything appealing left over in the fridge.

Cassie screamed and nearly jumped out of her skin when she rounded the corner and the lights suddenly came on.

"Relax," Jake said. "Your dinner is here."

Cassie doubled over in laughter at the sight of him. He wore a surgical mask over his face and carried the unopened box of pizza toward her at arm's length as if it were some kind of hazardous material.

"What in the world?" Cassie asked.

"I took the liberty of ordering your favorite pizza: a medium pepperoni, pineapple, and onion." Jake made a gagging face while he described it.

"Shut up! You didn't?"

"Oh, yes, I did. Mama Jo's latest food item: The Pregnancy Special."

Cassie couldn't control herself. She flipped open the box, delighted by what she saw and smelled. She was about to dive in when she hesitated.

"Wait. What about you?"

"Oh, don't worry. I got one for myself and made sure to keep it a safe distance from that." Jake wrinkled his nose.

"Aw, c'mon; it's not that bad."

"You're right. It's worse."

"Don't knock it until you've tried it."

Cassie flashed him a mischievous grin before taking an enormous bite of her pizza.

"Oh, no." Jake backed away as Cassie came closer and tried to pull his mask down. "Don't even think about kissing me right now."

"But I love you," she cooed.

"And I love you too."

Jake wrapped his fingers lightly around her wrists, but it did him no good.

Jake's laughter turned to panic once he realized she had backed him into a corner. Cassie's eyebrows shot up in glee; victory was hers.

"Then…kiss me!"

She broke free from his grasp, yanked down his mask, and planted an open-mouthed kiss on him.

Adrian stepped aside as their playfulness accelerated. She ran her hands slowly up and down her arms while her lips curved up into a half-hearted smile.

"You okay?" Kevin asked.

"Mm-hmm," Adrian said with her chin up.

This wasn't the first time Kevin had seen her like this. It seemed to happen more frequently since Cassie had become pregnant.

He studied her closely.

"What?" Adrian asked him.

"Nothing."

There was no trace of green around her, but that may have been worse than if she were illuminated by it.

You're keeping it under control really well right now, Kevin thought, *but it's still there inside you. I can feel it, and that's what scares me.*

"Okay," Cassie said to Jake after he tried to wash the taste of her pizza out of his mouth with a swig of his beer, "since I sabotaged your taste buds, I'll let you pick what we watch tonight."

"Really? Whatever I want to watch?"

"Yep." Cassie swallowed hard. "Whatever you want."

Moments later, they lay on the couch together—Cassie in front of Jake with her box of pizza balanced on her lap—and settled in for a Rocky movie marathon.

Cassie groaned. "The least you could've done was make it a Creed double-feature."

"And the least you could've done was developed a craving for something other than a dragon-breath pizza," Jake teased her.

"That's beyond my control," Cassie said as she leaned back and breathed heavily into Jake's face.

"Now you made us miss a classic scene in the movie," Jake told her after he tried to wave the smell of her breath away. "I have no choice but to rewind it."

"Hey, before you do that," Cassie's hand hovered over the remote, "did I mention I have the next four days off?"

"Four days?" Jake raised an eyebrow skeptically at her. "Free and clear? No on-call?"

"No on-call. See, that's one of the perks of picking up extra shifts when I'm needed," she added with a broad grin.

"Good. That means you and our little bambino can finally have some downtime."

"Our little bambino?" Cassie stared curiously up at him. "Your mom was here, wasn't she?"

"She may have delivered the pizzas."

"Uh-huh. I figured as much, because the only time you start calling the baby 'bambino' is after you've been around your mom."

"You don't like 'bambino'?"

"I didn't say that. But, since we're on the subject," Cassie hit the pause button on the remote, "we really should start thinking of some legitimate names for our child."

"I think Bambino Riley sounds pretty legit."

"You think you're funny, don't you?"

"Or how about Bambi for a girl?"

"Absolutely not."

"Or better yet: Miley."

"You're kidding, right?"

"What?" Jake asked.

"You really want to name our daughter Miley Riley?"

Cassie felt a strange pain in her stomach as Adrian got up and brushed by her.

"Oh, uh-oh," Cassie said while her hand splayed protectively over her belly.

"What's wrong?"

Adrian stopped in front of the window, her head whipped around toward the sound of her husband's distraught voice.

She shot Kevin a desperate look that started a conversation between them through their thoughts.

I didn't cause that, did I?

Kevin responded with a reassuring look of his own.

No, absolutely not.

Adrian leaned against the windowsill with a sigh of relief once she felt her friend's pain go away.

"Nothing," Cassie answered Jake's question. "I just don't think our little bambino cared for that name either."

"Oh, okay," Jake replied. "Well, let's try out some more names and see what our little bambino thinks of them. I've got plenty of ideas, especially for a boy."

"Oh, I'm sure you do," Cassie mumbled while she turned the movie back on.

Chapter Fifteen

Daytime TV is overrated.

Cassie came to that conclusion, much to her disappointment, during her time off.

She couldn't wait to get sucked into outlandish soap opera plots and talk show tragedies, but by the middle of day three, Cassie was ready to slap the stupid out of every real or fictional television personality she saw.

"All right, that's enough of this."

Cassie aimed the remote at the flat screen and hit the off button with a decisive click.

"We need to cut ties with the TV," she continued as she looked down at her stomach, "before we both lose vital brain cells."

"But what else is there for us to do?" Cassie asked herself while she shuffled to the window.

"I'm not really feeling the whole 'get outside and go for a walk' vibe," she said as she stared out into the gray, dismal day. "How about you, little one?"

Cassie waited for a sign from the baby, but she got nothing, not even a little gas or a touch of indigestion.

"Really? Nothing, huh?" she spoke to her stomach. "Okay, well, I guess it's up to me then, so don't give me any grief if you don't like what I decide."

And that's when she got struck with inspiration.

"And I say," her eyes brightened with excitement, "we need to go on an ice cream run."

*

Julia tossed her pencil on the desk and leaned back in her chair as the door shut behind the last set of parents she had to speak with today.

Who knew, she thought, *that parent/teacher conferences for first graders could be so grueling?*

Julia did because she had been teaching since before she had even had kids of her own.

And if there was one thing she had learned in all that time, it was that some parents could be way worse than the most difficult child in her classroom.

Julia prayed at the beginning of each new school year for a good group, but there was always one set of parents who managed to get under her skin.

She dealt with them as tactfully as possible each and every day, but the conferences were her real test.

She was relieved once they were all said and done, but they also left her so mentally and physically exhausted.

Julia sighed as she glanced at her desk calendar.

Well, only two more weeks until Thanksgiving break, she thought. *We can hang on until then.*

But tonight, her sights were set on going home and drinking a very large glass of wine.

Or two. Okay, maybe three. Oh, who am I kidding? This may be an entire bottle night.

"I hate to break it to you," Kevin told Julia, "but your wine-drinking may have to wait."

Adrian wrinkled her eyebrows in confusion.

"For what?" she asked Kevin.

Adrian hadn't even finished uttering her words before she knew exactly what Kevin would say.

"You'll see," she impersonated him.

*

Cassie sat inside her parked car in the front of Coldstone Creamery and gave her stomach an irritated look.

"I told you no griping. You had your chance; now settle down."

Cassie's grimace coincided with what was happening inside her.

"Maybe if we just sit here for a little while longer and relax," she told herself, "it'll go away."

She was right. After about ten minutes of fiddling with the radio dial and scrolling through Twitter on her phone, the pain stopped. And her craving for ice cream grew ravenous.

"Hot fudge and sprinkles here we come," Cassie said as she got out of the car.

"You coming?" Kevin poked his head back inside the car at Adrian.

Adrian sat in the backseat, her body numb with anger.

"What is happening?" she asked, her voice frighteningly calm.

"Nothing. Now c'mon."

"Not until you quit lying to me!"

"Adrian," Kevin groaned, "now is not the time to start this."

"I'm not starting anything! I just want you to tell me the truth instead of keeping me in the dark."

Something came over Adrian then. She forgot everything—her righteous indignation, even Kevin—and was suddenly compelled to get inside that ice cream shop as fast as she possibly could.

She flew through the front door and came to a screeching halt. The sound of a ringing bell would forever be associated in Adrian's mind with the moment she saw her best friend doubled over in agony on the stark, linoleum floor.

*

Julia drove calmly through the traffic, despite how congested it was.

She was happy. She was on her way home; The Beatles sang "Can't Buy Me Love" on whatever Sirius station she had stumbled upon, and the stress of the day was a million miles behind her in the rearview mirror.

Life is good, she thought.

Her lips even curled up into a smile as she glanced at all the familiar mini-malls and restaurants she passed on a regular basis. That is, until something else caught her eye.

A red flashing light.

But it wasn't the light so much as the vehicle parked alongside it that really got Julia's attention.

Her head and her mind moved in slow motion while she tried to process it all.

That's not...no, it can't be, can it? It sure looks like Cassie's car parked next to that ambulance. It's got to be a coincidence though, right? But what if it's not?

Julia flipped her car around in the opposite direction as soon as she was able to. She almost caused an accident of her own in the parking lot when she saw her daughter being rolled outside on a stretcher.

Julia slammed on her brakes, catapulted out the door, and ran straight for Cassie.

Cassie had insisted they didn't need to call an ambulance, but the manager of the ice cream shop wouldn't listen to her.

She felt arms around her—she didn't know whose, much less that they were Adrian's—trying to help her up off the floor, even though she didn't want to stand.

"C'mon, Cass," Adrian urged her. "You have to get up. Please."

No, Cassie thought as she felt the blood surging uncontrollably out of her body. *No, no, no! Don't make me get up; just leave me here.*

She wanted to push all the comforting arms away, but she didn't have the strength.

Just leave me here with my baby. Maybe if we just sit here a little while longer it'll stop and she'll still be okay.

Adrian gasped while her hand flew up to her face to cover her mouth.

But if I get up, Cassie's thoughts raced on even after the blood seeped through her jeans and pooled around her on the floor, *that's it. It's over. She'll be gone, and that can't happen. It just can't.*

"No!" she cried out, her arm stretched out toward something she would never reach as the EMTs lifted her gently onto the stretcher.

Cassie barely acknowledged her mother, who threw her arms around her as soon as she was close enough to.

All Cassie could think about was being separated from her child and how empty she suddenly felt inside.

Chapter Sixteen

JAKE SAT IN THE BACK of the room, slumped down in his chair, his fingers at his temple, trying to hold his head up during the monthly safety meeting at work.

Charlie sat beside him and elbowed Jake every so often whenever he saw his friend's eyes start to droop.

And when that didn't work, Jake's cell phone buzzed in his pocket, jolting him awake and nearly causing him to spill his entire cup of coffee all over the table in front of him.

Jake flipped up the collar of his Carhart jacket and sank a little lower in his chair while his supervisor gave him the evil eye. He put his hand in his pocket to silence his phone.

The meeting resumed only to be interrupted a few minutes later by a tentative knock on the door.

"I'm sorry," Valerie, the receptionist, apologized as she poked her head in the room, "but Jake has a phone call. It's an emergency."

Jake and Charlie exchanged subtle glances.

Thank God, Jake thought as he hurried out the door.

"Thanks, Val," he said once they were out in the hallway. "You're a lifesaver."

"I wasn't trying to save you this time, Jake." Valerie's face turned bleak as she spoke. "It really is an emergency."

Oh, shit! Cassie!

He stared, frozen by panic, at the portable phone Valerie held out to him.

When Jake finally grabbed it, all he heard was Cassie's mother's voice.

"Jake. We're in the emergency room at St. Anne's. Get here now!"

*

Jake gripped both hands together into a ball in front of him, rolled his shoulders back, and steeled himself for the inevitable tidal wave of emotions about to hit him.

I hate hospitals; I hate hospitals, he thought as he trudged up the sidewalk to the emergency room entrance.

"He always has," Kevin told Adrian as they followed behind him. "Ever since he was a little kid. He went head over heels on his bike when he was about seven or eight. Broke his arm and spent most of the summer in a cast."

"I vaguely remember Laura mentioning something to me about that." Adrian grinned. "He missed an entire season of baseball, and still blames the doctors to this day for ruining his chances of becoming the next Ryan Braun."

"Yep." Kevin laughed. "That he does."

Jake stopped to make sure he had his phone completely shut off before he went inside. He glanced up at the sign above the sliding doors and let out a deep breath.

Out of all the hospitals in Green Bay, Jake thought, *they had to bring you here, to the one where it all happened.*

Adrian lowered her eyes as she leaned into Jake.

His jaw slackened when he felt goosebumps prickling up on both of his arms.

Damn, Jake thought. *It's almost like I can still feel her next to me.*

"Almost." Adrian smiled.

Jake quickly shook the notion off, even while memories of Adrian and that day swirled around him as if it were happening all over again.

He stood up even straighter just as his father clapped a hand down on his other shoulder.

Sorry, Sweet Thing, Jake thought, *but today is not about you.*

"Understood," Adrian replied.

She and Kevin released Jake and he was off, flying down the hospital halls in search of anyone who had any information about Cassie.

"My wife," he spoke breathlessly to the first person he saw behind the nurses' station. "She's here and I need to know how she is."

Jake's voice caught in his throat while his mind threatened to be overtaken by a memory he would have much rather forgotten.

He had awoken in a hospital bed in a room here—319 to be exact—groggy and in excruciating pain, with only one question on his mind.

How is she? I need to know she's okay.

"Sir," the nurse behind the desk brought Jake back to the present day. "What's your wife's name?"

Jesus, why is this happening again?

Adrian folded her arms and bit her tongue as she shifted her weight from one foot to the other.

"Cassie," Jake answered the nurse. "Her name is Cassie Riley."

"Jake."

His blood went cold at the sound of his mother-in-law's voice. He turned to her ever so slowly, as if he were being called out by his archenemy.

Jake knew the second he saw Julia's face. She tried to put up a brave front, but her quivering lips gave her away.

"She's been asking for you," Julia told him.

No one would know by looking at Jake that his heart had sunk like a stone, except for Kevin and Adrian.

"He's got a gift," Adrian said.

"Passed down from one Riley man to another," Kevin added.

Jake gave Julia a nod before he brushed past her, only to stop inches away from the door when he heard her not-so-subtle scoff.

"If you have something to say to me," Jake said through clenched teeth, "please, don't hold back."

"This is your fault," Julia replied, not missing a beat.

"Is that the doctor's professional opinion, or just yours?"

Her eyes narrowed into thin slits.

"I blame you. My daughter wouldn't be here if it weren't for you."

Jake stared complacently at his mother-in-law and said nothing, which only seemed to infuriate Julia all the more.

He was about to turn his back on her, but she refused to let him off that easy.

"If you love her as much as you claim to, you wouldn't have let her work herself to death like she did."

"I did not *let* Cassie do anything," Jake said, cutting her off.

"Oh, damn," Kevin and Adrian said simultaneously as if they both knew the worst was about to happen.

Julia raged on, deaf to anything Jake had to say.

"A better man would've found a way to convince his wife to slow down. A better man would've made the woman he loves stay home and rest. But no, not you. You didn't do a damn thing, and now my grandchild is gone!"

"And so is our baby."

Julia and Jake both turned toward the sound of Cassie's voice. Neither one had even known she was there, standing in the doorway of her room and listening to every word.

Julia started toward her and opened her mouth to speak, but Cassie stopped her with a raised hand. She didn't yell at her mother, but there was enough adamance in her voice to make Julia listen.

"Mom, stop. You've said enough. All I want to do is go home with Jake."

The hurt was evident in Julia's face. Even Adrian felt sorry for her as she backed away from her daughter.

"Oh, all right. Whatever you want, sweetheart. You, um, you just let me know if you need me for anything, okay?"

"Mm-hmm," Cassie muttered.

Adrian felt everything Cassie felt so strongly that it overwhelmed her.

Cassie couldn't hold on much longer either. But she did, just until her mother slunk away like a reprimanded family pet.

Once Julia was gone, Jake reached for his wife. Cassie took his hand and led him back into her room. Then, after the door shut behind them, she turned to face him and fell apart in his arms like the petals of a wilting flower.

Jake held her tight and cradled her head in the palm of his hand. His face twisted in pain while Cassie sobbed into the folds of his work shirt. He stood strong and silent, never once shushing or trying to quiet his wife.

And so they remained, melded together by their own private grief until both Cassie and Adrian could cry no more.

*

A stabbing pain woke Cassie. She shot up in bed, her hands wrapped protectively around her stomach.

She cringed and touched her forehead to her knees as she waited out another wave of punishment.

Damn, baby, Cassie thought, her eyes open to the darkness while her mind remained in a dream-like fog. *Did I eat something you didn't like, or maybe we just need to go to the bathroom?*

She prayed for the latter as she threw the covers gently off her, careful not to wake Jake.

Why worry him if we don't have to, right?

Cassie stumbled around the bed and into the bathroom. Her brain fully awakened the second she saw the blood.

Once the shock wore off, she searched frantically in the back of the cabinet for the box of tampons she thought she wouldn't need for a while.

A chill ran through her afterwards as she stood in the bathroom doorway and stared longingly at their bed.

Maybe this is a nightmare. Maybe if I just go back to sleep....

But she just couldn't convince herself, no matter how hard she tried. Nor could she make her feet move back into the bedroom. She found herself downstairs on the couch before she knew it.

Cassie turned on the TV, but nothing she found held her attention. She stared out the window into the darkness, the same question replaying in her mind with no answer:

Why?

Adrian sat across from her best friend, wracking her own brain.

"I've got nothing," she said out loud as she ran her hands backward through her hair. "Please, Kevin, give me something."

Adrian looked around when he didn't answer her to find he was gone.

"C'mon, Kevin. You can't do this to me! You can't leave me to figure this one out on my own!"

"I didn't."

She heard him, but she didn't see him until she felt the sun begin to rise above the horizon.

Adrian turned to the window, unable to take her eyes off Kevin, who stood bathed in the rays of sunshine that swept across the sky and erased the darkness.

"There's someone here I'd like you to meet before I have to bring her home."

Her mouth dropped open at the sight of the tiny bundle Kevin held swaddled in his arms.

"Is that?"

Adrian took a tentative step forward. Her hand reached through the window before she faltered.

"It's okay," Kevin said as he curled his fingers around Adrian's and brought her closer to him. "You should see her; she's absolutely perfect."

"Oh I'm sure she is," Adrian replied.

Kevin unwrapped the blanket. Adrian's heart soared with joy as soon as she saw her best friend's baby girl's blissfully happy face.

She couldn't resist kissing the baby softly on her forehead, and as she did so, the sky erupted in a pallet of brilliant colors Adrian remembered seeing on the day she left this world.

"Safe journey, baby girl," Adrian said. "You're in good hands." At that exact moment, Cassie felt strangely at peace as she watched the sunrise.

Maybe it was Jake's arms around her shoulders after he came downstairs in search of her, or the kiss he placed ever so delicately on the base of her neck. She couldn't say for sure.

All Cassie knew, as she stretched her arm behind her to give her husband a hug, was that she wasn't alone. And for that, she was grateful.

Chapter Seventeen

JAKE STRODE DOWN THE STEPS of the spiral staircase in his bare feet and Packer sweatpants. His eyes were glued to his cell phone until Cassie popped up from behind the refrigerator door.

Jake looked up, then couldn't take his eyes off his wife.

"Whoa!" he said as his foot missed the last step.

"What?" Cassie asked anxiously while she set the carton of milk down on the counter.

"Have I ever told you how hot you look in your work clothes?"

Cassie's worry lines ironed themselves out as she put her hands to her hips and tilted her head at her husband.

"Oh please."

"I'm serious," he replied, his voice an octave lower and huskier in a way that normally would have melted her faster than chocolate on a humid day.

Jake stood tantalizingly close to Cassie now.

"You know, I've always had a thing for a woman in uniform."

He stroked her cheek with the back of his fingers. She leaned into the palm of his hand before suddenly pulling away.

"Well, as much as I'd love to continue this," Cassie said before she kissed him, "duty calls."

"But what about breakfast?" Jake asked, his eyes darting to the carton of milk she had taken out.

"No time now," Cassie said while she dashed to the front door. "I'll see you tonight. Love you!"

"Love you too," Jake mumbled, dazed and confused as the door clicked shut.

Cassie stood on the other side of the door and relished the taste of her husband's lips, which still lingered on hers.

Some day, she thought, *but not today. Not yet.*

Damn, Jake thought while he rubbed his fingers across his forehead. *I really thought I had her this time.*

Jake was pouring himself a glass of milk when it dawned on him. He grabbed his phone and swiped over to the calendar.

"Jesus!" he yelled.

You are such an asshole! Trying to seduce your wife on the anniversary of the day you lost your child!

"Three months today, to be exact," Jake mumbled with a heavy heart.

He could only imagine what Cassie was going through.

"If you ask me," Adrian told Jake, "she's turning into the female version of you."

Jake saw it too. Every day since the miscarriage, Cassie had added another brick to her rising wall. He knew he needed to do something before it got too high around her, but what?

"He's never had to deal with anything like this before," Kevin told Adrian.

"What?" Adrian asked as she hopped up on the barstool beside him. "You mean, being on the receiving end of someone who's becoming as emotionally closed off as him?" She flashed Kevin a big, toothy grin after this last question.

"Yeah," Kevin replied. "Anyway, he's going to need help."

"Which he'll be too stubborn to ask for."

"Exactly."

"Hmm," said Adrian. "Do you mind if I try something?"

"No, go right ahead." Kevin waved her on.

Jake's phone rang. He tipped his head back and sighed.

"Hey, Mom," he said in his best 'act casual' voice. "What's up?"

Kevin stared curiously at Adrian.

"What?" she asked him.

"His mother is your answer?" he asked skeptically.

"No, she's just the first phase."

"The first phase," Kevin repeated, intrigued.

"You'll see."

"Oh, I can't wait."

"Not much," Laura answered her son's question. "I just thought I'd check to see if you and Cassie want to have dinner with me tonight at Mama Jo's?"

"Um, tonight's really not a good night for us."

"Why? Do you guys already have plans?"

"No, but—"

"But nothing! It'd be good for the two of you to get out and have a good time together."

Shit, Jake thought, *pinching the bridge of his nose. She knows! How in the hell did my mom remember but not me?*

"I just don't know how Cassie's going to feel after work," Jake said, throwing out another feeble excuse.

"Okay, well, why don't you just come over then?"

"Mom," he snapped. "I told you. Not tonight."

"Was this part of your plan too?" Kevin teased Adrian. "Because if it is, it seems to be working like a charm so far."

"Shhhh!"

"Okay, *fine*," Laura replied to Jake's outburst.

"Oh, no," Kevin said. "She threw out the 'fine' card."

"I'll still keep your table reserved in case you change your mind," Laura continued in a voice she reserved specifically to make her son feel guilty. "Love you," she added as she abruptly hung up the phone.

"Love you too," Jake said flatly to the dial tone.

Great, he thought, *now I've managed to piss my mom off on top of everything else. What the hell next?*

"I'm fucking late," he grumbled after he looked up at the clock on the wall.

"And now," Adrian said as she rubbed her hands together in glee, "it's time for phase two."

Charlie sat in the truck outside Jake's apartment and laid on the horn. Jake finally came out ranting and raving the entire way.

"Jesus," Charlie said after Jake slammed his door shut. "What's up with you? Cass kick you to the couch last night or something?"

"Just drive."

"Sure thing. Do you need me to stop at the drugstore on the way so we can pick up some Midol for you?" Charlie grinned.

Jake glared daggers into Charlie, which had no effect on him.

"Or better yet," Charlie suggested, "how about we have a long overdue guys' night out?"

"What the hell is with everyone trying to get me to go out all of a sudden?"

Charlie just stared at his friend.

"Oh, I don't know," Charlie finally said, "maybe it's your sparking personality?"

Jake's head hung low. "Sorry," he muttered.

"Yeah, you are," Charlie replied, "but I'll let it slide this time."

"Exactly how many more phases are there to this plan of yours?" Kevin leaned in to ask Adrian.

"Enough," she replied with a knowing smile.

*

Jake returned home that night to a silent, empty apartment.

"Of course she's still working."

And that's when the ghosts came alive.

Jake saw himself and Cassie facing off against each other in the living room, her stance matching, if not surpassing, his own.

She tightened her grip on the handle of her suitcase. Jake inched closer to his wife and laid his hands on her arms. Cassie flung them off with a roll of her shoulders. Jake flinched as if she had slapped him across the face.

"You're right," Jake said, holding his ground. "I don't want you to keep working, but not because I want to control you, but because I love you and want to keep you and our baby safe. And I will not apologize for that."

Jake saw the suitcase fall over onto the floor, and he swore he still felt the soft touch of his wife's hand on his cheek as she guided his face to hers and kissed him tenderly on the lips.

Jake looked up to the top of the spiral staircase and watched another ghost of himself staring down at Cassie on the couch.

The vacant look in her eyes haunted him and left him feeling powerless.

He sunk down onto the steps and intended to stay there until something inside of him compelled him to go to her.

Jake couldn't—even now—conjure up the right words to describe how he felt when he finally saw that spark of life reignite in Cassie's eyes.

Thank God, he thought as he leaned in to kiss her.

Jake blinked, and the ghosts scattered into the air like dust.

"Maybe a boys' night out wouldn't be such a bad idea after all," Jake said while he pulled his phone out of his pocket. "Right after I get something to eat."

*

Jake walked through the front door of Mama Jo's Pizzeria to find his mother in the center of a perfect storm.

A long line of people were waiting at the register; a harried young girl was behind it, her palms up in a total loss. Laura stood beside her—calm as always—trying to fix whatever was wrong with one hand while taking an order over the phone, and cracking jokes that magically put all the impatiently waiting customers instantly at ease.

To say his mom was distracted was an understatement. Jake couldn't pass up this rare opportunity to mess with her.

He snuck up to the bar by her and disguised his voice.

"There's someone at my table," he said in a thick Chicago-style accent.

"I'm sorry, what?" Laura asked politely, her eyes still focused on the register.

"There's a specific table I sit at every time I come here, but tonight someone else is already there!"

"I'm sorry, sir, but we can't guarantee tables unless you reserve them ahead of time."

"Maybe for other people, but not me. I want to speak to the man in charge. Now."

The young girl beside Jake's mother looked up, her eyes enlarged with horror. She hadn't worked there long enough to know who he was, but she was well aware of how Laura would react to that comment. And it wasn't going to be good.

Jake saw the tension rise in his mother's shoulders as she stood up straight, poised to do battle with this male chauvinist monster, until she saw her son laughing at her instead.

"I'm sorry, Mom, but I had to do it."

"Sure. Just like I had to give away your table tonight." Laura lifted her chin with a confident air as she rounded the bar and moved swiftly past Jake.

His laughter quickly subsided.

"Wait...what?" he stammered while he trailed behind her.

"You heard me," Laura called over her shoulder, unable to prevent the smile forming on her lips.

"But that's my table."

"I know."

"You've never given my table away, not when I'm supposed to be here."

"You said tonight wasn't going to be a good night, remember?"

"So you just gave it away?"

"To a paying customer? Absolutely."

By this time, they had reached the dining room where Jake's regular table was nestled in a secluded corner of the pizzeria.

Laura stopped, blocking Jake's view of the table.

"Besides, how could I possibly say no to her?"

Laura stepped aside to reveal to her son the woman who had stolen his table.

Jake's jaw dropped when he saw Cassie waving her fingers at him with a sheepish grin on her face.

He stuttered worse than Elmer Fudd, which only made Cassie's grin broaden.

"I thought you were working late again?" he asked her.

"I was going to," Cassie said, "until someone convinced me my time might be better spent out with you for a change."

Jake followed his wife's gaze onto his mother.

"And I told you tonight wouldn't work. How'd you know I'd show up?"

Laura chuckled as if the answer were obvious.

"Oh, my sweet boy," she said as she cupped his chin in her hand, "don't you know by now? I know you better than you know yourself. Now sit down and enjoy."

A thought suddenly struck Jake after he slid into his seat and took the menu his mother offered him.

"What about Charlie?"

"What about him?" Laura asked.

"Oh, don't worry," Cassie replied from behind her menu, "we're still meeting up with him later."

"We?" Jake asked with raised eyebrows.

"Mm-hmm. Hope you don't mind, but you're going to have a third for boys' night." Cassie lowered her menu to give her husband a playful wink. "So what do you think? Should we start with a pitcher of beer or a bottle of wine?"

*

That is such a beautiful sound; music to my ears, Jake thought.

Cassie couldn't stop giggling. It was something he hadn't heard from her in a very long time, and he couldn't get enough of it.

The three of them were at a bar—one of Charlie's choosing—downtown. Jake and Cassie sat together and watched Charlie in action. His moves on the ladies seemed to be what set Cassie off, but her husband had a different explanation for it.

"Ah," Jake said with a voracious smile as his wife snuggled up to him, "I think my girl may be just a little bit drunk."

"Drunk?" Cassie feigned indignation while she locked eyes with Jake. "Me? Oh please."

"Yes, you."

"Well, two shots are usually all it takes to do that to her," Adrian agreed.

Jake wanted to act on his instincts—press his forehead against Cassie's, trace the frame of her face with his fingertips, cup her chin in his hand and lift it up to his lips—but he knew she wasn't ready for that yet, so he resisted.

"Jake?"

The way she spoke his name was like an aphrodisiac to him.

"Yeah?" He bit his lower lip and shifted around on his barstool.

"You're right; I am drunk."

Cassie held her finger up to Jake's lips to keep him from gloating.

"And I want you to take advantage of that. And me."

"Wait." Jake shook his head like a dog who had just come out of the lake. "I must be drunk too because I swear I just heard you say you want me to take advantage of you."

"I did and I do."

"Are you sure? Because this morning—"

"No," Cassie cut him off with a vehement shake of her head. "No more mourning. I'll always miss her—our baby girl—but I need to start living again. With you. Right now."

Cassie motioned for Jake to bring his lips to hers, and when he did, she gave him a kiss that took him completely by surprise.

"Aw, c'mon you two!" Charlie shouted as he elbowed his way through the crowd to his friends. "Go get a room."

Jake grinned. "We thought we'd save money and just use your truck. You don't mind, do you?"

"Nah," Charlie winked as he pulled his new female acquaintance closer to his side. "Just don't take too long."

"The last phase of my plan is now complete. And that," Adrian said, as she swiveled around on her barstool with a triumphant smile for Kevin, "is how it's done."

Chapter Eighteen

"WHAT'S THE MATTER?"

Maggie had just delivered a steaming hot plate of double-decker nachos. Cassie wrinkled her nose at it as if it were the most unappetizing food she'd ever smelled.

"I thought you said you were craving these," Maggie said.

"I have been, but now that I've got them...." Cassie's voice trailed off as she gave Maggie an apologetic shrug.

"Mm-hmm."

Cassie's eyes narrowed suspiciously onto Maggie.

"What?" Cassie asked.

"Nothing," Maggie said while stealing a nacho off Cassie's plate. "It's just that I can only remember one other time when my double-decker nachos made you sick to your stomach."

Cassie's eyes nearly bugged out of her head as Maggie popped the nacho into her mouth.

"No," Cassie responded in disbelief.

"Why not? Unless you and Jake haven't...."

"Oh, we have."

Cassie blushed as fond memories of that night raced to the forefront of her mind.

"That night?" Adrian asked Kevin, her ears perked up as she scooted toward the edge of her barstool. "What night? Which one?"

"Oh." Adrian's mouth formed into a perfectly shaped letter "O" when it dawned on her. "It was the night of my plan, wasn't it?"

"Maybe," Kevin replied.

"So, Cassie is pregnant again?"

Adrian reminded Kevin of a child trying to get information out of a parent about their Christmas presents. He was almost about to give in to her too. Almost.

"Possibly," he said.

Adrian groaned. "Why do you do this to me?"

"Because I can," Kevin replied with a sly smile.

He slid his thumb underneath his chin while he appraised Adrian with his eyes.

"What?" she asked.

"You," he said.

"What about me?"

"I'm impressed by how you're handling all of this."

Adrian gave him a sideways glance.

"What do you mean by that?"

"I mean," Kevin said as he leaned forward, "a year or so ago, you would've completely Hulked out over this, but not now."

"Cassie's my best friend," she replied.

"And Jake was your husband."

"But now he's Cassie's."

Adrian glanced over her shoulder at her friend. "They deserve this, and I'm happy for them."

Lines of concern appeared on Adrian's face once she saw Cassie's cloud over.

"Although I'm not sure 'happy' is the word I'd use to describe Cassie right now."

No, Cassie thought. *I can't be pregnant again—already—can I?*

The rush of hope she felt nose-dived into crippling fear as her thoughts became consumed by loss.

What if it happens again? What if I lose this baby too?

"Uh-oh," Adrian said to Kevin. "She's swimming in the dark pool. We need to get her out before she drowns."

Maggie to the rescue.

"It's okay to be scared," Maggie said, covering Cassie's trembling hands with her own. "And who knows? I could be way off-base here. I mean, there has been a major flu bug going around, right, Tony?"

"Sure," Maggie's boyfriend replied, his mind obviously distracted as he snuck around behind her.

Maggie gave him a light kick in the shin, which started a facial fight between the two of them that ended with Maggie appearing to be the victor.

"I mean," Tony quickly backtracked, "yeah. Biggest flu outbreak in like a decade."

He looked to Maggie for approval. She sighed and turned back to Cassie, who seemed not to have heard any of their conversation.

"Have you talked to your mom lately?" asked Maggie.

That got Cassie's attention. Her eyes darkened while her expression transformed into a "You've got to be kidding me?" look.

"Okay, I'll take that as a 'no'."

"You know I have a better relationship with you than I do with her."

"Yeah," Maggie said as her mind drifted back to the morning Cassie had called her to pick her up from Jake's apartment, "I know. That's why I'm going to do a very motherly thing right now. Tony?"

"Yeah, babe?"

"Can you hold down the fort for a little while so I can go help Cassie with something?"

"Yes, ma'am, I can."

"Thanks, babe." Maggie stood on her tiptoes and gave Tony a kiss on the cheek. "All right," she said to Cassie, "let's go."

"Go where?" Cassie asked.

"To put your mind at ease."

*

"I can't believe you just did that," Cassie said as she sank back onto the headrest.

"I can," Adrian said as she popped up between the front seats of Maggie's vintage pickup truck.

"Well, someone had to," Maggie replied as she slipped behind the wheel, "since you wouldn't."

They were parked in a Piggly Wiggly parking lot, the closest store to the bar Maggie could think of. Cassie thought she could put an end to this game by refusing to play it, but she should've known better with Maggie.

"It was worth it, though," Maggie added with a devilish grin, "just to see the cashier's face when I came up to the checkout with all of these."

"How many did you buy?" Cassie asked while she stared openmouthed at the small paper bag that dangled from Maggie's fingertips.

"Enough so that we know for sure," Maggie said as she threw her truck into gear.

A brief, terrifying thought crossed Cassie's mind once she realized they were heading back down the same route they had taken to get there.

"We're not going back to the bar, are we?"

"Do you really think I'd make you do this there?"

Cassie remained awkwardly silent while her face spoke volumes.

"Wait; don't answer that," Maggie said.

Cassie laughed despite herself.

"So where are we going then?"

"My place. It's not far from the bar."

"This is kind of exciting," Adrian said to Kevin.

"Why's that?" Kevin asked.

"Because, in all the time Cass and I have known Maggie, we've never seen where she lives."

"Close your mouth," Maggie teased Cassie after they pulled into the underground, heated parking lot, "before you start catching flies."

Cassie's bottom lip eventually met with the top, but she remained in awe.

"You live in Party Harbor?"

"That's not the actual name of the condos," Adrian explained to Kevin, "but it is what everyone calls it."

"The Downtown Oasis—the perfect escape in the center of it all for the young, urban professional," Kevin recited. "Isn't that the tagline for it?"

"Yeah, it is," Adrian replied, her skeptical eyes still trained on Maggie. "But that is so not Tony and Maggie."

"What?"

Adrian jumped; Maggie's question sounded more like a response to her than to Cassie's reaction.

"Did I disappoint you?" Maggie joked. "Were you expecting something else, like a double-wide trailer or maybe a commune of hippie bikers?"

"N-o," Cassie stammered as she struggled to find the right words to explain herself.

"It's okay." Maggie smiled while she parked the truck in her designated spot and cut the engine. "I get it. If I were you, I'd be questioning it too."

"So?" Cassie asked, eagerly awaiting an explanation.

"Why here?"

"Uh…yeah."

"Well, it's close to the bar and it just works for us."

Cassie felt like she had crossed over into *The Twilight Zone* as she watched Maggie give a friendly wave to a young man in a three-piece suit who had just stepped out of the black BMW parked beside them.

"The place is full of mostly single, insomniac twenty-somethings who never complain about us coming in after two or three in the morning and making a bunch of noise because they're all still awake too."

"I guess you can't argue with that," Cassie said.

"Hey, like I always say: If it ain't broke, don't fix it right."

"Right."

"Now, let's get back to the real reason we're here, shall we?"

"I'd much rather keep learning more about you."

"I'm sure you would and you can, right after we get upstairs and you take your tests."

Cassie's heart sank, and it showed all over her face.

"It'll be all right," Maggie told Cassie, giving her hand a reassuring squeeze, "no matter what happens."

I hope you're right, Cassie thought as she nodded at Maggie just before Maggie gave her a gentle nudge forward.

Maggie unlocked the front door and ushered Cassie inside a condo that more closely resembled Maggie's lifestyle.

The floor was done in a deep brown hardwood. The efficient kitchen had all black appliances with a small, marble, granite-top island in the center with two black leather barstools positioned on its opposite side.

Beyond the kitchen was a space most people might have used as a dining room, but Maggie preferred to put her custom-made pool table there.

Cassie wanted to explore more, but Maggie prevented it by handing her a large, cold bottle of water from the fridge.

"Drink up," Maggie told her. "Bathroom is to your left."

Cassie uncapped the bottle and reluctantly began to chug the water while she grabbed the paper bag from Maggie, then headed begrudgingly down the hall.

A few minutes later, Cassie opened the bathroom door and was about to walk out when she looked back at the plastic stick on the counter that held her fate.

Part of me, Cassie thought, *wants so badly for that to be positive. But,* a deep sense of dread seized her while vivid memories of that moment in Coldstone—an ice cream shop she had refused to step foot inside since—grabbed hold of her and wouldn't let go, *there's a bigger part of me that's terrified it is.*

"Hey, Cass."

Maggie had kept her distance, but she felt as if Cassie might need her now.

"Yeah?" Cassie answered, her mind still diverted elsewhere.

"I forgot to tell you before that we have one rule here. You need to leave all negative vibes at the door; only positive energy is allowed inside."

"I don't think I can follow that rule right now."

"Sure you can. I'll even help you out. Just imagine," Maggie said as she placed her hands delicately on Cassie's stomach, "there may be a little mini-you or mini-Jake growing inside of you right now."

That made Cassie's lips twitch up into an irresistible smile.

"See, it's working already. Now, c'mon; let me show you around the rest of the place."

"What? Now?"

"Why not? You said you wanted to learn more about me, right?" Maggie raised an eyebrow.

Cassie strolled behind Maggie and found herself taking everything in. One thought lingered as she admired the framed posters that hung in the bedroom from every Sturgis Motorcycle Rally Maggie and Tony had rode to, and the pictures on the mantle of the solid rock fireplace of each of their motorcycles.

"Hey, Mag, can I ask you something?"

"Shoot," Maggie said while she racked the pool balls up for a quick game.

"Did you ever want to have kids of your own?"

"Sure I did," Maggie said as she handed Cassie a stick, "but thankfully, God knew none of the assholes I dated in the past had little swimmers smart enough to break through to impregnate me."

Adrian and Cassie burst out laughing.

"What?" Maggie grinned. "It's the truth."

"Oh, damn," Adrian said, wiping a stray tear of joy from the corner of her eye, "how I miss Maggie."

Oh, damn, Cassie thought as she regained her composure, only to be reminded of the absence of her best friend, *how I miss Adrian. You should be here right now, laughing your ass off right beside me.*

Cassie leaned over the pool table and pretended to set up her shot. She took aim and broke the balls apart, much like how she tried to separate Adrian from her mind and return to the subject at hand.

"But," Cassie asked Maggie, "what about Tony?"

"Ah, well, Tony," Maggie said as she sunk a striped ball into the corner pocket, "came into my life well after I made peace with all of that."

"And he's okay with it?"

"Yeah, he's cool with it. He's got to be," Maggie added with a wink, "if he wants me to keep him around. And," she paused to watch the cue ball she had shot graze the nine ball and stop a hair short of falling into the side pocket, "it all worked out in the long run for me anyway."

"How's that?" Cassie asked while she leaned against her pool stick.

"Because," Maggie slung her arm lovingly around Cassie's shoulders, "I got to be you girls' adopted mom instead."

"Aw." Adrian's hand flew over her heart.

The moment was interrupted by Cassie's cell phone ringing.

"Speaking of mothers," she said, sounding less than thrilled as she ignored the call. "I'm really not in the mood," Cassie said in response to the look on Maggie's face, "to listen to one of her uplifting sermons right now."

"Well, you would've had to cut her off even if you were because," Maggie's eyes darted back and forth between the directions on the box to the Harley Davidson clock on the wall, "it's time."

Chapter Nineteen

MAGGIE AND CASSIE HOVERED OVER the bathroom counter like a pair of scientists waiting to see if their lab experiment had actually worked.

Cassie's mouth went dry, even after all the water she had just drank.

"That can't be right; it's got to be a mistake."

"Well," Maggie said, "I'm no expert, but I would think four tests all with the same result is pretty accurate."

Cassie put her hand to her forehead and collapsed onto the toilet seat until the heat that scorched through her finally rescinded.

"So," Maggie treaded lightly as she knelt down beside Cassie, "are congratulations or condolences in order?"

"I don't know." Cassie sighed. "Let me get back to you if I make it to the delivery room."

"Hey, positive thoughts, remember?"

"Yeah, I know."

"Well, just wait till Jake finds out. He'll have more than enough positive energy for the both of you."

"No," Cassie said fiercely while her head snapped up to meet Maggie's eyes. "I do not want Jake to know anything about this yet. Promise me you will not say a word to him."

"Cassie!" Adrian and Maggie objected simultaneously.

"Maggie, please. Not one word."

"Maggie," Adrian warned, "don't give in to her. This is not a good idea. You have to know how wrong it would be to keep this from him."

Maggie was torn, but in the end, she was persuaded by Cassie's earnest, puppy dog eyes.

"All right, my lips are sealed, until you tell me otherwise."

"Ah, Maggie, no!" Adrian shouted, disappointed as her head flung forward into her hands.

"But," Maggie said, "if you drag this out like some worn-out soap opera storyline, I swear I'll sing like a canary to Jake the first chance I get."

Cassie held back her urge to laugh.

"I promise I'll tell him soon."

As soon as I know it's safe.

*

"What's up with Cass?" Jake shouted over the crowded bar to Maggie.

"What?" Maggie yelled back. She leaned as far forward as she could and even turned her ear toward him, but with all the people and the band kicking into high gear, it was pointless.

She gave Jake a sympathetic look of confusion before she got dragged back into the chaos of the impatient patrons desperate for another drink.

Fuck! Jake sighed as he backpedaled away from the bar. *Now what do I do?*

He raked his hands through his dark blonde hair while scanning the room for his wife.

She was still there, sitting on her stool, moping around like a teenager who just had her phone taken away from her and was now forced to actually communicate with the real world.

I don't get it. This is her favorite band; they're playing in her favorite bar. I even made sure to get us a table as close to them as possible, yet she's still pouting. What. The. Hell?

"Yeah, what the hell," Adrian said as Jake trudged over to Cassie. "I can't believe she still hasn't told him yet," Adrian went on before turning to Kevin. "I mean, it's been—what—at least a month now?"

"At least," Kevin said.

"And what's worse," Adrian was on a roll as she spoke to Jake, "is how clueless you are! It's so obvious. The signs are all right there in front of you, but you still can't piece them together."

Typical man, she thought, which resulted in a scowl from Kevin.

Adrian blew it off, her attention focused on Jake and what he was about to say.

"Don't do it," she warned him. "Don't let her bad mood seep into your words because once you say something, you can never take it back. Stop and think first, please."

Jake put his fist to his mouth.

"Can I get you something to drink?" he eventually asked Cassie, much to Adrian's relief.

It seemed to take all the energy in Cassie just to squint at him.

Jake forced himself to calm down long enough to make a drinking motion with his hands. She nodded; he waited for more but got nothing.

"Choose your words wisely," Adrian said.

A little more information would be nice, Jake thought, but what he said was:

"What would you like?"

"Sprite," said Cassie.

"Sprite?" Jake asked as if he had heard her wrong.

"Mm-hmm."

"With nothing else? Just Sprite?"

"Just Sprite."

"Okay."

Just Sprite, Jake thought as he zig-zagged through the throngs of people back to the bar. *Really? She's that pissed off at me that she won't even drink?*

Adrian groaned. "See, this is what I'm saying! You're looking at two plus two, but you keep coming up with eighteen!"

"It's not always about you and, even if it was, don't you think she'd be downing shots or something?"

Jake's thoughts leaned more toward his frustration in reaching the bar than the obvious explanation for his wife's behavior.

Damn people; damn lines. Is there even a fucking line, or is it just who can muscle their way in the fastest? Jesus, all this for a damn stupid Sprite.

Adrian went wild. Kevin took a step back, just in case her head really did explode.

"I can't believe it. He's totally tuned me out!"

"Well," Kevin put his hand over his mouth to hide his smile, "figure out a way to tune him back in to you."

He half-expected the heat from her glare to obliterate him.

"You're right."

"What?" he asked shocked that she agreed with him. "I mean, of course I am. Now what are you going to do about it?"

"Make him remember."

Jake suddenly spotted an opening—a clear path to the bar that wouldn't last long. He made a break for it, unaware that Adrian stood with her arms spread out in a brief barricade.

Jake was wedged neatly into the bar, like an involuntary member of a mosh pit. Maggie tried to keep the irritation out of her eyes while she waited for him to regain enough air in his lungs to give her his order.

"A Bud and a Sprite."

"A what?"

"Sprite!" Jake shouted as loud as he could.

The look Maggie gave him made him suspicious.

"What?"

Maggie faked hearing impairment before she disappeared to get his drinks.

"I know you hate going back," Adrian said as she squeezed in beside her husband, "but, Baby, you have to so you can understand."

The memory came to him from out of nowhere.

They were sitting at the bar at Valentino's—he and Adrian, Laura and Clint—ordering drinks.

It had been a tense night to begin with.

That night.

"Don't stop," Adrian told him. "Don't shake off the memories."

My mom was relaying everything everyone wanted back to the bartender....

"And?" Adrian coaxed him.

Adrian ordered the same thing.

Adrian flexed her fingers like a magician's assistant, revealing the end of an elaborate trick, but instead of applause, she got silence. She watched the wheels turning in her husband's mind as all the pieces started to fit together.

Adrian said it was because she was driving, Jake thought, *but I wasn't buying it. I wanted to call her on it too, but I never got the chance.*

"One Bud; one Sprite," Maggie announced as she set Jake's drinks in front of him.

The answer struck him like a bolt of lightning. His eyes leapt to Maggie's.

They were both thinking the exact same thing:

Oh, fuck.

Chapter Twenty

"JAKE!" MAGGIE SHOUTED. "WAIT!"

I am not missing another chance, Jake thought.

He snatched his drinks, then fought his way through the sea of people back to their table, determined to get a straight answer from his wife.

Unfortunately, Cassie had other ideas.

She stood up before Jake could even say a word.

"I'm ready to go home."

"What? Already?"

"Jake, please."

"You're kidding, right?"

"Jake." Adrian sensed some thoughtless words were about to come flying out of his mouth, but it was too late to stop him.

"You're ready to go home after I just spent a fucking lifetime waiting in line to get your damn soda?"

"Oh, shit." Adrian grimaced. "This isn't going to be good."

Cassie said nothing as she reached for her red solo cup. She chugged the soda down like a pro before she threw it—ice and all—

at Jake. Then Cassie turned on her heel and headed for the door without so much as a glance back at her husband.

Tony rushed over until Jake held up his hand to keep him back.

"Kevin?"

"Yeah?"

He could hear Adrian struggling to formulate her real question in her mind, plus find the courage to ask it out loud.

"I had a feeling," she began while she watched Jake jam his fists into his pockets and leave the bar with his chin up.

"But that's all it was, right?" She wouldn't turn around to look at him, afraid his eyes would give everything away no matter what he said. "Just a feeling?"

Adrian got her answer by the way Kevin set his hand on her shoulder. She shut her eyes, her head bowed slightly.

"Adrian," Kevin gently spoke her name.

She took a deep breath before turning to face him.

It took everything in him not to look away from her.

"We need to go after them," Adrian said.

"Whenever you're ready," Kevin replied.

"We can go now."

*

Cassie went straight to bed as soon as she and Jake got home. She didn't even bother kicking him to the couch. It didn't matter anyway; after tossing and turning for what felt like forever, Cassie gave up and went downstairs on her own where Adrian was waiting for her.

Babies were keeping both women awake.

Adrian hadn't really thought about it—the possibility of being pregnant. So much had happened since then, but now she couldn't switch her mind off it, just like Cassie.

Except Cassie knew she was carrying her baby, and now her mind wrestled with whether or not to tell Jake.

Cassie finally came to the conclusion, during the wee hours of the morning, to forego whatever sleep she may have gained to seek a Higher Power.

*

She parked her car in a spot as far away from the church as possible. It was about a half hour before the earliest morning Mass. Cassie knew her mother wouldn't be there; she always preferred the later services.

Cassie intended to go inside, but for some reason, she couldn't bring herself to get out of the driver's seat.

She sat with her hands around the steering wheel and stared up at the massive steeple as if seeing it for the first time.

Adrian sat beside her in the passenger seat, the same look of awe on her face.

Why? both women thought.

This place, Cassie thought wistfully, *was my everything when I was a kid. I can remember running up the aisle of this church every Christmas morning to show Jesus my new dolly, and sometimes,* Cassie laughed, *I'd make my parents take me to all the weekend Masses because there was always something else I forgot to tell Him after we left His house the last time.*

But now....

Cassie's eyes drifted slowly down from the steeple and onto the congregation that filtered through the parking lot.

A parade of Volvos, BMWs, and Mercedes were rolling in. Their owners stepped out wearing three-piece suits and fresh-off-the-runway dresses; their children followed behind them in single file, portraits of perfection without a wrinkle in their clothing or a speck of dirt on their wholesome faces.

Now, Cassie continued as she averted her eyes away from the red-carpet ceremony, *it feels like it's all for show.*

Adrian pushed herself up in her seat, shoved aside her self-pity, and looked at her friend as if she had just declared country music the root of all evil.

"Whoa."

"What?" Kevin played along from the backseat.

"I don't know about you," Adrian replied, "but I've never had any illusions about organized religion."

"I can't say I've ever really been a fan of it myself," Kevin replied.

"So you and I are on the same page, but Cassie...she's never been like that. She may not be a devout Catholic, but she's always had faith. Until now. And to see her like this...it's just not right."

"So," Kevin asked while he rested his chin on his arms, "what do you think we should do to fix it?"

"Well, getting her out of here would be a good start."

Cassie glanced down at her sweatshirt, blue jeans, and sneakers.

I don't fit in here anymore, she thought.

She turned the key in the ignition and let the car idle for a moment before she eased out of her parking spot.

Cassie locked eyes with a common, middle-aged woman who bolted out in front of her car as if she were afraid Cassie might run her over.

The woman looked vaguely familiar, but Cassie couldn't remember why. It bothered her until she reached the exit, then was immediately forgotten when she pulled into oncoming traffic and proceeded down the busy street.

Adrian felt her friend's mind clutter with doubt and worry again. She wanted to help her clear it; the problem was how.

Adrian touched her friend's shoulder; Cassie swiped at it, thinking an annoying fly had landed there.

Then Adrian sat sideways in her seat and stared directly at Cassie, her eyes narrowing more the harder she tried to telepathically send her positive vibes into her best friend's mind, but all she did was make Kevin bust out laughing.

"What?" Adrian asked, rolling her eyes in his direction.

"Nothing," Kevin replied as he wiped the tears away with the curve of his finger. "I've just never seen you use that technique before."

He was dangerously close to losing it again when Adrian glared at him.

"Well, what else am I supposed to do? I've got nothing," she told him.

"How about not trying so hard and just going with whatever feels right?"

"Oh, of course," she said. "Why didn't I think of that?"

He lowered his eyes. "Just relax and quit putting so much pressure on yourself. This isn't a game show; you don't have to have the answer within a minute or less."

"I know." Adrian sighed and ran her fingers through her hair. *I just wish I did.*

She sat back in her seat and watched the traffic turn into a gridlock at the red light.

Cassie leaned over to change the radio station, and that's when it hit Adrian.

I've got it!

She sprang forward and lunged for the radio dial.

The signal faded. Cassie gritted her teeth while she punched several other buttons to no avail.

That's what I get for trying to listen to local stations, she thought before she switched to Sirius.

And that's when she heard it: Blake Shelton's "God Gave Me You."

The song made her think of Jake, and it swept away all of the clutter that had built up in her mind.

Cassie remembered the night of Adrian's show and the moment Jake first saw the last photograph she had taken of him.

He fell apart that night, she thought. *He trusted me with that, and he didn't care who saw it or what anyone thought about it. So, how can I possibly keep this from him now? He'll be there to catch me just like I was for him.*

Adrian folded her arms with a triumphant grin.

"See; I told you," said Kevin, gloating.

"Lucky guess," Adrian replied with a wink.

A horn honked behind Cassie to remind her of the green light. She waved her hand out the window in apology as she sailed through the intersection, her heart lighter now that she knew what to do.

Cassie pulled into the garage, energized and urgently needing to use the bathroom.

She wasted no time waiting for the elevator and flew up the stairs to their apartment. She flung the front door open, careful not to let it bang against the wall, even though she knew Jake would still be out like a light.

Then Cassie made a mad dash to the bathroom, unaware that her husband had been watching her from the railing the entire time.

Cassie was relieved she had made it in time, until she saw the spotting.

It wasn't much blood, but it was enough for her to know.

Her head fell into her hands and remained there until a knock at the door startled her.

"Hey," Jake called from the other side, "what did you do? Fall in?"

"No." Her voice was barely audible. She cleared her throat and tried again. "No."

She stood up and checked her reflection in the mirror before she opened the door.

"I'm good," Cassie said with a tight smile.

Jake studied his wife's face for a moment before he replied.

"No," he said, "you definitely are not."

He opened his arms to her, and she fell into them without a second thought.

Adrian glanced over her shoulder to ask Kevin something, but he had vanished from sight. She faced forward, refusing to see what she felt was happening beyond those walls.

Kevin immersed himself in the warmth of the strengthening sunlight as he clutched a tiny bundle close to him. The horizon exploded into a breathtaking array of colors when he brought him home.

Tears welled up in Adrian's eyes and her heart filled with emptiness while she wondered if he had done the same for her and Jake's child.

I wish I would've known sooner, Jake thought as he pulled his wife closer to him.

I wish I would've told you sooner, Cassie thought to herself.

Chapter Twenty-One

"ARE YOU SURE YOU WANT to do this?" Jake asked as he came slowly up behind his wife and wrapped his arms around her waist.

"I have to," Cassie said with a defeated shrug.

"No, you don't." He turned her away from their bedroom mirror so she was facing him. "You can tell them you're sick, or that your husband needs you to stay in bed with him."

That prompted a flicker of a smile from Cassie.

"Nice try," she said as she stood on her tiptoes to kiss him, "but I can't miss Dominick's first birthday."

It's bad enough I've barely seen him as it is, Cassie thought.

She had planned on spending so much time with little Dom.

But that was before.

Cassie had gone over to visit a few times, whenever Mama Bear Kathleen wasn't around, but seeing Dominick just hit too close to home for her.

Every baby quality he exuded, from his little mousy cries, to the sudden smiles that may or may not have been gas, and even the scent of him caused her mind to go to a place she didn't want to travel to.

All the what ifs and maybes; all the possibilities lost. Once Cassie went there, it could be a very long road back.

Even Benji's girls—Kayla and Caroline—were asking where Auntie Cass had been. Benji could only use the "She's not feeling good" card so much.

There were no more excuses. It was time for Cassie to face all of it: baby Dom, the kids, her family, and the glaring fact that none of them were aware of her second miscarriage.

Telling Jake had drained Cassie, and the thought of reliving it every time she told the tale did not appeal to her, so they agreed to keep it to themselves.

Which was why today was more stressful than it should've been.

But Jake promised to be there with her for as long or as short of a time as she wanted to stay there.

The party was at Nicky and Kathleen's house, and knowing Kathleen, she'd have everything planned right down to the last second. Cassie hoped they could make a quick appearance and sneak out as soon as baby Dom dug into his cake, wearing as much protective gear as Kathleen could possibly put on him to keep him clean.

That was the plan anyway.

And we all know how much God loves plans, Cassie thought anxiously.

*

Cassie felt the shift in affluence the moment the tires on Jake's truck rolled into De Pere. She crouched down lower in her seat, feeling smaller and smaller with each mansion they drove past.

Heads turned—and not in admiration—at the sound of the truck's pipes roaring through the quaint, residential neighborhood.

Jake fed off it, rising higher in his seat, and nudged Cassie to do the same.

She stared at him—her cheek smooshed comfortably into her fist—as if he were her happy place, her home.

"What?" Jake asked when he caught her looking at him.

"Nothing." Cassie blushed like a lovesick teenager. "Just that I love you."

"Love you too." Jake winked at her. "So quit acting like you're embarrassed to be seen with me. Besides, we're almost there."

That seemed to suck the joy right out of Cassie's smile. Her stomach lurched, like she was riding in a roller-coaster car that was just about to drop off the edge, as they wound their way past the soccer field and into the familiar cul-de-sac.

The life snuck slowly back into her smile when she saw the basketball hoop in the driveway.

Nicky put that up as soon as he found out they were having a boy, Cassie thought.

She was still fascinated by it when she jumped out of the truck, which left her completely unaware of the tag team that planned to plow into her until she heard their warrior cry:

"Auntie Cass! Auntie Cass!"

There was no time to brace for impact. Cassie felt the full weight of both of her nieces upon her after they launched themselves at her. She couldn't maintain her balance, and all three of them toppled over onto the perfectly manicured lawn.

The silence that followed was deafening. Jake came around the front of the truck, then stopped shocked, both because his wife had just gone down like a WWE wrestler, and it was the first time she had really interacted with the kids since....

He didn't know what to think when he heard the laughter.

Oh, shit; she's lost it. She's hysterical.

But then, after Jake really listened to it, he realized it was more of a joyful noise. Something so infectious even he wasn't immune to it.

"Okay, okay," Cassie said between gasps. "I give."

"All right, girls, c'mon," Jake intervened. "It's time to let Auntie Cass up and give her some air."

They reluctantly rolled off her and were getting back onto their feet when Sara came outside.

"Girls! What in the world is going on out here?"

"Nutting, Mommy," Kayla said.

"We're just playing with Auntie Cass," Caroline chimed in.

"Mm-hmm," Sara replied while she folded her arms. "Playing."

"It's all good, Sara," Cassie said while she brushed the grass off her jeans. "They were just excited to see me."

"I got that," Sara said, smiling. "But we need to dial down our enthusiasm a notch or two, especially," she leaned conspiratorially closer to Cassie, "before the photographer comes and Queen Kathleen decides it's off with our heads."

"What now?" Cassie asked.

"A photographer," Adrian repeated, not believing what she had heard, "for a one-year-old's birthday party?"

"Yep," Sara replied to Cassie. "She hired a professional photographer for the day. Which is why," she knelt down beside her daughters to talk to them, "we need to be on our best behavior today, okay?"

"Okay, Mommy," Kayla said, nodding her head.

"We'll be good," Caroline followed suit.

"Thank you, babies," Sara said, wrapping her arms around both of them in a quick embrace.

"Now, why don't you two go find something quiet to play in the backyard until it's time for baby Dominick to wake up from his nap?"

Cassie shot Sara a look; Sara shrugged.

"Apparently he can't veer off his schedule, even on his birthday," Sara explained once the girls were out of earshot.

"Well, of course not," Cassie replied. "One missed nap will make him crabby for the rest of the day, and that'll wreck Kathleen's perfect family photos."

"Oh, God," Sara laughed while she slung her arm around Cassie, "how I've missed you."

They continued up the balloon-lined path to the front door, leaving Jake behind with his hands full of food and presents.

"No, no, that's okay," he told them, even though he knew they weren't listening, "don't worry about me. I don't need any help. I can carry all of this myself."

Cassie made it through the front door and halfway down the hallway before she froze like a deer sensing the presence of a predator.

"She's here, isn't she?" Cassie asked Sara.

Sara was struggling to come up with an answer when the smell of Julia's barbeque and her distinct voice drifted toward them from the kitchen.

"You okay?" Sara asked. "We could sneak out to the backyard if you want."

"No. Thanks," Cassie replied with a reassuring smile. "I'm going to have to face her sooner or later."

"She hasn't seen her mom since that day in the hospital, right?" Adrian asked Kevin.

"Right," Kevin quietly concurred.

"Oh, boy."

"Yeah. Oh, boy."

Cassie rounded the corner into the kitchen and came head to ankle with baby Dominick, who had gone beyond the perimeters of his freshly washed flannel blanket on the floor.

He looked up at her with his soft, innocent brown eyes and said, "Ma-ma."

Cassie became paralyzed by her emotions. The room went devoid of sound. She felt claustrophobic, as if the walls had closed in around her. Baby Dominick zoomed into close-up range of her, but instead of seeing him, all Cassie saw was the baby she had lost. Then she blinked; her vision doubled and both of her babies appeared before her eyes.

Instinct took over once the shock wore off. Cassie fled, knocking Dominick gently over onto his heavily cushioned, diapered butt.

The baby cried—more from surprise than harm—which caused Kathleen to bolt out of her chair and straight to her son.

Jake had just entered the hallway when he jumped out of his wife's way, seconds before she barreled past him.

He continued cautiously forward until he locked eyes with Kathleen.

She held her baby protectively to her chest as if Cassie had purposely harmed him. Her jaw was set in a hard, stern line as her eyes went dead cold. She flicked her chin at Jake as if she were a queen and he a mere peasant unworthy of an explanation for her actions.

And that set Jake off.

"Jake," Adrian put her hands on his shoulders and tried to push him back, but it was like trying to move a brick wall.

"Jake, please don't—don't give in to this. Walk away; go check on Cassie. Please."

Jake felt the push and pull of his conscience pulsating through him, but in the end, he didn't follow it.

"Here's your fucking food," he said as he slammed the bowl of potato salad down onto the kitchen table. "I hope you choke on it."

He didn't stick around to hear Kathleen's response, but Sara did.

"What kind of man uses that kind of language at a child's birthday party?" Kathleen asked, her voice filled with disapproval.

"The kind," Sara replied, "whose wife had a miscarriage and expected people not to be so thoughtless."

Sara said this before she realized Kayla had just come in from the backyard through the sliding door.

"Mommy, what's a miscarriage?"

*

Cassie sat rim-rod straight in the truck's passenger seat, zombified. There was so much raw emotion charging through her that her entire body trembled as if it couldn't find an outlet for all of it.

Adrian sat cross-legged in the driver's seat, facing her friend with her fingertips meeting on the bridge of her nose. "So there's nothing we can do for her?" she asked Kevin hopelessly as she lowered her hands.

Kevin sighed. "We can't always take their pain away from them. That's not our job."

"Then what exactly is our job then?" Adrian snapped.

"Our job," Kevin replied, "is to be there for them through the process."

Adrian let her head fall back against the seat just as Kevin yanked her into the back beside him.

Adrian was ready to let Kevin have it when she saw Jake storming toward the truck.

"Jesus fucking Christ," Jake muttered under his breath after he practically tore the door open, "that bitch is a real piece of work. Strutting around like a fucking queen bee. Who does she think she is, Beyoncé?"

That elicited a loud snort of laughter from Cassie that caught them both off guard.

They stared awkwardly at each other for a moment. Adrian leaned forward to place her hands and head lovingly on her friend's shoulder.

"Well," Cassie replied, "I guess we better get out of here before she sicks the cul-de-sac security team on us."

Adrian grinned at the same time Cassie did.

"And we can't have that now, can we?" Jake asked as he reached for his wife's hand.

*

"What are we doing back here?" Adrian whined to Kevin as they stood in Kathleen and Nicky's backyard. "Cassie needs me."

"You're needed more here," Kevin replied.

"To do what? Give pointers to the photographer?"

Everyone had gathered in the backyard where Kathleen held Dominick on her lap in a chair surrounded by presents in all different shapes and sizes. The photographer staked her claim on the perfect spot in front of them so she wouldn't miss a single moment with her camera.

"It's not up to me," Kevin said as he leveled his glare at Adrian. "If you have a problem with it, you have to take it up with Him."

Adrian sighed as she sat down on the end of the miniature plastic slide.

"Fine," she pouted with her chin in her hands. "I'll just sit here and wait till I'm needed."

Adrian suddenly felt the cold draft of a shadow fall over her. She looked up to see Caroline standing before her with her arms crossed and her foot tapping loudly on the lawn.

"S'cuze me," she said angrily.

Caroline was staring right at Adrian. Adrian looked back at her in confusion.

"Move, now," Caroline said louder this time, causing some of the guests to stare their way, "so my baby can slide!"

Adrian was speechless; it had been a long time since anyone other than Kevin had actually seen her, much less spoken to her.

Kathleen had gotten wind of the commotion and did not look happy about it. Sara rushed over to her daughter to diffuse the situation before it got any worse.

"Caroline Rose Adler, what is going on over here?"

"She won't move, Mommy!"

"Who, baby?" Sara asked as she knelt down to be eye-level with her girl.

"The dark-haired lady. Right there!" Caroline pointed at the bottom of the slide where Adrian sat. "Make her move, Mommy! Make her move!"

Okay, Sara thought as she stood back up, her eyes focused on the empty slide. *Now her imaginary friends are at the party too. Why not?*

Sara covered her mouth with her fist while she tried to figure out the right way to handle this.

Like a parent, she thought before she took a deep breath and dived in.

"Caro, what have I always told you? If you want something, don't be…"

"De-anding," Caroline mumbled unhappily.

Sara stifled a laugh at her daughter's pronunciation.

"That's right. Don't be demanding. So maybe if you ask the dark-haired lady nicely, she'll move for you. Okay?"

"Okay, Caroline grumbled.

Adrian watched Caroline in awe as she kicked the toe of her sandal into the ground before she turned to Adrian with her eyes on her feet.

"Sorry, lady." Caroline raised her eyes up to meet Adrian's. "But could you p'ease move so my baby can slide?"

Adrian pressed her lips together in amusement. She glanced at Kevin, who returned her expression with a playful wave of his hand, indicating she should move along.

"Oh!" she said first to Kevin before turning to Caroline. "Oh, yes! Sure. I'm sorry. I didn't realize I was in your way."

"Thank you." Caroline beamed after Adrian stood up and made her way to Kevin, just as Julia was approaching Caroline and Sara.

The wind picked up as the two women crossed paths. Julia rubbed her arms; the breeze sent chills through her body.

"Caroline, aren't you cold?" Julia asked.

"No," Caroline said while she pushed her baby down the slide. "I'm good."

"Well, Grandma's not. I need you to come sit on my lap and warm me up while Dominick opens his presents, okay?"

"Okay. Can my baby Chloe come too?"

"Of course she can, sweetheart."

And off they went, leaving Sara staring at the slide, wondering who her daughter saw and why.

"C'mon, Mommy!" Caroline shouted.

"I'm coming, baby," Sara answered while she tore her eyes away from the spot where a dark-haired lady had supposedly sat.

There's nothing to worry about, Sara thought. *It's just her imaginary friend. That's all.*

"I'm coming," Sara said, not as loudly this time.

*

"How many more presents are left?" Adrian asked as she threw her head back listlessly.

"Only one," said Kevin, "and it's big."

His tone caused Adrian to snap to attention.

She hung back beneath the weeping willow tree along the fence line so as not to disturb Caroline again, but now she was drawn to the main attraction.

Nicky and Kathleen sat close enough together to be joined at the hip. Kathleen held Dominick on her lap while Nicky held the last, small, slim, perfectly wrapped gift on his.

Dominick lunged for the shiny gold bow on top.

Nicky tugged the box closer to him and just out of his son's reach, which made Dominick erupt with laughter.

That's when Adrian caught the look that passed between Nicky and Kathleen, and her heart took a freefall.

"Oh no. Don't tell me."

Chapter Twenty-Two

KATHLEEN LOOSENED HER GRIP ON Dominick so he could attack the bow and flip the top of the box off along with it.

Nicky peeled back the white tissue paper, and in his most animated, baby-like voice—which normally would have irritated the hell out of Kathleen—revealed the gift to Dominick before holding it up for everyone else to see.

It took a moment for most of the people to understand what was so special about the dark blue onesie, until they read what it said:

I AM THE BIG BROTHER

The backyard erupted into shrieks of joy and thunderous applause. Nicky and Kathleen were instantly mobbed, bringing Dominick to tears that could only be quieted by his being placed into Grandpa Benny's arms.

No one seemed to notice the more reserved partygoers except for Adrian.

While Benji was slapping his little brother on the back and teasing him with inappropriate jokes, Sara stayed back as one thought wormed its way into her mind:

Thank God Cass isn't here.

Adrian felt a similar vibe across the yard where Julia sat with Caroline still on her lap.

"Okay," Adrian said, "Sara, I can understand, but why isn't Julia doing cartwheels across the lawn? She is Kathleen's second mother after all."

"Grandma," Caroline said, "aren't you 'cited?"

"Oh yes, honey; I am excited," Julia replied.

"Then why do you look so sad?"

"Everything okay over here?" Ben asked as he came over, bouncing Dominick on his shoulder.

"Grandma's sad."

"No, Grandma's not sad," Julia corrected her. "I'm just not feeling well."

"You were fine earlier," Ben said.

"I know. Maybe I've just been out in the sun too long today."

"Do you want me to take you home?"

"That might not be a bad idea."

"Oh, please," Adrian scoffed. "Too much sun, my—"

"Adrian," Kevin cautioned.

She pressed her lips together tightly while she searched for a better choice of words.

"...good God."

"Do you mind if we make one stop on the way?" Julia asked her husband.

"Where is she planning on stopping?" Adrian asked, her eyes bugged out in horror.

*

"You sure you don't want me to run in and get your ginger ale for you?" Benjamin asked Julia as they sat in the grocery store parking lot.

"No offense, but I think I can find it way faster than you could."

"All right. I tried."

"I won't be gone long. I promise."

Julia wasn't lying. Her stomach really hadn't been feeling good, ever since Nicky and Kathleen had made their big baby announcement.

It had just triggered something inside of her. Julia thought if she broke away even for just a few minutes inside the grocery store, it might help her regroup, clear her mind, and calm her churning stomach.

And then she ran into Lydia.

Julia snagged the last bottle of Vernors on the shelf and was on a mission to the checkout when Lydia and her cart came at her from out of nowhere.

"Oh, hey, Julia!" Lydia exclaimed. "How are you?"

Julia manufactured a smile she hoped Lydia couldn't tell wasn't real.

"Good," Julia replied.

Keep it short and simple, she told herself.

Julia knew all too well that Lydia was the biggest gossip this side of the Fox River, and anything she said to her could and would be used against her somehow.

"Good," Julia said again as she tried to come up with an exit strategy.

"Well, I have to get going. Ben's waiting for me, but we'll have to catch up sometime after Mass again soon."

Julia thought that was it. She was walking away when she heard Lydia call out like an eager reporter with a juicy tidbit:

"Speaking of Mass, I could've swore I saw Cassie in the church parking lot—alone—not too long ago."

That stopped Julia in her tracks.

Keep it together, she told herself while slowly turning around to face Lydia. *Don't lose it in front of her.*

"My God," Kevin said, "she sounds just like me."

"Hmm, a woman putting up a brave front," Adrian replied with a raised eyebrow. "Imagine that."

Kevin let her comment go; he was too caught up in the very convincing performance Julia was putting on.

"Really?" Julia asked Lydia. "When was this?"

Lydia became tongue-tied by Julia's assuredness.

"Oh...um...I don't know, not too long ago. Maybe a week or two. It was right before eight o'clock Mass. I...uh...I was on my way inside when I saw her in her car."

"Oh, yes," Julia acted as if it were all coming back to her now. "We were going to go to church together, but we got our wires crossed on the time."

"Hmm, well it looked like more than just wires crossed to me. In fact, I was going to go over to check on her, but she flew out of the parking lot before I had the chance."

"Poor thing," Lydia continued on after Julia didn't respond, "she's been through so much lately. Give her my best the next time you see her, would you please? And let her know we're all praying for her."

Lydia's words struck Julia like a bolt of lightning, knocking down her shield.

"Julia," Lydia reached out to her, "are you all right?"

"What just happened?" Adrian asked Kevin.

Julia found herself back in time, holed up in her bedroom after she had come home from college. She could hear people talking about her in hushed voices just beyond the door:

"The poor thing. Has she told you anything yet?"

"No, not a word."

"Well, just let her know we're all thinking about her and praying for her."

"Yeah right," Julia had thought as she buried herself deeper under the blankets, *"like all your prayers are really going to help."*

Adrian's jaw dropped at that. She turned to Kevin, her face twisted in confusion. She couldn't even find the words to express it. Every time she tried, it came out sounding like a dying car trying to sputter to life one last time.

Kevin appreciated the show, until he saw Julia doing the same thing.

She backed away from Lydia like a cornered criminal.

"Julia?" Lydia asked, her voice filled with concern.

Julia still couldn't speak. She gave Lydia an apologetic wave as she dashed for the exit, then suddenly rerouted to the checkout to pay for her ginger ale. She didn't even care what Lydia thought or reported to everyone else about this incident. All Julia cared about was getting home.

Benjamin was shocked when he saw her.

"My God, Jules, you look worse than when you went in!"

"I feel like it too," she mumbled.

Benjamin sighed. "I knew I should've gone in."

"Can we just get home please?" Julia asked as politely as she could.

"I'll go as fast as I can."

"All right," Adrian said to Kevin, "you need to explain that to me now, please."

"All in good time," he replied.

"No, that's not an answer."

"Well, it's the only one I've got for you."

"Why is it you can know everything but I can't?"

"Who says I know everything?"

"You know more than I do."

"Patience, my dear," Kevin said with an inkling of a smile, "patience. You'll know when you need to know."

"And until then," Adrian groaned, feeling as worn-out as Julia, who pressed her forehead against the window, "you're just going to leave me hanging, aren't you?"

"'Fraid so," said Kevin.

Chapter Twenty-Three

"**M**OMMY?" CAROLINE ASKED.

"Yes, baby?" Sara replied while attempting to buckle her youngest into her car seat.

"Can we stop and tell Auntie Cass and Uncle Jake about the new baby?"

"Yeah, Mommy," Kayla interjected, "can we please?"

"*Please*?" both girls drew the word out into one long, loud syllable.

Sara and Benji shot questioning looks at each other between the front and back seats. Neither knew how to respond, but the girls' incessant plea was becoming unbearable.

"Okay, okay," Benji finally gave in. "We'll go see Auntie Cass and Uncle Jake."

Sara eventually shook off her stunned expression to add, "but we're not going to stay if Auntie Cass isn't feeling good. Understood?"

"Understood," the girls replied together in disappointment.

"Mommy?"

"Yes, Kayla-bear?"

"How come everybody's getting sick today?"

"I don't know," Sara said, looking directly at her husband as she slid into the passenger seat beside him, "must be a bug going around."

Benji fell into a loud coughing fit before he pulled their vehicle away from the curb.

*

Jake and Cassie had been doing a strange dance ever since they had gotten home. They weren't mad at each other, but they were communicating only in hand gestures or muffled grunts and groans.

So, when the buzzer went off, Cassie let out a desperate moan. When it rang again, Jake emerged from the kitchen with his plate in hand, his half-made sandwich on it, and grunted at his wife as if to ask her what she wanted him to do.

Cassie shook her head vehemently to ignore it until she heard her nieces.

"Auntie Cass, Uncle Jake, are you there? P'ease let us in! P'ease!"

Cassie smiled and nodded her approval to her husband.

"T'anks!" the girls yelled after Jake pushed the button to let them in.

Cassie eased herself off the couch and made her way to the door to unlock it, the sound of little feet making a big impact down the hallway.

She flung the door open mere seconds before the girls got there.

"Auntie Cass, are you feeling okay?" Kayla asked.

"'Cause Mommy says we can't stay if you're not," Caroline said.

Cassie glanced up at Sara, who rolled her eyes at her daughters' lack of subtlety.

"I am much better now," Cassie said.

"Yeah! That means we can tell them, right, Mommy?" Kayla asked.

Sara and Benji exchanged a nervous glance.

"What?" Cassie asked.

"We're gonna have a new baby cousin!" Caroline blurted out before her parents had a chance to stop her.

"Really?" Cassie asked, acutely aware of her brother and sister-in-law's eyes avoiding hers.

"Yeah," Kayla said, "and this time I hope they have a girl!"

Cassie tried to disguise her reaction, but it didn't work.

"Auntie Cass, you look just like Grandma did when she heard," Caroline said. "You're not getting sick again, are you?"

"Sick? Me? No, honey. I'm just really tired is all."

Caroline made a face as if Cassie had just told her a complicated riddle she couldn't figure out.

"What's that face for?" Cassie asked.

"Nutting," Caroline answered just before her face cleared with clarity.

She had an idea and was quick to share it with her big sister, who instantly approved.

"Mommy," Kayla asked, "can we go get something out of the car quick, p'ease?"

"As long as you have an adult go with you, sure," Sara said.

"I'll go," Benji offered.

"Oh, my God, I am so sorry," Sara apologized to Cassie the second the girls were out of earshot.

"It's all right," Cassie replied. "They were excited."

"I know, but still."

"It's okay. Really."

Cassie truly believed that too, especially when she felt Jake squeeze her shoulder, making all the tension in her muscles just seem to melt away. Her euphoria didn't last long.

Kayla and Caroline bounded triumphantly up the stairs with their dad lagging behind them.

"Close your eyes, Auntie Cass!" Kayla shouted.

"We have a sup-ise for you," Caroline said.

"A surprise?" Cassie turned her head curiously behind her to Jake. "For me?"

"Well, I guess it can be for Uncle Jake too, right, Caro?"

Caroline nodded her head eagerly.

"So should I close my eyes too?" Jake asked the girls.

They looked at each other before giving their unanimous response. "Uh-huh!"

Jake arched an eyebrow inquisitively down at his wife. She shrugged, just as clueless as he was.

"C'mon, guys," Caroline whined. "You got to close your eyes... p'ease."

"Okay," Cassie told her while she elbowed Jake. "We're closing our eyes."

She didn't know what to expect when her nieces told her she could open them again, but nothing could have prepared her for it even if she had.

"Surprise!" the girls shouted seconds later.

Cassie stared blankly down at the baby doll Caroline held out to her.

"Caro, that's your baby Chloe doll; the only thing you asked Santa for last year for Christmas. *And the only thing your mom and I drove all the way to Toyland in The Mall of America for, after we camped out in front of The Fox River Mall on Black Friday only to learn they were all sold out of them, and the backorder list was a mile long on Cyber Monday.* Don't you want her anymore?" Cassie asked.

"Yeah, but I want to share her with you too, but just until you and Uncle Jake have another baby of your own. Then maybe you won't feel so sad about God having to take your first baby back home to heaven with him."

Her niece's words—so simple and innocent—nearly knocked Cassie off her feet. Jake captured her in his arms, his lips on her cheek the only comfort she craved.

"Are we in trouble?" Kayla asked as she glanced nervously around at her parents, "'cause if we are, it was all Caro's idea."

"No, baby," said Sara, smiling, "you're not in trouble."

"We're so proud of both of you in fact," Benji said, "that we're going to stop at Dairy Queen on the way home."

"Really?" the girls squealed with excitement.

"Yes, really," Benji told them, "but we have to leave right now, okay?"

"No," Caroline said, "not till Auntie Cass says she'll take care of baby Chloe for me."

"Oh, my gosh," Cassie said as she knelt down to accept the baby doll from her niece. "Yes, I promise I'll take very good care of her for you."

"I know you will." Caroline beamed before she turned to her parents with a confident air. "'Kay, we can go now."

Cassie watched in awe as Caroline skipped out the front door ahead of her mom and sister.

"You have amazing daughters," she told her brother.

"Yeah, well," he paused to squeeze his sister's shoulder, "they learned from their amazing aunt."

Cassie responded to him with a "mmph" and a half-hearted smile.

She remained down on bended knee long after Benji left.

Oh, God, please, no, Cassie thought. *I don't have the strength to face him now.*

Please, Jake thought, *help me come up with the right thing to say to her.*

"You know," Adrian told Jake, "we don't always need to hear the right words; sometimes we just want arms."

Cassie bowed her head and kept her eyes closed as she felt her husband draw nearer to her.

No, no, no, Cassie thought.

"C'mon, Cass," Jake said while he crouched down before his wife and lifted her chin up slowly with his thumb and forefinger. "Look at me."

She begrudgingly obliged.

"You are amazing."

Cassie tried to shake her head in denial, but Jake wouldn't let her.

"Truly amazing."

"And there it is," Adrian said to Kevin.

"There what is?" Kevin asked her.

"That…thing…he does when he speaks to you that just sucks you in. I…I just can't explain it."

Neither could Cassie, but she felt it too, and it compelled her to look deeper into Jake's eyes.

It was like two live wires crossing paths during the height of a violent storm. Everything that had built up inside of them all day long since they had left for the birthday party boiled over into a passionate rage that neither could control.

Jake kissed Cassie voraciously, as if her lips were a long-awaited craving he could finally consume.

Cassie responded by ripping Jake's shirt apart. Her hands roamed wildly over his chest. She wanted to touch every single inch of him, but her mind reeled as to where to start.

They toppled carelessly backwards onto the floor, their lovemaking temporarily halted by the sound of a crying baby.

Their heads turned toward the source of the sound: Caroline's baby Chloe face down on the floor beside them.

Cassie started to reach for it when Jake grabbed her wrist and held her arm firmly in place over her head.

"Oh, no, you don't," he told her as his lips brushed against her ear and sent shivers down her spine.

"But I promised Caroline," Cassie groaned.

"Her doll is fine right where she is. Trust me."

"But...."

Cassie's protest turned feeble after Jake leaned heavily into her. She gasped in ecstasy, the doll's welfare long forgotten.

"You know," Adrian said to Jake, "when I told you sometimes we just want arms, this isn't exactly what I had in mind."

Chapter Twenty-Four

C ASSIE SAT ON THE EDGE of her seat in Dr. Kerrigan's office, her knee jittering worse than if she had just drank an entire pot of coffee.

This is ridiculous!

Cassie had been seeing Dr. Kerrigan ever since she had hit puberty, but this was the first time the doctor had asked her to come back to her office.

But that doesn't necessarily mean bad news, right...? Oh, c'mon; who am I kidding? Of course it's bad news. Cassie groaned. *It was stupid of me even to make this appointment. What was I thinking?*

Adrian sat down in the chair beside her friend and argued compassionately with her.

"You were thinking you might be pregnant, and there's nothing wrong with that."

I still should've known better.

Adrian tipped her head back and growled at the ceiling just as the door creaked open.

No expectations.... Cassie prepared herself while she discreetly tried to slide her hand over her knee to calm it.

Her leg steadied as soon as she saw the sympathetic expression on her gynecologist's face.

...no disappointments.

Cassie pressed her lips together into her patented, practiced smile.

Yeah, right.

She stood up to leave when Dr. Kerrigan stopped her.

"Cassie, wait, please."

"Why? What else is there for us to talk about?"

"Your options."

"Options."

The word split in two as it fell flat from her lips like a deflated balloon.

Dr. Kerrigan was quick to comfort Cassie, but her words fell on deaf ears. All Cassie heard was that one single word that only grew uglier the louder it rang out in her mind:

OPTIONS.

Cassie cringed. It was the like the word was mocking her, telling her she had failed.

Your dream is over, it told her. Done. Finished. You have no choice now but to discuss your options. Go with Plan B—the one thing you never wanted to do unless there was absolutely no other... OPTION.

"No, no," Adrian protested, rising beside Cassie like a Phoenix from the ashes. "Stop this. I know what you're trying to do to her, and I'm not about to let it happen. I will not let the darkness take you," Adrian said as she looked down into her best friend's eyes. "But I need you to fight for yourself too. Now, c'mon! Stop listening to the darkness and start hearing your doctor. Now."

It was as if Dr. Kerrigan had been underwater and just now come up to the surface where Cassie could hear her loud and clear.

"I'm not saying you and Jake can never have kids of your own."

"So," Cassie dragged the word out as if afraid to finish her question, "what are you saying then?"

"I'm saying," the doctor explained while she reached across her desk to place her hand over Cassie's, "you're going to have to keep an open mind."

Keep an open mind.

Cassie stood in the waiting room after her appointment ended, her purse stuffed with pamphlets and her dream still a possibility.

That's exactly what I'm going to tell Jake tonight, and hopefully, he will.

"Damn," Adrian said to Kevin as she watched her friend stride to the elevators, "I really thought she would go in with a better game plan than that."

Chapter Twenty-Five

JAKE TRUDGED UP THE STAIRS to their apartment with every muscle in his body aching, even his brain. All he wanted to do was crash and forget this day had ever happened, until the succulent scent of baby back ribs lured him in.

"Is that...?" Jake asked his eyes now wide open as he walked through the front door.

"Ribs from Valentino's? Yes, it is."

Jake was so focused on the food that he didn't pay any attention to his wife until he heard her.

Cassie stood in their candlelit kitchen in her favorite pair of skinny jeans and a form-fitting gray T-shirt.

"What?" she asked, feigning innocence, her eyes locked onto her husband's while she slowly licked the barbeque sauce off her fingertips.

"Well played," Adrian nodded in approval.

"Very well played," Kevin agreed.

Jake cleared his throat and looked anywhere except at his wife's lips. Then it dawned on him.

Oh, shit! What did I forget? A birthday? An anniversary?

He wracked his brain, but nothing came to him.

Damn it! There's only one way to find out.

"What's the occasion?"

"No special occasion. I swear," Cassie replied as her fingers leisurely intertwined themselves around her husband's neck. "Maybe I just wanted to do something nice for you."

"Like drive all the way out to Valentino's for ribs?"

"And tiramisu for dessert."

Cassie looked up at Jake, her eyes projecting an irresistibility he couldn't deny.

He was about to profess his love for her when skepticism set in.

"Wait. Tiramisu and ribs?"

"Yeah." Cassie's voice faltered while her eyes drifted away from his.

"No, no, no," Adrian pleaded with her. "You were doing so well. You've got him right where you want him. You can't fall apart now. Stay strong; stay confident and, above all else, maintain eye contact with him."

"For no reason at all?"

Jake took her chin between his fingers and lifted it gently so they were eye-to-eye once more.

"On second thought," Adrian said nervously, "avoid eye contact at all costs."

"Just because?" he asked his wife.

"Well," Cassie stammered as she watched her hands unlace and fall listlessly down to Jake's forearms, "there is something I need you to do for me."

"So close," Adrian whispered with her hand pressed against her forehead.

"Uh-huh," Jake replied as if he had known all along. "Like what?"

"It's not that bad; I promise."

"Yeah right. You wouldn't have gone all out like this if it weren't...." He paused, his eyes round with shock. "You're not trying to get me to do something with my mom and Clint, are you?"

"What?" Cassie stared at him in confusion as if that were the last thing she would have even thought of. "No, no, it's nothing like that."

"Oh, thank God," he replied half-seriously.

Then he thought about it some more.

"So then, what do you need me to do?"

"The best way to do this, Cass," Adrian leaned over her friend's shoulder, "is just to tell him straight out. You've got nothing to worry about; it'll all be good."

"Well, I need you to get tested. We both do actually," she quickly added.

"Tested? For what?"

"I had my appointment with Dr. Kerrigan today."

Jake didn't need to ask. The look on his wife's face said it all.

"And she...um...she told me we could still have kids of our own, but that we should also keep an open mind."

Cassie took a deep breath before she continued.

"There's a lot of great options out there." She tried to pour as much optimism into her words as possible. "More than I ever realized, but before we even think about trying any of them, she suggested we both get tested."

Jake grew quiet.

Damn it, Cassie thought. *I knew it. I just knew it.*

"You really don't want to do this?" Adrian yelled at Jake before turning to Kevin. "What possible reason could he have for not wanting to do this?"

Her eyes darted inquisitively back and forth between father and son.

"Okay, what am I missing here?" she asked.

Kevin ignored her. He gave his full attention to his son, who was now doing battle with childhood memories that insisted on resurfacing.

"Jake," Kevin begged him, "don't go back to all that."

"Back where?" Adrian asked. "To all of what? What's going on?"

"Jake?" Cassie spoke his name tentatively. "Say something. Please."

Kevin knew what was about to come out of his son's mouth, but as hard as he tried to prevent it, he couldn't stop it.

"So you want to find out who's to blame?"

"What?" Cassie replied with a mixture of anger and shock.

"Damn it," Kevin mumbled.

"What did he just say?" Adrian sounded appalled.

Cassie felt as if the breath had been knocked out of her, but she managed to speak anyway. "You really think I'm looking to blame one of us?"

"Please, son," said Kevin, "just quit while you're ahead."

"No," Jake answered his wife.

"Oh, thank God," Kevin said.

"I think you need a reason; you need to know why and…."

"And what?"

"I don't know; maybe I'd make the perfect scapegoat for you."

Cassie's jaw dropped. She was so furious with him that she couldn't even speak. She glared at her husband, her eyes ignited with rage, before she vehemently shook her head at him and stormed upstairs.

Jake didn't bother to chase after her. He turned toward the front door and sighed, his shoulders slowly rolling back into his Riley stance with every step he took.

The door shut quietly behind him; the breeze from it snuffed out the solitary candle on the kitchen table beside the plate of steaming hot ribs that sat untouched.

Chapter Twenty-Six

"WHAT THE HELL WAS THAT?" Adrian asked as she whacked Kevin in the arm.

"Ow! What was that for?"

"Because you did something to cause all of this. I know you did!"

Kevin didn't look away from Adrian, but he didn't answer her either.

"Go on," she demanded, getting up in his face, "tell me I'm wrong."

"No," he answered, his voice barely audible, "you're not."

Adrian backed down. His pain was evident, no matter how hard he was trying to disguise it.

"C'mon," she said, her voice more sympathetic, "you can try to explain yourself on the way."

"On the way?"

"Yeah, to wherever Jake's going. I'm assuming we're going to go after him, and not just put up our feet, and binge watch Netflix until Cass decides to come back downstairs."

It was as if Adrian's words had summoned her best friend to appear at the top of the staircase.

Cassie was wrapped in her favorite pink camouflage blanket. She bounded down the first few steps, but then her feet grew heavy when she reached the last one and realized no one else was there.

She gripped the railing, determined not to give into the devastation she felt.

"Ass! Why do you have to be such an ass?"

She thrust her chin up to keep the few tears that had escaped from rolling down her cheeks. Adrian rushed over to wrap her arms around her just as Cassie let go of the railing to pull her blanket tighter to her.

"Don't worry," Adrian told her. "We're going to fix this. Right?" she asked Kevin.

"We're going to do our best."

*

The hum of the motorcycle engine was like a cherished lullaby being sung to Jake by his mother. It soothed him and allowed him to take in the tepid blue sky and the cool, autumn air that invigorated his soul until he reached his destination.

Jake parked his bike in the lot. His heart grew heavier with each step he took along the path. The guilt sank deep down inside of him, like a ship that had hit the ocean floor, by the time he reached the ancient, moss-laden oak tree.

This was it. The place where every Riley man had been laid to rest.

"I'm an ass," Jake muttered to himself as he marched blindly around the head stones to the trunk of the tree. "Such an ass!"

He proceeded to kick the mighty oak as hard as he could.

"God-damn, son-of-a-bitch!" Jake screamed as his foot exploded in pain.

"Yep," a voice from somewhere behind him spoke, "you're an ass all right."

Jake hobbled over to the bench closest to his family's plots. He sat down and rubbed his foot, oblivious to the fact that his father sat right beside him.

"Just like your old man," Kevin said before he took a drink from his can of Pepsi. "A real horse's ass."

Jake sat back with his arms crossed and stared intently at his father's grave.

"This is all your fault, you know."

"I know," Kevin replied, his head bowed heavy with regret. "I didn't know that then, but I sure as hell do now."

Jake closed his eyes, but the memory returned to him anyway.

He was twelve years old—the age when his mom and he never saw eye to eye about anything anymore.

It was a warm, sunny spring day. Jake was in a relatively good mood on his way home from school, until he saw his dad's semi parked in their driveway.

Normally, Jake would have been thrilled, but all week long, his mother had been threatening, "Just wait until your father gets home." And now he was here.

Jake froze when he saw his dad waiting for him at the side door.

"Jake." Kevin gave a curt nod to his son.

Jake gulped before he could reply.

"Dad." He returned the nod.

"Go bring your bag up to your room; then get straight back here to me."

"Yes, sir."

"You and I are going for a ride."

"I'll admit," Jake said now as he leaned forward on the bench with his elbows on his knees, "I was scared to death."

"That's what I was going for," Kevin replied with a slight smile. "I wouldn't even say anything to you until after we got to that truck stop in Cecil."

"You ran inside and got us each a bottle of Pepsi. Then we sat on the tailgate of your pickup and you dropped the bomb on me."

"I gave you The Talk."

Jake cringed.

"Your version of The Talk. I blocked most of it out, except for the part where you told me the greatest gift I could ever give the woman I chose to spend the rest of my life with is the family she wants."

"That's all I could think about when Cass asked me to get tested." Jake's hands combined into one large fist that he rested his chin upon. "That, and those few rare times I overheard you and Mom fighting about this exact same thing."

Kevin flinched as his son's words struck him harder than any punch he could have thrown.

"Your mom kept trying to convince me it was no big deal. We had you; we had our family, but I knew she always wanted more kids." Kevin finished off his soda, then crushed it in his hand. "And that's something that just kills me, even to this day, to know I couldn't give her that."

"Dad, I let the 'what ifs' take control of me. I lashed out at Cass because I'm afraid of what we might find out. I turned it all on her, and then I took off and ended up here."

"So you ran away," Kevin stated.

"I ran away," Jake concluded, averting his eyes from his father's headstone in shame.

Kevin's can of soda fell to the ground while he slid closer to his son.

"Now go back."

Jake's head perked up as if he had heard someone call out to him.

"I need to go back."

Jake stood up to leave when he caught something out of the corner of his eye beneath the bench. He bent down to see what it was and discovered a crushed Pepsi can.

He smiled wistfully as he picked it up and tossed it in the recycling bin on his way back to his bike.

*

Cassie couldn't take it anymore—standing there, waiting in their apartment for whenever Jake might come home. She had to go find him.

She snatched her purse off the back of the kitchen chair and pulled the front door open. But she jumped back when she saw him standing in front of her.

"Hey," Jake mumbled.

"Hey," Cassie replied coolly.

"Going somewhere?"

"To look for you." Then she added under her breath, "God only knows why."

"Cass, I'm sorry."

"Mm-hmm."

"I love you so much. You're my girl, and I just don't want to let you down."

"Let me down?"

Jake motioned to come inside. Cassie stepped aside and swung the door open wider.

"Yeah." He came into their kitchen and cleared his throat. "I mean, you know."

"Oh," Cassie tried not to roll her eyes at him, "you're talking about that whole Riley men code thing."

"It's not just a Riley men thing." He paused to keep his defenses under control. "It's my thing."

"You think I'm not scared too? That it might be me?" Cassie grasped her husband's hands in hers. "All these tests are going to do is let us know what our next steps need to be. Together. That's it; nothing more."

"Okay."

"Okay, like yes, you'll do it?"

"Yes, I'll do it."

Chapter Twenty-Seven

THE ONLY GOOD THING ABOUT Wisconsin winters to Jake was the overtime he got paid. And this weekend was no exception.

Snowstorm Annie—the first storm of the season—blew through Brown County just as all the meteorologists predicted she would. There had to be a good foot of snow already and counting. This forced Jake to be up behind the wheel of a snowplow way earlier than he wanted.

The snow was coming down so hard he could barely see in front of him. His eyes were so strained by the time he pulled back into the city garage that the words from Cassie's text all seemed to blur together.

Jake shut one eye, then rubbed them both with his fingertips before his wife's message finally made sense to him.

"Jesus," Jake grimaced. "Really? Now?"

He sighed heavily while his hand slid down to his stubbled chin.

A couple of months had passed since Jake had agreed to Cassie's plan for them both to get tested. He hadn't thought it would take this long. He had assumed one trip to the doctor's office would do it, but he had been wrong.

Cassie's doctor had informed them that to get an accurate reading from Jake, they would need to get at least three samples, each approximately one month apart.

And, as if that weren't enough, Cassie took it upon herself to start tracking when she was ovulating. That was where the texting came in.

But not just any texts. Cassie wanted to have fun with it, and Jake was all for that.

It could be anything: a line from a song, some movie quote, a popular catchphrase. Whatever she could think of to keep it interesting for them.

Today she was in a *Top Gun* mood.

Goose, you big stud, she had written, *take me to bed or lose me forever.*

Show me the way home, honey, Jake half-heartedly wrote back.

"All right boys," he said while he looked down between his legs, "this isn't our first mission. Let's try not to crash and burn."

Jake barely made it through the front door before his wife was all over him.

"What took you so long?"

She never gave him a chance to answer her question.

Cassie's kisses—as intense as they were—felt different to Jake now. They seemed to be fueled more by necessity than passion. That did nothing to inspire his enthusiasm.

She wasn't interested in foreplay either. That much became obvious to Jake as her fingers furiously unfastened the buttons on his work jeans. Then she yanked them off him faster than a male stripper wearing breakaway pants.

Holy shit, he thought. Is she going to fuck me right here on the kitchen floor?

Which he normally wouldn't have argued with, but now...he wasn't so sure he'd be up for it.

Cassie wrapped her hands firmly around him and took great care to massage every single inch. She was about to kneel down when he stopped her.

"What's wrong?" she asked.

"Cass," Jake gritted his teeth as he stared up at the ceiling. *I can't believe I'm saying this.* "Stop."

"Why?"

"Cass." He tilted his head at his wife while he placed his hands over hers. "Really?"

"Yes, really. C'mon, baby; please just let me keep trying."

Jake protested until Cassie tried a new tactic with her tongue.

Holy... fuck yeah, he thought. *I do believe the boys are staging a comeback.*

His back was pressed up against the wall. He grabbed hold of her hair as his body became wracked with spasms of desire.

Jake glanced down at Cassie. She couldn't resist seeing his reaction, her eyes filled with wicked determination.

And then the magic vanished just as quickly as it had come.

What? No! C'mon boys; you can't do this to me now!

"It's all right," Cassie told him as she slowly rose to her feet.

But it was obvious to both of them that it wasn't.

"Cass."

He wanted to explain, needed to explain to her. *I've been awake since 2 a.m., out plowing for the last ten hours, living on nothing but beef jerky and Mountain Dew.*

But she wouldn't let him.

"Jake, really, it's all right," Cassie said as she gave him a peck on the cheek. "I need to get ready for my shift anyway."

Jake nodded with downcast eyes as if he understood, but all he felt was his own despondency.

He didn't move until after Cassie shut the bathroom door and he heard the shower running.

Jake catapulted away from the wall and headed straight for the couch.

"Damn it," he muttered as he fell backwards onto the cushions, the heels of his hands pressed into his eyes. "God damn it!" he screamed while he slammed his elbow into the arm of the couch.

Adrian and Kevin sat at the bottom of the spiral staircase. Her jaw dropped.

"I'm going to go check on Cass," she finally said.

Adrian breached the door to the bathroom to hear her best friend softly sobbing in the shower. She took a few tentative steps forward, then stopped as soon as the crying did.

Cassie swore she heard someone come in.

"Jake?" she anxiously called out.

No one answered. She shut the water off and peeked around the curtain to find the room empty.

Thank God, Cassie thought. *That's all I need right now.*

She grabbed a towel off the hook and proceeded to dry off.

What if, she felt the tears welling up in her eyes again as she spread her hand over her stomach, *nothing was ever meant to grow inside of me?*

"Oh, Cass, no," Adrian told her.

*

"So, how's she doing?" Kevin asked after Adrian returned.

"This goes way beyond just manhood issues," Adrian replied.

"Yes, it does," Kevin agreed.

Adrian heard something in his voice and gave him a sideways glance.

"But you knew that already, didn't you?"

"Just waiting to see how long it would take you to catch on," Kevin said with a sly smile.

Chapter Twenty-Eight

CASSIE SAT ON THE BENCH in front of her locker and stared blankly at her cell phone.

Benji had been blowing it up ever since the storm began. She told herself she hadn't responded because she was working and had no time to check in with him.

But what was her excuse now? She couldn't come up with one except for the truth.

Her fingers kneaded the back of her neck while her mind reluctantly brought her back to this afternoon with Jake.

How could she possibly talk to Benji with all of that still bothering her?

But Cassie also knew if she didn't soon, he'd call the authorities, or worse.

Too late, Cassie thought as she continued to scroll through her phone.

C'mon, Soap Star, Benji had written about two hours before, *shoot me an emoji—something, anything—so I know you're okay.*

Then an hour ago:

All right, you've left me no choice. Don't say I didn't warn you.

Sure enough, she had a voicemail.

Cassie brought the phone anxiously up to her ear and listened.

Hey, Cass. It's your dad. We need to hear from you. Your mom and I are worried about you, with this storm and all. Okay...just call us as soon as you can. Love you. Bye.

"We," Cassie scoffed while she deleted the message, "yeah, right. I'm sure Mom's really wringing her hands and starting a prayer chain for me as I speak."

They hadn't seen each other since Dom's birthday party back in August, and they hadn't spoken to each other in forever.

"And I'm sure if they had," Adrian spoke up, "Julia would've done nothing but lecture Cassie anyway."

Cassie shrieked when she heard her phone go off. It was Benji trying to FaceTime her.

"Ugh." She raked her fingers through her hair, dreading this unavoidable conversation.

"Hey, Benji," she said doing her best to look and sound as normal as possible.

"Hey, Soap Star, you are alive!"

"Yeah, and I've been working nonstop to make sure everyone else stays alive through this stupid storm. So you can call off the bloodhounds and let Mom and Dad know I'm just fine."

"You don't want to call and tell them yourself?" Benji asked sarcastically.

"No, smartass, I don't," Cassie snapped, adding under her breath, "especially not today."

"Okay, what's wrong?"

"Nothing. It's just been a really long day. I'm fine."

"Fine, huh?"

"What?"

"Lose the attitude, little sister. I've been around women long enough to know that when they say they're fine, they're really not. So why don't you just cut to the chase and tell me what's going on?"

"Benji, I love you, but you wouldn't understand."

"Try me."

Cassie was tempted, but this was one of the few things she just couldn't share with her big brother. Benji knew it too.

"Or is this something you'd rather talk to someone else, like Sara, about?"

"Don't answer him right away!" Adrian jumped in. "Think before you speak."

"Sara?" Cassie mulled it over for less than a minute. "Yeah, sure. I suppose."

Adrian slapped her forehead with the palm of her hand.

That was all Benji needed to hear.

"Okay, hang on a second. I'll be right back."

"Where are you going?" Cassie asked him.

"To get Sara."

"What? Benji, no, you don't have to do that."

Benji paid no attention to her. He was too busy trying to track down his wife.

"Sara, where are you? Cass is on the phone. She needs to talk to you."

"No, I don't. We don't need to be doing any of this. Not now. I can call her later."

Much later.

"I tried to warn you," Adrian told her. "You know how he gets, like a dog with a bone."

Cassie gave up. She knew it was a lost cause. Benji wouldn't stop until….

She heard her nieces shouting her name before she saw them come flying over to the phone.

"Auntie Cass! Auntie Cass!"

They were so excited and so loud. Each girl was so desperate to be heard over the other that Cassie couldn't understand a single thing either one was saying.

That's when Sara broke in.

"Girls…girls! Her voice rose sharply as she knelt down between them. "This is Mommy's time with Auntie Cass."

This was met with resounding and simultaneous groans, which had no effect on their mother.

Sara promptly shooed her daughters away, causing more moaning and whining until she came up with an idea.

"Why don't you go down in the basement and play circus acrobats with your dad?"

It got so quiet so suddenly that Cassie thought the sound went out on her phone.

"But Mommy," Kayla spoke up, "you always yell at us when we play circus acrobats with Daddy."

"Yeah," Caroline chimed in.

"Well, today's your lucky day, girls. Now you better hurry up and get to it before I change my mind."

They scrambled out of the living room as if their feet were on fire.

Sara made herself comfortable on the sectional once they were finished laughing at the girls.

"So," she said to her sister-in-law after she heard the last pair of feet descend the basement stairs, "what's up?"

"Ah," Cassie responded with a dismissive wave of her hand. "You know how Benji is when he's on the phone."

"Oh, yeah, all too well."

"So, when I told him there was something I might be more comfortable talking to you about..."

"He took it to mean get Sara on the phone now," Sara finished.

"Exactly."

"So, what's the something?"

"Huh?" Cassie asked while she pulled her hair free from its bun.

"That you're more comfortable talking to me about?"

"Oh, that." Cassie tried to act nonchalant. "It's nothing. Really."

"Uh-huh." Sara answered like a mother listening to one of her children's tall tales.

"So, everything is all right with you and Jake?"

"Yeah," Cassie's voice cracked. She cleared her throat and soldiered on, praying her sister-in-law hadn't noticed. "Yeah, we're good."

"Uh-huh." There was a longer pause between syllables this time.

Sara's coffee-colored eyes stayed trained on Cassie, even as she pulled her dark, curly hair up into a ponytail.

Cassie felt the heat from Sara's eyes as if they were a spotlight aimed at her during an interrogation. It didn't take long for her to break.

"Okay," she admitted, "we're not good right now, but we will be...eventually." *I hope.*

"What happened?"

"Uh." Cassie sighed as she looked anxiously over her shoulder to the locker room door. "This really isn't a good place to be talking about this."

"All right, I get it, but you better not be playing me just to get me off the phone."

"No." Cassie looked away from her phone as her voice grew somber. "I'm not. I swear."

"Well, I'm telling you right now we will finish this conversation, even if I have to drive up there and throw you into my car so we can be alone. You hear me?"

"Yeah," Cassie replied with a meager smile. "I hear you."

"Good. You hang in there. Stay strong, and I'll talk to you again soon."

"Okay. Bye."

Cassie hung up her phone and drew it close to her chest along with her knees. She bowed her head and allowed the tears to fall until she heard voices drifting through the recently opened door.

Cassie jerked her head up and swiped the droplets roughly from her cheek.

Stay strong, she thought.

*

The only thing Cassie dreaded more than whatever awaited her at home was driving there in this storm.

When she ventured outside, she was pleasantly surprised to find that Snowstorm Annie had lost her edge. The snow drifted down to the ground now in the type of large, fluffy flakes that people wrote Christmas songs about.

It covered her car, and she knew it would probably take forever to clear it off, but that was all right.

Prolong the inevitable as long as we can, she thought as she reached over Adrian for the snowbrush she kept in the backseat.

"Hey," Adrian teased her, "I was able to tone down the weather for you, but I can't control what Jake's going to do. Right?"

Adrian looked for Kevin, but the seat beside her was empty.

"Now, Kevin on the other hand…."

*

Kevin sat back in the oversized chair, one hand behind his head while the other aimed the remote at the TV and scrolled through Netflix.

His son lay on the couch across from him, his face pressed into the pillow. His snoring still louder than any freighter crossing The Fox River.

Kevin sighed.

"How long are you going to sleep?"

"Not much longer now."

Kevin turned toward the window when he heard Adrian's voice. He couldn't see her, but he could see the storm was letting up. "Good job, Adrian." He grinned like a proud papa before he pushed himself up out of the chair.

Kevin went on a scavenger hunt throughout the apartment for Jake's phone. He finally found it peeking out from underneath the refrigerator, inches away from a discarded pair of blue jeans.

He raised an eyebrow but made no judgments as he retrieved the phone and proceeded back into the living room.

"Showtime," Kevin said as he set the phone down on the floor beside the couch.

The phone rang the moment Kevin took his hand off it. The noise startled Jake out of a sound sleep. His eyes were half open while his mind struggled to escape from its dreamy haze and reorient himself enough to figure out where in the hell the sound was coming from.

"Your phone," his father instructed. "It's your phone; on the floor; right there."

The wires finally connected, much to Kevin's relief. Jake stretched out his arm; his hand fumbled around all over the floor until he got it.

"Yeah," he grumbled into the receiver.

"Dude!"

"Charlie, you better have one damn-good, fucking reason to be calling."

"I do man, I swear."

Jake's eyes were fully open now. He had never heard that level of desperation in his best friend's voice.

"You're not in jail, are you?"

"No. Worse."

What the hell could be worse than jail? Jake thought.

"I need you to get over here now, man. Please."

"Dude, no offense, but it's a shit show outside right now."

"Not where I'm at."

"What?"

Jake raised himself up on one arm as if he were doing a push-up. He craned his neck to peer out the window and was shocked to discover the storm was more or less over.

"Damn," he told Charlie. "You're right."

"Just get the fuck over here as fast as you can."

"Yes, sir," Jake said to the dial tone.

*

"So where's the fire?" Jake asked after Charlie hurried him into his apartment.

"Dude," Charlie responded. "I'm freaking out!"

Jake watched in shock as his friend paced back and forth between the kitchen and living room like a caged animal. Charlie seemed to be rubbing the palms of his hands so hard against the sides of his head that Jake half-expected to find them bald.

"Yeah, I can see that," Jake said. "You need to calm down."

"I can't. I don't know what the fuck I'm going to do."

"About what?"

"Janiece."

Jake bit the inside of his cheek and did his damnedest not to roll his eyes.

"You mean to tell me I hauled my ass all the way over here for some girl?"

Charlie quit pacing and looked his best friend straight in the eye.

"She's pregnant. With my kid."

Jake's body went numb while his mind stayed active.

Way too active.

Pregnant. He got a girl he barely even knows...pregnant. Without even trying; without even wanting to. What. The. Fuck?

"Dude!" Charlie said. "You better sit down before you fall down."

He grabbed the nearest chair and set it behind his friend. Jake sunk into it as his thoughts spiraled down into self-pity and injustice.

Most people would've rushed to the sink for a glass of water at this point, but not Charlie. He pulled a cold bottle of beer from the fridge and put it in Jake's hand.

"You..." Jake said, his voice apathetic, his eyes on the counter while he nudged the bottle away with the back of his hand, "a dad."

"Shit!" Charlie reacted as if he were just hearing the words for the first time.

His nerves drove him right into the chair across from Jake and caused his mouth to go on another uncensored rant.

"I'm going to be a dad. Me! What the hell kind of twisted, parallel universe did we beam up into where I'm going to be a parent? You're better daddy material than I am...."

Jake raised his head up with amazing restraint, and that's when Charlie realized his mistake.

"Jesus, I am such an ass! Why didn't you tell me just to shut the fuck up?"

"Because," Kevin said from his vantage point between the two men, "then he'd have to admit he cares."

Charlie knew some of what had happened with Jake and Cassie, but not everything, and Jake had no intention of enlightening him anytime soon. He chose to remain silent; his jaw clenched as his thoughts turned angrier and harder to contain.

Why? Why you: someone who never even wanted kids, who's done everything in his power his entire life to prevent having one? While I....

"Jake?" Charlie asked anxiously as he glanced at his friend's bright white knuckles. Jake kept his head up in a semi-Riley stance. His father stood beside him, his hand covering his son's fists.

"Take a breath; take a drink, but do not take this out on Charlie."

Jake uncurled his fingers and reached for his beer bottle. The anticipation was killing Charlie, like waiting to hear who was the winner of *The Voice*.

Jake knew it too, but it didn't make him respond any faster. The bottle made a soft popping sound as it parted from his lips. He set the bottle down and casually wiped his mouth with the back of his hand.

"Dude, c'mon!" Charlie said.

"You," Jake replied allowing a slow onset of a smile, "a dad. God really does work in mysterious ways, doesn't he?"

*

Cassie stood before the front door of her apartment for so long one of her neighbors stopped to ask if she had forgotten her keys.

"No," she said with a polite smile. *I'm just too chicken shit to go inside.*

"You just have to rip off the Band-Aid, Cass," Adrian told her.

Cassie's hand thrust the key into the lock before she even realized it. The next thing she knew, she was inside and still alone.

She didn't spot the note on the fridge right away.

Had to go. Charlie needed me. Be back as soon as I can. Love, Me.

"Well, she said as she detached the note from its magnet, "at least he still loves me."

Cassie opened the door, dying for a beer, but she didn't want to chance it.

We haven't stopped trying...yet.

She grabbed the jug of juice instead and poured herself a glass. Her thoughts were wrapped up in baby blankets the entire time.

Which reminded her of Sara.

"Oh, c'mon," Adrian lamented when she saw Cassie sit down at the kitchen table. "Don't tell me you're going to stare down your phone now?"

Cassie shifted around uncomfortably in her chair.

"Would you rather talk to Sara or Jake right now?"

Cassie snatched up her phone and hit Sara's number.

"Good choice," Adrian said.

"Hey," Sara said after the second or third ring. "So, does this mean you're in a better place where we can talk now?"

"Yeah," Cassie replied, though she still felt uncertain. "Jake's out with Charlie, but who knows for how long."

"Well, let's get to it then."

The words came slowly to Cassie at first, but then—maybe because she was saying them for the first time out loud to anyone—

they seemed to rush out of her like water flowing toward the edge of a fall. And once it started, she couldn't stop until it all poured out of her.

Sara never interrupted her. There was silence on both ends of the line after Cassie finished. Cassie was grateful she had chosen not to FaceTime her. Hearing the tears in her voice was bad enough; there was no need for Sara to see them too.

"The way I see it," Sara replied gravely, "there's only one thing you and Jake should do."

"What's that?" Cassie sniffed.

"Come down and stay with us for a while!"

"What?" Cassie shrieked in disbelief.

"Why not? A break could be just what you guys need."

"Hmm." Sara could hear the thought going into her sister-in-law's voice, so she persisted.

"And, I happen to know someone's thirtieth birthday is coming up soon."

"Ugh."

"All the more reason we need to get you down here! You can't stay up there moping on your birthday. It's just not healthy."

"I will not be moping."

"Because you'll be here celebrating with us!"

"Celebrating what, Mommy?"

Cassie heard Kayla's voice in the background. Her eyes grew huge. She knew exactly what her sister-in-law might do next, and she didn't hesitate to stop her.

"Sara, don't you dare! Don't do it. Sara…."

"Auntie Cass's birthday," Sara responded to her daughter without missing a beat. "She and Uncle Jake might come down for a visit."

"Sara!" Cassie threw her head back in frustration. Then she lowered her voice and added, "I haven't even said anything to Jake yet."

"And now you have to." Cassie could practically hear Sara grinning through the phone. "Let me know what he says. We'll start making more concrete plans after that. Okay? Bye! Say bye to Auntie Cass, girls!"

"What was all that about?" Benji asked after Sara hung up the phone.

"Oh." Sara leaned casually back against their bed's headboard. "I was just trying to get Cassie and Jake to come down for a visit."

"And?"

"And, maybe talk them into seeing Madeline."

"Madeline, huh?" said Benji as he climbed into bed. "Care to elaborate?"

"Only if you swear on your life not to tell another soul, especially your sister."

"I swear," Benji crossed his heart, "on my life."

Chapter Twenty-Nine

SOMETHING ABOUT RIDING SHOTGUN IN Jake's pickup, cruising down a stretch of open highway on a brilliant, sunshiny summer afternoon with Garth Brooks blaring out of the speakers, put Cassie completely at ease.

"I hear you," Adrian said blissfully as she set her chin in her hands on the upraised armrest. "It's like heaven on earth."

Cassie took in a deep, full breath of summer air from her wide-open window, glad she and Jake had decided to do this.

She had no idea how he'd respond to the idea of taking an extended weekend away to go down to Madison. He'd never really been one for vacations, unless it involved going to Sturgis or to visit The Harley Davidson Museum.

But this time—after some careful consideration and her honest opinion on the subject—Jake agreed. And now here they were, humming and tapping in time to the music on the first leg of their two-and-a-half-hour drive.

Maybe this will be good for both of us, Cassie thought while staring pensively at her husband.

*

"Hey, how was your trip?" Benji called out when he met them in the driveway.

"Have I ever told you how glad I am you don't live downtown?" Jake replied.

Benji laughed. "Had your fill of roundabouts, have you?"

"If I see another one," Jake said while grabbing their luggage out of the back, "it'll be too soon."

"I keep telling him," Cassie paused to sip the remnants of her Cherry Coke, "there's nothing to it. You yield; wait for any oncoming cars, and just follow the rest of the traffic."

"That's driving like a bunch of fucking maniacs," Jake grumbled as he slung his duffel bag over his shoulder.

"I give up." Cassie groaned with a roll of her eyes.

"I think you should, Soap Star, and get over here and give your big brother a hug instead."

"Ah, it's been too long, Benji," she said as she hugged him harder than she would have her husband.

After she let him go, Cassie asked, "Where's Sara and the girls?"

"The girls conned Sara into taking them for ice cream while they were waiting for you guys to show up," Benji said. "I'll text her to let her know you're here."

"Before you do that, could you please direct me to the nearest cold beer?" Jake begged.

"Absolutely. C'mon inside. Let's get you settled in and relaxed before the tiny terrors get a hold of you."

No more than fifteen minutes later, they were sitting on the reclining couch in the living room watching a few stray deer grazing in the backyard when the sound of slamming car doors frightened the animals away.

Cassie sat up eagerly to be instantly embraced by sticky fingers and covered in Superman ice cream.

"Girls," Sara scolded them, "you're getting Auntie Cass all messy."

"It's okay," said Cassie, laughing. "I'm still in my road trip clothes anyway."

The girls begged and pleaded with Cassie to sleep with them in their room that night. Cassie caved; Sara warned them: one night, no more.

"This is Auntie Cass's birthday weekend. She should get to do whatever she wants."

The girls happily agreed.

*

Cassie woke up early the next morning wedged between her two nieces on an air mattress.

"Now I know what the cream inside an Oreo feels like," Cassie said to herself while she carefully stretched.

She kicked her legs out slowly from beneath The Trolls blanket as if recreating moves from *The Matrix*.

Any quicker and her bladder would have exploded. She was relieved to have made it off the air mattress without too much disruption.

"Bathroom," she whispered like a woman on a mission, "and then caffeine."

Cassie padded barefoot down the hall—after she made her bathroom pitstop—to the stairs. She paused midway and found herself back-pedaling toward a closed door on the left-hand side—their room, the one she and Jake were supposed to be sleeping in together.

Cassie put her palm up against the door and gave it a gentle push.

She stood on the threshold for just a moment, so tempted to go in and lay inside her husband's arms, but not now. Her hand dropped to the doorknob, which she then pulled softly shut.

The sound jolted Jake awake. He sat up and stared bleary-eyed at the door, uncertain if what he had seen was real.

"Good morning."

Cassie stifled a scream when she reached the bottom of the stairs and found Sara sitting at the kitchen table scrolling through her phone.

"What are you doing up already?" she asked Sara.

"Force of habit I guess," Sara said with a shrug before she took a sip of her coffee. "You?"

"Bathroom."

Cassie turned her nose up at Sara when she motioned toward the coffeepot.

"There's a case of Mountain Dew on the bottom shelf." Sara's eyes never left her phone, but she knew Cassie had just gone over to the refrigerator.

"Benji knows me so well," she said, grinning.

"That he does," Sara agreed while she swung around in her chair to face her sister-in-law. "So, how'd you sleep last night?"

Cassie shut the refrigerator door, popped the top of the soda can, and took a long drink before she answered.

"Let's just say one of my top priorities today is to have a nice, long massage."

"Oh, c'mon," Jake interrupted them as he halted halfway down the staircase, "you can get a massage anywhere, any time. We're in Madison; it's your birthday weekend. You can do whatever you want."

"Anything I want?" Cassie clarified.

"Anything. You name it; we'll do it, with no complaints from me."

Both women exchanged raised eyebrows.

"Go on," Adrian said. "You may never get another opportunity like this!"

"Well," Cassie replied to her husband, "there are a couple places I've always wanted to go...."

*

"Man, you must really love my sister," Benji told Jake later that morning, "if you're willing to spend the entire day wandering through Olbrich Gardens with her."

"I did tell Cass we could do whatever she wanted. And besides, it'll all even out later when we go for drinks at Noel's."

"All right, boys!"

Both men turned to the stairs at the sound of Kayla's voice. She and Caroline strutted down like they were on a catwalk in their stylish sunglasses, sandals, and floppy straw hats.

"We're ready to go see all the pretty flowers!" Caroline announced much to the amusement of Sara and Cassie, who trailed behind them.

"Lead the way, ladies," Benji said with a flourish of his arm.

*

"Who knew," Jake said to Benji, his voice filled with disappointment as they came upon yet another garden to walk through, "there were so many damn different flowers?"

"Isn't it cool, Uncle Jake?" Caroline asked as she skipped up alongside him and took his hand.

"Very." Jake cleared his throat in order to bury his sarcasm. "Where are we headed to now?"

"Don't know," Caroline shrugged, "but we got to catch up to Auntie Cass and Kayla fast!"

The next thing Jake knew, he was having trouble keeping up with Caroline while she ran as fast as her little legs would carry her to reach her big sister.

Cassie grinned when she saw him doubled over and gasping for breath.

"Caroline give you a workout, did she?"

"No," Jake said while he immediately straightened up. "She just caught me off guard."

"Uh-huh, sure she did," Cassie said with a wink.

"What are we going to see now?" Caroline asked her auntie before Jake had a chance to defend himself.

"Now," Cassie replied as she bent down so she could be face-to-face with her niece, "we're going to see the best part!"

"Which is?" Jake asked expectantly.

"You're going to have to follow me," Cassie said while she slowly rose, "to find out."

"Wow," Adrian said. "She sounded like she had channeled me for a second there."

"Or," Jake said as he took hold of her hand, "we could see it together."

"C'mon, girls," Sara told her daughters. "Why don't you hang back by your dad and me for this one."

"So, does this mean?" Adrian tentatively asked Kevin.

"Yep, it's showtime."

It was warm outside as they approached The Bolz Conservatory, or the glass pyramid as Jake referred to it, but it became downright unbearable once they stepped inside.

Jake never complained, though. He was sweating buckets the farther they ventured into the tropical gardens, but if that was the price he had to pay to see the pure joy on his wife's face, it was well worth trudging through the jungle.

Especially when they reached The Blooming Butterfly exhibit.

They were surrounded by large, leafy, green plants. One wall they walked past was lined with cases—chrysanthemums, or something like that Jake thought they were called—where the butterflies actually hatched from. And then there were the free-flying butterflies themselves.

The animals snuck up on them. Their wings fluttered soundlessly through the air, their presence only felt after one landed unassumingly on Cassie's shoulder.

"What the...?" she asked in shock.

"Don't move," Jake told her.

She had to see it, though; she just couldn't resist. Cassie turned her head slowly, but it didn't matter. The butterfly fanned out its black wings as casually as if it had landed on one of the garden flowers. Cassie's entire arm tingled, and Jake wasn't even blowing in her ear.

"Wow," she whispered.

"Cool!" the girls exclaimed while they rushed over to her.

"Slow down, girls," Benji told them, but the butterfly never moved.

"You know what they say about black butterflies," Sara said.

Apparently, no one did. They all stared baffled at her, waiting to hear the explanation.

"They're the souls of the departed who haven't moved on to the afterlife yet."

"Jeez," Benji said, laughing, "for a well-educated woman—"

"Hey," Sara stopped him right there, "don't you be disrespecting anything my grandma told me."

Jake and Cassie both stared intently at the butterfly before their eyes suddenly locked as if each one had heard the other's thoughts and they were eerily the same:

That's Adrian!

Sara's lips curved up into a secretive smile she wasn't even aware of until Benji pointed it out to her.

"What's that smile for? You know something we don't?"

"Nope," Sara said. "Not at all." *Just that my grandma also believed black butterflies are a sign of renewal and rebirth. Oh, how I hope to Jesus she was right.*

*

"We'll have a round of apple pie shots," Sara told the bartender at Noel's, "and keep 'em coming!"

Noel's Bar was another one of Cassie's go-to places. She had always heard her big brother talk about it. Noel's was well-known for its spectacular display of year-round Christmas lights. And now Cassie was here looking around in awe like she was in New Orleans experiencing Mardi Gras for the first time.

"Apple pie?" she stammered.

"Mmm." Adrian smacked her lips. "Apple pie. Goes down so good you don't even know it hit you until it's too late."

That's exactly what Cassie was afraid of.

"You know," Cassie tried again, "you don't have to do this on my account."

"I hate to tell you this, Soap Star," Benji leaned over the bar so his little sister could see him, "but this is not all about you. Today may be your thirtieth birthday," he put a loud emphasis on the number, "but it's also the first night in a very long time that Sara and I are childless!"

"Here's to my parents for taking the girls overnight!" Sara shouted before downing her shot with wild abandon.

"I'll drink to that!" Benji followed suit.

Then all eyes turned to Cassie and the full shot glass that sat in front of her.

"Oh, all right," she moaned, her head hung low in defeat.

New life came to her the second she felt her husband's fingers kneading into her shoulders.

"C'mon, champ," he whispered into her ear. "You got this."

Cassie looked at Jake as if it were the first night she had ever seen him back at The Borderline.

"I got this," she said as she grabbed the shot glass off the bar and tossed it back in one gulp.

"That's my girl." Jake cheered her on amid all the hooting and hollering that came from everyone within earshot of them.

Cassie could not have cared less about all the commotion and attention being showered upon her. She only had eyes for Jake, who kissed her at that moment in a way he hadn't in a long time.

*

About an hour later, Jake leaned back on his barstool at the high table they were all sitting around to admire the *Dirty Dancing* routine Cassie was performing for him along to Luke Bryan's song, "One Margarita." He also noticed some of the younger guys at the bar were enjoying her show.

"Hey!" Jake shouted at them. "That's my wife you're ogling."

"And my baby sister!" Benji chimed in.

The boys immediately put their eyes back into their sockets and focused on the big screen TV above the bar.

"Oh, c'mon," Cassie said as she yanked Jake off his feet. "Don't be like that."

"What?" he asked good-naturedly, their bodies so close no one could cut in if they tried. "You don't like it when I defend your honor?"

Jake interwove his fingers behind Cassie's back and took a firm hold of her ass.

"Well, on second thought," she teased, "if it makes you behave like that."

"Where are you taking me?" Jake asked as she pulled him around the floor.

"I'm trying to find some mistletoe," she said. Her eyes narrowed while she stared straight up at the ceiling. "You wouldn't think that would be so hard to find in a place that's filled with Christmas lights!"

"Hey, baby." Jake stopped her to cup her face in his hands. "We don't need any fucking mistletoe."

He smiled wickedly at her before kissing her like he was trying to funnel her soul through his lips.

It created the desired effect. Cassie stood there, after they broke apart, looking like she had just gotten off a super-speed Tilt-a-Whirl ride.

"Are you all right?" Jake asked.

"Oh, yeah."

"Good. So, I'm thinking it might be time for me to take my girl home."

"If it means more of that, then hell yes!"

Jake laughed as he slid his arm around Cassie's waist, and they sauntered back over to their table.

"I hope you guys don't mind," Jake said to Benji and Sara, "but I'd like to call an Uber and give my wife a private birthday celebration at your place."

"We have no objections at all!" Sara shouted. "In fact, we would be honored if our place is where you conceive your first child."

That nearly knocked an already teetering Cassie off her feet. Jake held his head high like an esteemed soldier, then gave a polite nod.

"We shall do our best. And with that, we bid you adieu."

He bowed as gracefully as possible before he scooped Cassie up in his arms and carried her out of the bar.

Sara couldn't quit laughing until she saw her husband's angry eyes on her.

"What?" she asked innocently.

"What? Really?" Benji fired back at her.

"Oh, stop." She waved him off. "It's all good. They were fine."

"That's because they're plastered! What are they going to do when they're sober and we 'bump into' Madeline?"

"We'll deal with that when it comes, okay. Right now, let's just focus on us."

Sara leaned over to nibble on Benji's ear, rendering him virtually powerless.

Chapter Thirty

ADRIAN STARED DISCONCERTINGLY UP AT the large, black clouds that seemed to hover over the bar.

"This isn't good," she said, voicing her concern.

Jake was thinking the same thing, but not because of the weather.

Something was off with Cassie; he could just sense it, even though she'd never admit it.

What is it? he thought while he helped her into their Uber. *Too much fresh air too fast? One too many shots of apple pie maybe?*

Cassie buried her head into the crook of Jake's neck the second he climbed in behind her.

"Or maybe somebody got her thinking," Adrian stated.

That's when it hit him: what Sara said to them before they left the bar.

I blew it off, but maybe Cass didn't, or couldn't. Now what do I do?

"Don't let her dwell on it. Right?" Adrian looked to Kevin for support.

"Mm-hmm," he replied.

"Hey," Jake said gently.

He lifted Cassie's chin up to discover the saddest pair of eyes he had ever seen. He was so caught off guard that it took him a moment to remember where he was going with this.

"You know what I just realized?"

"What?" Cassie sniffled.

"I don't believe I've wished you a proper happy thirtieth birthday yet."

That made her smile, not too much but just enough to give Jake hope.

"And how do you plan to do that?" Cassie asked.

Jake raised his eyebrows mischievously before leaning down close to her.

"By telling you everything I wish to do to you once we get inside the house."

Color sprang onto Cassie's cheeks while she squirmed impishly around in her seat.

"There." Adrian let out a sigh of relief. "Crisis averted."

"Not quite yet," Kevin corrected her.

*

The heat between them was palpable even before they stepped out into the humid air.

"I'm amazed they were able to unlock the front door," Adrian said in amusement.

"It does take some skill," Kevin replied.

They continued to watch Jake and Cassie fumble their way through Benji and Sara's house. Adrian remained impressed, especially because they never took their lips off each other.

That is, until one of them stepped on one of the girls' toys. Cassie swore they were in the right bedroom, but they could have easily gotten turned around somehow.

The how wasn't important. What was important was when she heard a familiar baby doll suddenly cry out: mama.

Baby Chloe, Cassie thought just as she heard a low rumble of thunder.

Caroline had asked them to bring Chloe along—just to make sure she was doing okay without Caroline—and they had happily obliged. But now, the baby doll's voice brought raw emotions back up to the surface for Cassie.

She backed away from Jake and purposefully avoided his eyes.

"Hey," he said to her with a sideways glance.

Cassie bit her lip, hoping it would detain her tears, but it didn't.

"I can't," she said, getting all choked up. "I'm sorry."

"Don't be," Jake said.

The thunder grew from a rumble into a roar. Adrian panicked; she felt as if the darkness were starting to close in around them.

"We need to do something, Kevin, now! We can't let it end like this."

"Adrian, you need to calm down," Kevin told her, "and just trust in the light."

"What?" Adrian asked as if he had lost his mind.

"The light," Kevin repeated. "Believe in the light."

"What light? It's pitch dark in here!"

A flash of lightning suddenly illuminated the room. Jake saw Baby Chloe right away and bent down to pick her up.

"What if..." Cassie's lips began to tremble uncontrollably. "What if...she's the only baby I can ever give you?"

"Oh, God," Adrian said with her hand over her heart.

Jake stayed hunched over for a moment as if Cassie's words had left him frozen in place.

"C'mon, Jake," Adrian pleaded with him. "You can't just leave her standing there. You have to say something compassionate to her. Tell him, Kevin!"

"He already knows," Kevin said quietly.

"I don't care," Jake said, his voice monotone as he shifted the doll from one hand to the other.

"What?" He spoke so softly that Cassie couldn't hear him.

"I said, I don't care about this," Jake replied as he sat the doll down on the shelf behind Cassie.

"You don't?" Her voice rose slightly higher.

Jake stood over Cassie and stared so intently at her with those piercing blue eyes of his that she had to remind herself to breathe.

"All I care about…" he said as he pressed her back up against the wall.

"Don't say 'fucking or screwing you'," Adrian recited like a strange prayer.

"…is forgetting all about that," Jake's eyes darted toward the shelf, then back to his wife, "and concentrating on making you scream in the best possible way I can."

He took her breath away again so she could only respond with her body.

Adrian let out a sigh of relief when she felt the storm clouds roll by.

"Well, I think I've been enlightened enough for one night," she said to Kevin.

"Don't go too far," he replied.

"I won't. I'm just going to follow the storm for a little bit, now that I can enjoy it again."

*

Adrian drifted back in with the dawn. Cassie recoiled from the light that poured in through the window, which made Adrian bust out laughing.

"Oh, Cass, you got me flashing back to our college days."

Cassie felt like she was back there too at first. Her mind flowed between dreams and consciousness. She was lost in that place in her head just before wakefulness took over.

Is it time to wake up already? I don't have an early class today, do I? Wait. It's Saturday, right? Or Sunday maybe? Yeah...but I'm not in school anymore. I have a job. Oh, shit! What time's my shift?

Cassie sprang out of bed, much to the regret of her pounding head.

She pressed the palm of her hand to her forehead and stared wide-eyed into the blinding light.

Adrian?!

Adrian instinctively hid in the shadows. Jake flung himself forward at the sound of his wife's distressed shouting.

"What the...? Cass, are you all right?"

"Yeah," Cassie said.

She blinked her eyes repeatedly and saw the same thing every time: a solitary ray of light and nothing more.

"Yeah," she said again as she put her head on her knees and waited for her heart rate to settle back down.

"It was just a bad dream," her husband told her.

"But it felt so damn real. It was like...someone...was standing right there watching us."

"It's okay," Jake said while he eased Cassie back down onto the pillows. "I've got you."

He pulled her close into the sanctuary of his arms; his head rested protectively on her shoulder.

"Better?" he asked.

"Much," Cassie replied tranquilly.

"Now, what would you like to do today, Miss Birthday Queen?"

"Stay right here, and maybe get that much-needed massage I wanted."

"As you wish."

Jake lifted his chin off her shoulder and readjusted himself.

"In case you've forgotten," he said while he let one hand slide down below her waist while the other reached around her breast, "I'm an excellent multi-tasker."

Chapter Thirty-One

IN HONOR OF JAKE AND Cassie's last night in Madison, Benji and Sara treated them to dinner at Jimmy Bean's on State Street.

Kayla and Caroline were in seventh heaven playing The Claw arcade game in the corner while they waited for their food. Cassie couldn't get over the view of The Capitol or how much time her sister-in-law was suddenly spending on her phone.

"Are we keeping you from a movie or a World of Warcraft Tournament or something?" Cassie asked her.

"Huh?"

Sara glanced up from her phone to discover everyone at the table staring at her in various forms of judgment.

"Oh." Her cheeks turned crimson as she held up her phone and hit the silence button. "Sorry. Work. All done now; I swear."

Sara tossed her phone into her handbag and the relaxed atmosphere gradually returned.

The girls were eventually enticed away from their game by cheese curds and boneless wings. Everyone was so engrossed in their appetizers and drinks that they barely noticed the tall woman with long, curly red hair who approached their table.

"Sara? Hey, hi, I thought that was you!"

"Madeline," Sara mumbled as she stood up with her mouth full of food. "Hey! Everyone, this is a friend of mine: Madeline Frasier."

Madeline raised an awkward hand in greeting to the group.

"So, what are you doing here?" Sara asked.

Jake raised his eyebrow a hair, partly for the question and partly because of the way Sara had asked it. Something in Sara's voice just sounded insincere—practiced even—to him. That, and the subtle look Benji tried to give his wife, sealed it for Jake. *Something's up.*

"How does he do that?" Adrian asked while she turned to Kevin in astonishment.

"First rule of hunting," Kevin replied. "Always be aware of your surroundings."

"Yeah, well, he's too damn aware of his surroundings, if you ask me," Adrian muttered.

"What am I doing here?" Madeline replied to Sara as if she really had to think about it. "I'm...uh...just picking something up for dinner to bring back to the office."

It was at this point that Benji caught both of his daughters gawking at Madeline.

"Ladies," he said, "manners please."

"Sorry, Daddy," Kayla quickly apologized, "but she just looks so much like..."

"Are you Princess Merida?" Caro couldn't help herself.

"Caroline!" Sara reprimanded.

"I am so sorry," she said to Madeline. "They're really into the movie *Brave* right now."

"It's okay." Madeline laughed. "I get that a lot."

"So," Kayla ventured further, "if you're not a princess, are you a doctor like Mommy and Daddy are?"

"Why, yes, I am."

"What kind?" Caro asked.

"Yeah," Jake reiterated in a deceptively casual manner like a defense attorney smelling blood in the water, "what kind of doctor are you exactly?"

"Oh, no." Adrian's voice was filled with dread, yet she couldn't resist pulling up a chair to get closer to the action.

Adrian kept a sharp eye on Miss Frasier while a sudden sense of unease swept over their table.

"This Madeline woman may be an excellent doctor," she observed, "but she'd make a horrible poker player. Even I can tell she's hiding something!"

"Well...I...uh..." Madeline stammered.

Sara couldn't take it anymore.

"She's a fertility doctor, okay!"

Her voice was so loud that several people in the restaurant turned their way, much to Benji's chagrin.

It was like they were all sitting in the aftermath of a bombing.

The blood pumped so strongly through Jake's veins that he had to grip both arms of his chair in a desperate attempt to control it.

Fertility doctor, he thought. *A God-damned FERTILITY doctor!*

Jake wanted to unleash his fury, but he didn't because of the girls. It translated very well in his eyes, though. He shot death rays at Sara, Benji, and finally Cassie, who looked about as flabbergasted as the children did.

"Mommy," Caro cautiously broke the silence, "what is a fertilie doctor?"

Kayla rolled her eyes at her little sister. "She helps people have babies, right, Mommy?"

"Mm-hmm." Sara bit her lip and shut her eyes as if it hurt her to speak.

"Oh," Caro replied thoughtfully before turning to Cassie. "So does this mean you might not need to keep Baby Chloe anymore?"

Jake gritted his teeth and willed himself, through memories of the last time he barged out of a restaurant, to stay seated.

It didn't last long.

"Speaking of Baby Chloe," Cassie told her nieces as she rose swiftly from her chair, "I think it might be a really good idea for Uncle Jake and I to go check on her."

"Right now?" Caro asked, clearly upset.

"Yep, right now."

Cassie couldn't even look her brother or sister-in-law in the eye. She just continued talking to the girls.

"You guys stay here and finish your dinner with your mom and dad, okay? I'll give you a full report when you get home."

"Okay," the girls replied, clearly disappointed.

With that, Cassie gave them both a kiss and strode unsteadily out of the restaurant, never once looking back.

Jake took this as his cue and followed after her, but not before shaking his head in disgust at both Benji and Sara.

"Why does this keep happening to him?" Adrian asked, not really expecting to get any kind of answer as she hurried to keep up with him.

Jake was thinking pretty much the same thing, along with some other thoughts that even made Adrian blush.

Chapter Thirty-Two

J AKE AND CASSIE HAD TO wait for an Uber since they had all ridden together to the restaurant in Benji's Land Rover. They didn't say much—they were both isolated in their own personal thoughts—until after they got to the house.

It really didn't fully hit Cassie until after she crossed the threshold of the front door.

It was like she had entered into another realm that had stripped her bare, leaving her vulnerable for all to see.

"Oh, my God," Cassie said as she fell into the nearest chair with her head in her hands. "What just happened?"

Jake stood stoic and unfazed behind her.

"We got ambushed," he said matter-of-factly.

Cassie's shoulders sagged lower as if her husband's words added extra weight onto her shoulders.

"Why?" she asked.

"How?" The word came out of Jake's mouth concise and measured. It sent a spine-tingling chill down Cassie's back that caused her to raise her head up out of her hands.

Not one word, she thought to herself. *Don't say anything that might incriminate you.*

Jake waited for a response, and when there wasn't one, he asked again.

"How, Cassie? How did they even know?"

His words fell like hailstones down upon her.

What do I say? I have to tell him something. I can't just ignore him, but how do I tell him the truth?

"Just say it," Adrian said sympathetically. "That's all you can do."

Cassie's next words came out on the tail end of a deep, wavering breath.

"I only told Sara."

"Oh, shit," Adrian replied.

"*Only* Sara," said Jake. "And you really thought she wouldn't share that information with anyone else, including her husband?"

"Don't take the bait," Adrian warned Cassie. "Just stay calm. Don't engage."

But it was too late. Jake had already hit a vital nerve.

"I needed to talk about it with someone before it destroyed us."

"Well, bravo. Job well done," Jake replied, heavy on the sarcasm.

Cassie never turned around to face him. She didn't even see him until he started to climb the stairs.

"Jake…" She spoke his name feebly. "Where are you going?"

"Bed," he replied, staring straight ahead. "I want to be out of here with the dawn."

Cassie didn't say a word. She stayed at the kitchen table with her hands folded in prayer.

Adrian stood behind her and rubbed her shoulders as if she were a prize fighter who had just finished a brutal round.

Adrian's eyes darted frantically over to Kevin, who stood at the bottom of the stairs and watched. He rubbed his fingers back and forth across his forehead as his son reached the bedroom door and shut it behind him.

*

Cassie woke to the sound of a duffel bag falling hard onto the tiled kitchen floor the next morning. She rolled over on the couch in the family room and winced at the oncoming sun.

The second she heard footsteps coming her way, she buried her head in the firm, decorative pillow.

"No," she grumbled. "Not again."

It had been a rough night. Cassie thought it best to sleep in the family room, only to be intruded upon by Benji and Sara as soon as they came home.

She didn't really want to say anything to them, especially Sara, because she knew once she started, she wouldn't be able to stop herself. So, Cassie turned to the back of the couch with the blanket pulled up over her head and pretended to be asleep, even when the girls asked their parents nervously if Auntie Cass was all right.

"She's fine," Cassie heard her brother tell his daughters. "It's just been a really long night for her and she's really tired."

That seemed to appease her nieces for the moment since they obeyed their father when he told them it was time to get ready for bed.

Darkness engulfed the room, but Cassie knew she wasn't alone yet. She could still sense someone else's presence there with her.

Sure enough, Sara stood in the doorway and whispered to her, "I am so sorry. I was only trying to help."

Help? Cassie thought as she lay on her back once the room was hers again. *You call blabbing something I told you in complete confidence to your husband—my brother!—helping me? Not counting the fact that you conveniently had a friend—who just happens to be a fertility specialist—show up at dinner with us? No way that was a coincidence. And now I'm pretty damn positive that Jake thinks I was in on all of it somehow too. Yeah, thanks, Sara, for all your help. Thanks a lot.*

"Hey," Jake spoke coldly to Cassie as he stood before her now, blocking out the light. "I'm all ready to go. Just waiting on you."

He didn't stick around for her reply. Cassie sat up slowly, her mouth wide open in shock at his behavior.

"What the…" she began out loud, then finished her thought silently. *I knew it was bad, but I didn't think it was bad enough to descend to this level of hell.*

Cassie didn't have time to analyze any further. She knew damn well Jake wouldn't think twice about leaving without her if she wasn't ready soon.

She ran a brush through her hair, skipped the makeup altogether, threw on a T-shirt and shorts, and was back downstairs with her suitcase in fifteen minutes flat.

"Here," she said while she thrust her luggage at her husband. "All set."

"No," she heard a startled cry from the staircase behind her. "You can't leave already!"

Great, Cassie thought while she shut her eyes. *Just great.*

She turned around to see her nieces standing between the railing in their nightgowns and fuzzy slippers looking as if they were about to cry.

"I'm sorry, girls," Cassie said, trying not to cry herself, "but we have to."

"Why?"

The girls flew down the stairs and clung to Cassie's legs. Cassie glared at her husband who, merely shrugged her off as if to say, *not my fault*.

Caro looked up at her aunt with sorrowful, guilt-ridden eyes.

"It's not because I asked about getting Baby Chloe back, is it? You're not mad at me, are you?"

Cassie tipped her head back in agony before she could look her niece in the eye.

"Oh God, Caro, no, we could never be mad at you, either one of you. Uncle Jake and I just need to get back home to take care of something there right away, okay?"

"Okay," Caro said, not pleased at all with her aunt's explanation. "You are going to say bye to Mommy and Daddy, though, right?"

"Aw, sweetheart, there really isn't any time. But I did leave them a note."

She handed the girls a folded piece of paper, just as Jake said from the doorway:

"We really do have to get going."

"Bye," Cassie said as she kissed each of her nieces. "I love you."

As soon as Jake and Cassie had left, the girls wasted no time in racing upstairs to their parents' bedroom with the note.

Adrian stood in the kitchen, dumbfounded.

"I don't understand," she said to Kevin. "How can he be such an...?"

She bit her tongue hard.

"It's okay," Kevin told her. "You can say it."

"Asshole." The air came out of her lungs like a deflating balloon.

"Because that's how we taught him to be."

"What?" Adrian's head snapped to attention.

"Laura and I," Kevin said. "He learned to fight like that from us. We always tried to keep it civil, so we wouldn't say anything we might regret later, especially in front of Jake. In the end, a lot of things were never said; we gave each other the silent treatment."

"I'm guessing that was all Laura's idea?" Adrian teased him.

"She had good intentions, and it worked most of the time."

"It definitely left an impression, that's for sure."

*

Cassie had her elbow propped up against the passenger side door of the truck, her chin in her hand as they sped away from her brother's house.

Her head jerked up after they passed the very last Kwik Trip on their way out of the city. Her eyes zeroed in on her husband, but he kept his eyes on the road ahead of him.

Really? she thought. *No Kwik Trip pit stop? What about gas or, more importantly, a drink and some cookies or even a brownie, for Christ's sake?*

"I hate to tell you this, Cass," Adrian said to her friend, "but I'm pretty sure Jake filled up way before you woke up this morning."

The trip became excruciatingly quiet. First a half hour, then forty-five minutes, up to an hour in complete silence.

Adrian and Kevin sat stretched out in the cab of Jake's pickup, the wind whipping Adrian's hair around in all directions.

"This has got to stop," she said, clearing strands away from her eyes.

"Hey," Kevin replied, "it's the price you pay when you choose to ride in the cab."

"Not that," Adrian rolled her eyes before she flexed her thumb through the half-open window between them at Jake and Cassie. "That."

"They have to start talking to each other."

"Only one way that's going to happen," Kevin stated while he stretched his arms out over his head.

It took Adrian a minute to catch onto his meaning.

"No! Absolutely not."

"Well, I guess they'll just have to suffer in silence then."

"Really? Is that the only way we can get them to talk to each other?"

"Yep."

"Even though…"

"Yep." Kevin spoke more assertively this time.

"No." Adrian crossed her arms. "I can't do it."

"You mean you won't." Kevin sat up straighter. "You're acting like you have a choice in this, but you don't."

"What?" Adrian turned to him while her arms slowly untangled and fell to her sides.

"It's an order you can't refuse, unless you want to take it up with…" Kevin pointed up to the sky.

"Kevin!"

"Adrian!" he mimicked her. "Go do your job. Now!"

Adrian let out a low growl and lay the palms of her hands out flat on the truck bed. She looked over her shoulder at the traffic that streamed by them on the country highway.

"Fine," she huffed as she stood up and slammed her hands down on the top of the truck.

Jake and Cassie both jumped but wouldn't look at each other.

A bug, a bird, some kind of animal hit something back there probably. Maybe. Hopefully, they thought and continued on in mutual silence.

"But let the record show," Adrian finished her conversation with Kevin, "I am doing this under protest."

"Duly noted." Kevin nodded. "Now get on with it, please."

Adrian looked out into the fields until she saw a group of deer grazing close by. She raised her hand up over her head and, when she felt the traffic had lightened enough, motioned for one of the deer to cross the highway.

Jake saw it just in the nick of time. He slammed on the brakes and sent everything, from their luggage to themselves, flying forward.

The truck veered off onto the shoulder of the road and remained there until they got their bearings back.

Adrian lay across the top of the truck.

"Happy now?" she asked Kevin as she eventually rose to her full height to see the deer move casually onto the next clump of trees as if it were just another normal moment in its life.

"What the?" she heard Cassie exclaim.

"How's my girl?" Jake asked anxiously a few seconds later.

"Well," Cassie answered honestly, "I could really use a mega-cup of Mountain Dew and about a half-dozen double-chocolate-chip cookies from the nearest Kwik Trip, if there is one."

There seemed to be a delayed response, and then laughter. First from Jake, then it spread over to Cassie.

"Let me see what I can do for you," Jake said, "as soon as I can maneuver this old girl back onto the road."

Adrian sank back down into the cab while Kevin smirked at her.

*

"Want one?" Cassie asked while she waved a cookie underneath her husband's nose.

"Damn straight," Jake said before he took a huge bite. "I didn't drive half an hour out of our way just for you."

"Yeah, right," Cassie grinned as she climbed back into the truck.

Jake adjusted his seatbelt and was about to put the key in the ignition when he stopped to look at his wife.

"Cass?"

"Yeah?"

"I'm sorry."

"Me too."

Jake started the truck and they pulled out of the gas station and onto the highway again.

"Jake?" Cassie turned to her husband.

"Yeah?"

"I had nothing to do with any of...that."

"I know." *Now.*

They drove another couple of miles before Jake reached over for his soda. Cassie twisted off the cap and handed it to him. Their hands seemed melded together around the plastic bottle in mid-air for some time before Jake reluctantly pulled it away to take a drink.

"And that," Kevin said with a flourish to Adrian, "is the result of civilized fighting."

"That, and almost crashing into a deer," Adrian added.

Chapter Thirty-Three

"**I**SN'T IT JUST A TRULY gorgeous day today, Father?" Julia asked as she stepped out of the cathedral and into the sunlight to shake Father Andrew's hand.

"It is indeed," he agreed, pleased to see the blue, cloudless sky. "A perfect one to go out and spread God's joy."

Benjamin hung back in the crowd but could still hear their conversation. He brought his fist to his mouth, acting like he was about to cough, but he was really trying to conceal his snickering.

Oh, she'll be spreading something today all right, Benjamin thought, *but I don't think it's going to be joy.*

He put his hands in his pockets as he made his way down the steps to stand beneath the shade of the nearest tree while he waited for his wife.

Benjamin knew Julia was going to be a while. Socializing is what she called it; gossiping was more like it.

There she stood in the center of the circle of women who belonged to The Ladies Auxiliary, looking like their queen bee.

*I would kill to have a cigarette right abo*ut now. Benjamin hardly ever smoked anymore, but when the urge hit, it hit hard. *And God forbid I light one up out here.*

So he paced back and forth from the tree trunk to the parking lot until he saw a familiar hand extend a cigarette out to him.

Benjamin looked up suspiciously, as if he suspected a trap being set.

"Go ahead," his son Nicky told him, "before the guards catch on."

Benjamin glanced over Nicky's shoulder at Julia. It seemed like the group was gathering steam, too intent in their own conversations to notice anything that was happening around them.

"Thanks," Benjamin said while he snatched the cigarette out of his son's fingers.

Nicky swiftly produced another one for himself, along with a lighter from the pocket of his pants.

Benjamin raised an inquisitive brow, but then he looked at his granddaughter sleeping peacefully in the bunting strapped over Nicky's shoulders, and found the answer to the question he didn't ask out loud.

Both men kept their backs to the intermingling crowd, looking up into the trees as if they were discussing something they saw climbing the branches.

They could feel the women dispersing as if they had radar. They quickly flicked their cigarette butts into the tall grass while Nicky discreetly handed his father a Life Saver.

"Ready?" Julia asked Benjamin as she and Kathleen approached them.

"Whenever you are," Benjamin replied, swallowing the last of his Life Saver as he turned around to face his wife. "Did you ladies have fun socializing?"

"We did. I was looking forward to doing a little of that with my granddaughter here." Julia's voice trailed off while she gently stroked the baby's tiny hand.

"She held out as long as she could, Grandma," Nicky said with an apologetic shrug.

"I really wish you wouldn't have let her fall asleep so soon, Nicholas," Kathleen sighed. "Now she'll be a bear for me to deal with later."

"Sorry." His response this time sounded less sincere.

"Well, it's too late now," Kathleen replied tensely. "Do you think you can handle getting her into her car seat while I go retrieve Dominick from daycare downstairs?"

"Yes, dear."

Benjamin shook his head and flashed a devilish grin when they parted ways.

I'll never understand what you were thinking, son, but I'm glad it's you and not me.

"Well," Julia said after they got into their vehicle, "let's see if I can connect with my other grandchildren."

While most churchgoers flocked to their favorite restaurant after Mass, Julia made it a point to stay in touch with all of her grandchildren.

Nicky and Kathleen's kids were easy since they attended Mass on a regular basis. Benji and Sara were sometimes a little harder to track down.

Julia was still learning how to navigate her new iPhone, but if she were lucky, she could FaceTime with her granddaughters every once in a while. That wasn't the case today, though.

Both Benji and Sara's cell phones went straight to voicemail, leaving Julia no choice but to try the landline.

They had both agreed that since the girls were still young, they would keep their landline for emergencies. Julia dialed it now, hoping she wouldn't be thrown a second strike.

*

"Now this is the kind of fighting I'm used to," Adrian told Kevin.

They were standing in Benji and Sara's family room. The doors were shut. Caroline and Kayla sat on the floor with *Brave* blaring on the big screen TV. The girls could have cranked the TV up to its maximum volume and it wouldn't have mattered. Their parents were shouting so loudly at each other in another room that it drowned out their movie.

Caroline tried to put the sides of her pillows up over her ears while Kayla hugged her teddy bear tightly to her chest.

"You wanna go outside and play tag?" Kayla asked her sister while she stared longingly at the backyard.

"Uh-uh."

"Please?" Kayla begged.

"No! Mommy and Daddy will get madder."

"And this is why," Kevin explained to Adrian, "Laura and I preferred civilized fighting."

"Can't argue with you on that one," Adrian replied.

Just then, the cordless phone rang. The girls scrambled around the room in search of it; Kayla came up the winner.

"Hello?" she asked tentatively.

"Hey, sweetheart!" Julia's cheerfulness poured out through the receiver. "I'm so glad I got a hold of you."

"Grandma J!" Caro nearly did a somersault trying to reach her big sister's side.

"Caro, is that you? How are you girls?"

"Okay," they both replied less than enthusiastically.

"What's wrong?"

"Mommy and Daddy are fighting," Caro said.

"What? Why?"

"Auntie Cass and Uncle Jake got mad!" Kayla yelled while she tried to grab the phone away from her sister. "And they left really early this morning."

"Kayla, let me talk!"

"Girls, girls, one at a time please. I can't understand anything you're saying. So, Auntie Cass and Uncle Jake were there with you?"

"Girls!"

The loud, commanding voice of their father as he flung open the door silenced them both.

"What is going on in here?"

"It's Grandma J," Kayla said as she held the phone out to her dad. "She wants to talk to you."

*

"Jules?" Benjamin asked cautiously.

She stood with her mouth open and the dead phone gripped tightly in her hand.

"Julia?" he tried again.

Her mouth snapped shut and her posture became finishing school perfect. A rare look in her eyes made her husband want to flee as if she were channeling Cruella De Vil.

Oh, shit! he thought. "What's wrong?" he asked, dreading the answer.

"I need to go," Julia replied as if she were possessed.

"Go? Go where?"

She walked right past him as if he weren't even there.

"To talk to Cassandra," she said as she opened and shut the front door in one single, fluid motion.

Cassandra? Benjamin thought. *Oh, fuck!*

*

The tension left Cassie's body as soon as they drove onto the familiar freeway. They were almost home, and she couldn't wait. It wasn't even noon yet, but it had already been a long day.

All she wanted to do, as they reached the hallway to their apartment, was head upstairs to their bedroom to take a nice, long nap with her husband.

Unfortunately, that wasn't to be.

"Mom!" Cassie exclaimed when she saw her looming before their front door.

Jake instinctively drew his wife closer to him.

"What are you doing here?" Cassie asked.

Julia's response came out in a measured tone.

"A fertility doctor."

Cassie cringed with anxiety.

"Mom, please, I really don't have the energy for this…"

"Inside now, Cassandra."

Jake and Cassie were both taken aback by the fierceness in Julia's voice.

Jake looked to his wife for confirmation before he stepped forward to unlock the door. Cassie kept her distance from her mother as they all went inside.

"I had a very informative talk with my granddaughters after church this morning," Julia began.

Cassie slowly shut her eyes as it all began to sink in.

Kayla and Caro. Of course!

Cassie's phone had been buzzing in her purse like crazy all the way home, but she had chosen to ignore it. She couldn't deal with anything more right then, but she knew now it was probably her brother trying to warn her; not that he could've prepared her for this.

"Mom, I didn't invite you in to fight with you. This is my choice to make; not yours."

"Your choice?" Julia scoffed. "Oh, I highly doubt that," she added, looking directly at Jake.

Cassie slipped her arm around Jake to keep him from lunging at her mother.

His nostrils flared and the veins in his neck popped out, but he stood his ground, even as Julia continued to carry on.

"I know all about choices. I thought I made the right one a long time ago too."

Cassie's patience was wearing thin.

"I'm in no mood for games, Mom. So if you have something to say to me, could you please just say it?"

"You want me to say it? Fine, I'll say it: I got pregnant back when I was in college."

Julia's entire body shook from an adrenaline rush. She didn't fully realize what she had just revealed until it was too late.

Jake's face transformed from defiant to shocked faster than he could control it. Cassie was stunned into silence.

Chapter Thirty-Four

"WHAT THE...!" ADRIAN EXPLODED BEFORE she asked Kevin. "Did you know about this?"

"Does it really matter?" he asked quietly.

"Hell, yeah!"

"No, it doesn't. What matters right now is protecting Cassie."

Adrian turned to her best friend, who seemed catatonic. Adrian couldn't handle it and diverted her gaze, only to have it fall upon Julia.

The impact of her words slowly took their toll on her. Her lips trembled and her eyes flittered around as if she were a trapped bird trying to find an escape route.

She staggered toward the door, leaving Jake and Cassie stupefied behind her.

Once Cassie's brain allowed her body to move again, she sank to the floor and lurched forward, her arm over her stomach as if she were about to throw up.

"Cass!" Jake rushed to her side. "Are you okay?"

"Yeah," she mumbled weakly while her eyes searched around the room for something.

"Tell me what you need."

"My purse; my phone actually."

Jake didn't question her. He just went on the hunt for her phone, and once he found it, he obediently handed it over to her.

"Thank you."

"You're sure you're all right?" Jake asked as he cupped her head in his hand.

Cassie closed her eyes, so tempted to lean into his palm, but she resisted. One more thing needed to be done.

"I have to be."

She smiled faintly before punching her brother's number into her phone.

"Soap Star." Benji sounded relieved to finally hear from her.

"What the hell did you tell her?" Cassie snapped.

"Mom got to you already, I take it?"

Cassie let out an exaggerated laugh that almost sounded psychotic. "That's the understatement of the year, brother dear. Now, answer my question."

"Not much really," he replied. "I swear! She asked why Sara and I were fighting. I told her you guys came down for a visit and we were all having a great time until we ran into one of Sara's friends at dinner."

"And?"

"And," Benji pinched the bridge of his nose and sucked in some much-needed air, "one of the girls may have let it slip that she was a fertility doctor."

"Oh, Jesus."

"I know; I know. I tried to explain, but Mom wouldn't let me. All she heard was 'fertility doctor' and that was it. You know how she gets."

"Yeah. Yeah, I do." *Or*, thought Cassie, *at least, I thought I did anyway.*

"I tried to warn you; call and give you a heads-up at least."

"I know."

"So how bad was it?" Benji asked.

Cassie tried to smooth out the creases in her forehead with her fingertips.

"You wouldn't believe me if I told you. I still can't even believe it myself."

"You up for talking about it?"

"No, not now. I'm still trying to process it all, but thanks."

"I'm sorry again, Soap Star, for everything. If you need me, you know how to get a hold of me."

"Yep, I do. I'll talk to you soon, Benji."

Cassie remained on the floor for a few minutes more after she hung up her phone. Jake tried to help her when she rose to her feet, but she waved him away.

Cassie stared into her husband's beautiful blue eyes that were now swimming in concern for her.

"It's all right," she reassured him. "I'm going to be fine. I just think I need to go for a ride, alone, okay?"

"Okay." *I get the need to ride. Completely.*

Jake took his wife's hands in his and squeezed as if he were trying to send his energy straight through his hands into her.

Cassie's arms suddenly felt stronger to him. He watched in awe as her shoulders rolled back, and she stood regally before him with her held high in an exquisite version of her own Riley stance.

Jake kissed her. Cassie's urgency to leave, along with Adrian's hands, pulled her away first. Instinct screamed at Jake to go after her, but his gut and his father's strong hold on him prevented him from taking any impulsive actions until after Cassie left.

Kevin released his son. Jake grabbed the closest thing to him— his duffel bag—and launched it at the wall with a primal scream Adrian had only heard once before.

Jesus Lord, he begged, *please just let her be safe.*

*

Benjamin heard Julia's Equinox pull into the driveway, but she didn't come inside. He set his ham and cheese sandwich down on the counter, wiped the crumbs on his sleeveless, gray T-shirt, and headed outside to check on her.

He only had to go as far as the garage door. Worry couldn't begin to describe what he felt when he saw her.

It was Julia standing there just inside the garage, but it wasn't. She reminded him of a cornered animal, too terrified to make its next move.

"Jules."

Benjamin spoke her name in a subdued voice as he came down the three cement steps and made his way over to her.

He didn't think she had heard him. The closer Benjamin got, the more panicked he became.

Jesus, should I call an ambulance for her?

Benjamin wanted so badly to reach out to her, but he was afraid if he touched her, she might shatter right there in front of him. But he couldn't just leave her there either, staring blankly at his beloved Charger that took up most of the space in their garage.

"Jules…sweetheart…why don't you come inside with me?"

"Inside?"

Benjamin jumped at the sound of her voice.

"Yeah, c'mon."

He offered his hand to her, but she didn't take it.

"No."

Julia moved with halted steps as if she wanted to go somewhere but didn't know where or how.

"I need..." her voice broke off, unable to communicate her thoughts.

"Need what, honey?"

Her eyes roamed around the garage until she saw what she was looking for on one of the shelves. Julia walked purposefully toward it, grabbed the crowbar, and wielded it with all of her pent-up aggression at the Charger.

"Julia!"

Benjamin's only thought was to get the tool away from his wife before she did serious damage. Not to the car—he was years away from getting her back to her former glory—but to herself. Then he stopped to watch her and realized it might actually be helping her.

Damn you, Chris Bradley, Julia thought as she took a chunk out of the hood. *Damn you, Kevin Riley,* she thought before she took another swing. *Damn men; damn them all.*

Adrian sat on the bottom step with her cheeks in the palms of her hands while Kevin leaned against a shelf, lined with cans of car wax and old rags, beside her.

"Still think Julia got what she deserves?" he asked.

Chapter Thirty-Five

THE CABIN WAS ABOUT AN hour north of Green Bay, nestled within the woods of The Ottawa National Forest. It had been built on private land by Cassie's great-grandfather and had been her family's getaway place for as long as she could remember.

And she definitely needed a place to get away to now.

Cassie only had to stop once for gas and a Mountain Dew to help keep her awake.

Her thumb hovered briefly over her phone after she got back inside her car.

I know he's worried, but the connection's terrible out here anyway, Cassie told herself as she tossed her phone on the passenger seat. *I'll call him as soon as I get there.*

Everything went away the second Cassie turned onto the gravel road that led to the cabin. She became one with the music on the radio, even as it cut in and out, as the lake air drifted in through her window.

Her heart leapt when the cabin finally came into sight. Cassie forced herself to maneuver her car slowly toward the small garage her dad had built alongside the cabin.

"God," she said while she shut the garage door behind her and stared longingly at the water before her. "I so needed this."

She felt like she was six years old again. She could picture herself on the edge of her seat in the back of her parents' minivan, her hand on the handle, just waiting for the right moment to jump out.

All I ever wanted to do was beat my brothers out to the dock and be the first one to do a cannonball off it.

Cassie swore she could hear her mother yelling at her to put her life jacket on, while her dad tried to calm down her mother.

"Relax, Jules," he'd tell her. "Cassie is a good swimmer. She'll be fine."

Mom. Dad.

Cassie's heart grew heavy.

Jesus, Dad!

"No," she told herself as she made her way to the front door. "We're not going to do this now."

She fished around in her purse for her keys, pulled them out victoriously, and unlocked the door. She stepped inside, stood on the cement floor, and embraced the ruggedness of it all.

The cabin was never meant to be modernized. It was the place you came to get away from it all. There was no internet or cell phone towers, not even a dishwasher was allowed to be installed. The floors were covered with mismatched, multicolored rag rugs, and family pictures, dating back to the days when the cabin walls were being raised, hung on practically every wall.

Cassie flopped happily down onto the deep brown, flowered couch and was surprised to hear her stomach growling.

"Aw, shit!"

It never occurred to her to bring food, and she was pretty sure there was nothing here except expired condiments and stale potato chips.

The nearest grocery store was a half hour away, just over the Wisconsin/Michigan border.

A couple of bars were closer, but she wasn't really in the mood for a pizza and beer.

Either way, Cassie was going to have to go back out and get something. But before she did that, she had to call Jake.

"Hey!"

Cassie got giddy when she heard the joy in her husband's voice.

"Hey," she practically giggled. "So, I made it here, safe and sound."

"Good. I'm glad to hear that." Jake quickly regained his cool. "Now, you mind telling me where 'here' is?"

"What? Oh…Jake, oh my God, baby, I am so sorry! I never told you where I was going, did I?"

Because I didn't know myself until I got here.

"No, you did not, but it's okay so long as I know where you are now."

"I decided to come up to the cabin. I was just about to head out and get some food—"

"How long you plan on staying up there?" he asked, cutting her off.

"I don't know," Cassie replied honestly while she twisted the phone cord between her fingers. "Overnight at least."

"Oh."

"You're not going to miss me or anything, are you?" she teased.

"No, no, take all the time you need," Jake replied, then back-pedaled. "I mean, yeah, of course I'd rather have you here with me."

The smile on her face widened while her stomach rumbled louder.

"I'll give you a call first thing in the morning and let you know when I'm heading back, okay."

"Okay, sounds good."

"But right now, I have to get some food in me before I eat my arm off."

Jake laughed. "All right, I don't want you turning to cannibalism. Love you."

"Love you too."

*

"Never go shopping when you're hungry," Cassie lectured herself a little too late.

She came back into the cabin with a full paper bag cradled in one arm and about a half-a-dozen plastic ones dangling from her other one. She dropped everything at her feet in the doorway and worked up the energy to return to the car to grab the six pack of Mountain Dew and the takeout she had ordered for dinner.

A sign outside one of the bars she had passed on her way to the store had advertised charbroiled, angus beef burgers. So, of course, she had to stop on the way back to order one, along with some chili cheese fries that were just calling her name.

Cassie left the groceries in their bags so she could take an enormous bite of her burger.

"Oh," her eyes nearly rolled back in her head, "so good."

She turned the radio on in the living room—there was no television for background noise—and jammed out to the music while she put the food away and picked at her fries.

"Apparently," Cassie said out loud later as she made herself some Jiffy-Pop popcorn on the stove, "I'm a stress eater. Who knew?"

"Not me," Adrian said in amazement.

Cassie licked the butter off her fingers as she carried the popcorn with her into the living room. She browsed the wide array of books that lined the shelves and decided on a suspense thriller about a dysfunctional family that sounded way worse than her own did right now.

Darkness eventually engulfed the room. Cassie lay back in the well-worn recliner, the popcorn tin toppled over on the floor, the radio still blaring old country hits, and the novel she was reading split open across her chest.

"This is one of those moments," Adrian whispered as she watched drool dribble down the corner of her best friend's mouth, "when I wish I had a camera."

*

Benjamin didn't pull his wife away from the Charger until she didn't have the energy to swing the crowbar anymore.

Julia didn't fight him as he set her gently onto the floor. She never moved, but her eyes followed him as he cranked the volume up on his boombox and hit the garage door remote with his elbow on his way back to her.

"Keep the neighbors guessing," he replied to her puzzled expression as he helped her to her feet.

"How about I get some bath water running for you?"

Julia nodded while she let her husband lead her back inside the house.

She clutched her robe tighter to her while she padded down the stairs in her slippers about an hour and a half later.

She felt more like herself now that she had taken a bath. She lay in the tub until all the bubbles had disintegrated and the warm water had turned cold.

Julia only went under once, but then she thought about Benjamin. She popped her head right back up, slicked her hair back, and told herself what she always did whenever she reached this attack of conscience:

This is my cross to bear, not his. There's no reason for him to be burdened with this too.

"She's never told him?" Adrian asked Kevin in shock.

Kevin stood as solemn as one of the queen's soldiers outside of Buckingham Palace, which didn't surprise Adrian.

What did surprise her, though, and Julia too, was that the downstairs was empty.

"Benjamin?" Julia called out as she roamed around the living room and kitchen. "Hello? Benjamin, where are you?"

Julia stopped short of the entrance to the garage. She heard noises coming from inside. She turned the knob and opened the door just enough so she could eavesdrop.

Her husband stood by the hood of his Charger, surveying the damage she had done to it.

Julia put her hand to her mouth. She'd had no idea, in the heat of the moment, how much destruction she had caused. She watched Benjamin run a hand over every dent she had made, as if he were a doctor uncertain if he could save a patient he had grown too close to.

She had seen enough and knew what she needed to do.

Benjamin came upstairs a little while later to find his wife sound asleep in their bed.

He lifted the blanket up to her shoulders, kissed her head, and snuck quietly out of the room.

"To give his wife her space," Kevin said before Adrian asked.

Benjamin stepped out of the boys' old room the next morning, still half asleep from a restless night. He tiptoed down the hall to their bedroom to find it empty.

The bed was made, and a note was propped up between the pillows. It read:

Left for the cabin.
Be home before dark.
Love, Me

Chapter Thirty-Six

C ASSIE WAS STARTLED AWAKE THE next morning by the sound of a roaring lawn mower. She sat up in the dark room, disoriented until she finally found her cell phone.

"Who's the ass who's up mowing their lawn at the ungodly hour of..."

She stopped ranting when the phone lit up with the correct time.

"Nine a.m.! What? That can't be right."

She swung her legs over the edge of the bed, stood up, and stumbled over to the sliding door that separated the bedroom from the kitchen. Cassie tugged the door aside and looked up in shock at the huge clock on the wall.

"Damn," she said while she waited for the numbers to solidify before her eyes, "it really is that late already."

She ran her hand over her face before she yanked the refrigerator door open and reached inside for a Mountain Dew.

The bottle was halfway to her mouth when she came up with a better way to wake herself up.

"What the hell?" she said. "Why not?"

Cassie was outside on the front lawn ten minutes later in her board shorts and halter top swimsuit. She positioned her bare feet in a runner's stance and sharply eyed the lake.

"Ready…set…go!"

She gained speed as her feet switched from grass to the planks in the long, wooden, dock. Cassie was airborne before she knew it, her knees held tight to her chest as she plunged into the cold lake water.

It felt exactly the way she remembered it, even better maybe. She rose to the surface with a rush of exhilaration and a scream that released all her inhibitions.

Cassie didn't stop until she cleared the water from her eyes and saw the sun rising into the sky from the far end of the lake.

It left her speechless.

Wow, she thought. *I had forgotten how truly beautiful it is out here.*

Just then, she swore she heard a car door shut in the distance somewhere. Her eyes darted to the top of the hill while she treaded water until she reached the ladder alongside the dock.

Cassie's hands froze on the railing when she caught sight of a figure standing by the cabin.

"Who the hell is that?" she muttered. *One of the neighbors maybe? It couldn't possibly be Jake, could it?*

Cassie's question was answered a few minutes later. She was lying back on the wooden bench, drip-drying in the sun, when she felt a shadow hover over her.

"That still scares the hell out of me every time I see you do it."

Cassie's body went as rigid as a nun's ruler when she heard her mother's voice above her.

"What is she doing?" Adrian asked before she said to Cassie, "Do you think if you shut your eyes tight enough you can make her go away?"

The childish part of Cassie wished it could work that way, but she knew it wouldn't.

"She's right there, Cass," Adrian continued. "She sees you, and you're going to have to deal with her."

I know, Cassie scolded herself. *I know.*

"Cassie," Julia asked, hoping the fear wasn't evident in her voice, "may I join you?"

Cassie didn't say a word. She let out a deep breath as she grabbed her towel and slid down the length of the bench, as far away from her mother as possible.

Julia pressed her lips together and nodded.

I expected nothing less, Julia thought as she chose a chair on the opposite end of the dock.

"I'm sorry," Julia began, her eyes cast down onto her hands. "I never meant for you to find out like that."

"No," Cassie replied with amazing calmness. "You never meant for me to find out about it all, did you?"

"Cassie."

"And what about Dad?" she went on as if her mother hadn't spoken. "Did you ever intend to clue him in on any of this?"

"Cassie, please, just let me explain."

Adrian looked up to see clouds overtaking the sky. She glanced nervously at Kevin as a light breeze blew through the trees.

Julia felt the heat from her only daughter's eyes on her. She knew whatever Cassie was about to say next was going to hurt her like a son-of-a-bitch.

"No!" Cassie rocketed up off the bench. "I don't want to hear any of your hypocritical excuses. You've been on me my whole life to be this good Christian girl. Hell, you even managed to keep me from getting married in church because we were 'living in sin,' and now you tell me you got pregnant in college."

Cassie was about to storm off, but she only got as far as the end of the dock.

"Cassandra Ann Adler!"

She automatically froze in place at the use of her full name.

"You can judge me any way you want to," Julia said, "but not until you listen to me first."

Cassie sighed in defeat. She knew her mother was right, and she hated it.

"Fine." She whirled around with her arms folded.

"Sit," her mother ordered her as she pointed to the spot Cassie had just vacated.

Cassie gave a slight roll of her eyes while she trudged back to the bench.

They sat in silence while Julia struggled with where to begin.

"I told you Chris and I were serious."

"The hockey player?" Cassie asked in disdain.

"Yes, the hockey player. He wasn't just some guy I met at a party or a one-night stand or a mistake I made after having too many drinks. I was nineteen and madly in love, but I didn't do anything until I was absolutely ready. Chris never pressured me or anything like that. He didn't leave a trail of rose petals leading to the bed or anything like you see in the movies either. It just felt right, and it happened, but I suppose I can't expect you to understand that."

Cassie's cheeks grew red with shame as she fell hard off her high horse.

Oh, I know all too well, Mom.

Cassie remembered her first time with Jake. She had been angry at having her leave of absence from work extended; Jake was just angry. Their frustration connected them in a way she never could have imagined.

It just happened, Cassie thought now.

Her eyes carried a hint of sympathy with them as they drifted onto her mother. Cassie saw her, for the first time in her life, not as a strong, demanding woman, but a frightened young teenager, younger than she and Adrian had been when they first met Jake.

Something in the way her daughter looked at her made it difficult for Julia to speak.

"Anyway," Julia continued after she cleared her throat, "we thought we had all of our bases covered, but God had other plans, I guess."

"So, you got pregnant, but there was no baby?"

Cassie never had a harder time asking a question before.

"You didn't...?" she stopped and tried again.

Julia spared her.

"No. Lord, no! It never once crossed my mind to end the pregnancy."

Julia's stomach twisted and turned, and that's when the pieces started to come together for Adrian.

"Wait," Adrian said. "So she wasn't faking at Dominick's birthday party, was she?"

"Grief comes out of nowhere sometimes," Kevin replied. "No matter how long ago it happened."

"I even convinced myself," Julia continued to Cassie, "that the three of us could be a happy little family."

The sound of loons calling out to each other across the lake halted their conversation.

"Do you remember me telling you about the weekend of Winter Carnival?"

"Yeah," Cassie said uneasily.

"I was going to tell Chris then that I was pregnant."

"But you caught him with another woman instead."

"Yep."

"So he never knew?"

"No, but it really didn't matter because I...um...I...miscarried right before I went home for spring break."

Cassie had inched over to her mother throughout their conversation. She was right beside her now and reached her hand out to her. Julia accepted it gratefully.

"I can still remember sitting in church between my parents and listening to the priest's sermon like we were the perfect Catholic family."

"Oh, Mom." Cassie squeezed her hand.

"I wanted to bolt, but I couldn't. I had to stay in that pew with my parents till Mass ended, smiling away like everything was fine."

"Why are you crying now?" her mother whispered sternly to her midway through the service.

"My mother knew something was wrong, but I had no intention of telling her or my dad. So I suffered in silence the entire time I was home until my mom, in a last-ditch effort, gave me her rosary. I went back to school and prayed on that rosary every night before I went to bed. I asked for His forgiveness and promised never to lose faith in Him again. And I really do believe that faith is what brought me to your father a few years later."

"But you never told him about any of this!" Cassie said incredulously.

"Why?" Julia shrugged. "That was something that happened to the old me. I had worked far too hard for too long to get rid of her and become a better person. And besides that, there wasn't anything your dad could have done to fix any of it. And I was terrified that talking about it might bring the old me back for good."

The loons had landed. Both women's eyes were fixed upon them as they floated aimlessly along the water.

"So," Cassie broke the silence, "you promised never to lose faith in Him again?"

"Yes," Julia replied.

"You lied," Cassie said matter-of-factly.

"What?"

"If you did have faith you would've trusted me with Jake."

*

Benjamin was in the garage listening to Bon Jovi and doing what he could for the Charger when his wife pulled up in the driveway. He didn't see the vehicle at first that pulled in behind her.

"I thought you said you weren't coming home until tonight?" he asked as he searched for something inside the trunk.

"Change of plans."

Benjamin was peeking around the Charger in confusion when he heard his daughter's voice.

Is that? he thought. *No, it can't be. Not here with Jules.*

"Cassie?"

Benjamin picked a rag up off the floor to wipe his hands as he ambled over to the two women, each one standing alongside their own vehicle.

"Hi, Dad."

"Somebody want to tell me what's going on?" he asked.

"It's a long story," Cassie replied, "that Mom will tell you all about."

"Jules?" Benjamin looked to his wife.

"Come inside with me, please."

"Okay." The tone of her voice heightened Benjamin's anxiety, but he followed her into the house.

"What about you?" Benjamin stopped to ask Cassie. "Aren't you coming in too?"

"No," Cassie said. "I have my own sit-down I need to have with Jake."

"It'll be fine," Julia reassured her.

"Thanks, Mom."

Benjamin hid his shock over how his wife and daughter were interacting behind a poker face.

"I'll call you later," Cassie said as she got back into her car. "Love you guys."

Adrian and Kevin made themselves comfortable in a pair of lawn chairs left out on the front lawn.

"What are you grinning about over there?" Kevin asked Adrian.

"I'm proud of myself," she said. "Aren't you?"

"Why's that?"

"Did you not just witness the last few hours at the cabin?"

"I did. Yes."

"And did you not see how well I kept my composure? How I did not let my personal feelings interfere with my job?"

"Oh, yeah, that."

"That's all you have to say: 'Oh, yeah, that'?"

Kevin laughed. "I was very impressed. Good job."

"Thank you." Adrian sat back in her chair, satisfied.

"Now," said Kevin, "let's hope Jake handles his conversation with Cassie just as well."

"Oh, yeah," Adrian said, nervously standing back up. "I hadn't thought about that.

Chapter Thirty-Seven

JAKE STRETCHED OUT ON THE couch. Badger football highlights played out on the television from the day before, but he wasn't really paying attention to them. His eyes were on the TV, but his mind was on his wife.

Cassie called to tell him she was going to be leaving the cabin soon, but that now seemed like hours ago to Jake.

She should've been here by now, he thought.

He jumped off the couch every time he heard something outside in the hallway. Once, Jake even threw the front door open, expecting to see Cassie there, only to find a bewildered next-door neighbor coming inside with her mail.

Jake ducked humbly back inside and vowed not to venture back into the hallway.

So, he was maintaining a calm appearance when Cassie finally did come through the door.

"Hey," he said as he slid off the couch and strolled over to her.

Cassie didn't say anything; she just burrowed inside her husband's arms, which left Jake dumbfounded.

She didn't seem upset to Jake. All the more reason to give him cause for alarm and hold her a little tighter.

"You all right?" he spoke into her hair.

"Yeah," she said. "I just needed to feel your arms around me, to know we have no secrets between us."

Cassie lingered in not only Jake's, but Adrian's embrace until she found the courage to speak again.

"So, my mom showed up at the cabin," she said with her cheek pressed up against Jake's chest.

"What?"

Jake tried to step back so he could look into his wife's eyes, but she wouldn't let him yet.

"No, it's all right. Really. We ended up having a really good talk."

"Seriously?"

"I know. Shocking, right? But true, and it got me thinking."

"About what?"

Her hands left his back and grasped his arms for support. She had never been so afraid of his enticing blue eyes, but she had to face them.

"I can't do this anymore, Jake."

He opened his mouth to speak, but nothing came out. He just stared down at her with a look of hurt and shock that he couldn't mask.

Adrian slapped her hand to her forehead. "Rephrase, Cass!" she yelled. "Now, damn it!"

Her husband's misinterpretation of her words suddenly dawned on Cassie.

"Oh God, no! I didn't mean that."

"What did you mean?"

"I meant about us trying to have a baby."

"Oh."

"I still want to have kids with you, but I'd rather just let it happen."

"Just let it happen." Jake repeated the words as if the concept were foreign to him. "And if it doesn't just happen?"

"Not an option," she replied brazenly.

Jake arched a critical eyebrow.

"I'm not explaining myself right, am I?" she said.

"Did you breathe in too much fresh air up there at the cabin?"

"No." Cassie laughed, "I just want us to both think positive. Have faith in each other."

"Have faith? Is that you or your mother talking?"

Cassie resisted the urge to roll her eyes at Jake.

"I'd rather put my faith in us than in doctors. I don't want to pour money we don't have into treatments and procedures that may not work. I don't want us to end up resenting each other either."

"That's never going to happen; we won't let it."

"We can say that now," she replied, "but look at all the fighting we've done already."

Jake paused to ponder the situation.

"I am tired of all the drama," Jake said softly while he pulled her back into his arms. "I think we've been through enough." *You way more so than me.*

Chapter Thirty-Eight

"So, that's it?" Maggie asked Cassie as she slid a can of soda across the bar to her. "You're done trying?"

They were at The Borderline. Charlie and Jake were shooting pool. Cassie had offered to be their DD for the night. She was more interested in unwinding than tying one on.

And right now, she and Jake were confiding in their friends.

"Lights out? Game over? No sudden death?" Charlie asked Jake.

"Well, Jesus, when you say it like that, it sounds so...final," Jake replied.

"Well, it is, isn't it?" Charlie said.

"We're just taking the pressure off ourselves," Cassie explained to Maggie, "and letting it just happen."

"She asked me to have faith in her," Jake told Charlie. "Now, how was I supposed to say no to that?"

"You got me there," Charlie said while he bent over to take his shot.

Jake's timing was impeccable. He looked toward the bar at the same time his wife glanced over her shoulder at him.

She raised her can of Mountain Dew to him. He gave her a flirtatious smile in return.

"We're just going with it," Cassie told Maggie, "and letting whatever happens, happen."

"C'mon, Dude!" Cassie heard Charlie yell at Jake. "Get your mind off your woman and back on the game!"

"You should be glad I'm distracted," Jake teased. "It might give you the upper hand for a change."

Charlie waved him away as if he were a pesky fly bothering him while he tried to set up for his next shot. Jake took the hint and sauntered over to his wife.

"Now, what's a gorgeous woman like you doing sitting in a bar all by herself?"

"Waiting for my husband to quit concentrating on his pool game long enough to remember how gorgeous I am," Cassie replied.

"Sorry it took me so long. May I?" Jake motioned to the stool beside her.

"I don't know. What do you think, Maggie?"

"I think letting whatever happens happen is working well for you guys. Too bad you can't teach Charlie that."

They followed Maggie's eyes behind them to the pool table where Charlie had abandoned the game to flirt with a new, young beauty who had just entered the bar.

"So much for keeping his mind on the game," Jake joked.

"He's not showing her a picture of his baby's sonogram, is he?" said Cassie.

"He carries it in his wallet for just such an occasion," Jake replied.

Both women stared skeptically at him.

"I kid you not," Jake said.

"Only Charlie...." Maggie laughed before she took a swig of her beer. "I still can't believe how involved he's been with that girl throughout her entire pregnancy."

"He never missed a doctor appointment, did he?" Cassie asked Jake.

"Nope," Jake said as he tipped back his beer bottle. *He knows I'd kick his ass if he did.*

"How much longer does she have?" Maggie asked.

"Should be any time now," said Jake.

"Papa Charlie." Maggie shook her head in disbelief.

"How much you want to bet he'll be bringing that baby in here with him every weekend he's got her?" Cassie asked.

Jake took notice of his wife's reaction. *Look at her! It's not bothering her at all that Charlie's going to be a father. Hell, it doesn't even bother me that much anymore! She's joking around and happy. She's good and that's all that matters to me.*

"Fuck no!"

It wasn't just Charlie's foul mouth, but the sound of his pool stick crashing to the floor that caught everyone's attention. Even the girl he was trying to pick up backed skittishly away from him.

"Dude!" Jake chastised Charlie as he turned to him with his palms up as if to say, "What the hell?"

"The baby! He's coming. Now!"

All the bar patrons whooped with excitement for him.

"Well, why the hell didn't you say so!" Jake leapt off his stool and rushed over to Charlie. "C'mon, Papa; let's get you to that hospital!"

"No one is going anywhere without me," Cassie said while she jingled her car keys.

"Never a dull moment is there?" Adrian asked Kevin.

"Not as a guardian, no," Kevin said.

Just then, Maggie's attention was drawn toward the far end of the bar. She swore she saw one of the empty stools swiveling around.

"I've been working myself way too hard," she told herself as she downed a shot of tequila.

*

Never in a million years would Cassie have believed she'd be crammed inside Jake's truck driving Charlie to the hospital for the birth of his baby.

But here they were, Cassie trying to beat every red light in the city while Jake tried to keep Charlie calm.

"I can't do this!" Charlie sounded hysterical. "I'm not ready for this, man."

"You don't have to do anything but show up," Cassie snapped. "Sorry," she then mumbled while she gripped the wheel tighter and focused on the congested traffic.

She wasn't concerned about the beads of sweat that appeared on her forehead, but her husband was.

"You all right?" he asked her.

"No," Charlie yelled.

"Not you," Jake said.

"I'm fine," Cassie replied, hunched over the steering wheel. "It's just these stupid drivers. I swear, they must give licenses to anyone nowadays."

"Maybe I should drive," Jake suggested.

"No, with our luck we'll cross paths with a cop who needs to meet his quota today. And besides, we're almost there."

They made it to the hospital without incident. Charlie nearly jumped out of the truck before Cassie could stop.

"Good luck, man!" Jake called out as he slid over to the passenger seat. "We'll go park and meet you inside."

"Jesus," Jake said, laughing. "I've never seen him like this before. They may have to sedate him."

Cassie didn't respond, not even a chuckle. Jake turned to his wife, who was staring vacantly ahead of her.

"Cass," Jake asked, "you sure you're okay?"

Her reaction was delayed and did nothing to reassure Jake's concerns. Cassie eventually muttered an affirmation before she put the truck into gear and maneuvered it into the nearest empty parking space.

It felt like déjà vu to Jake and brought back vivid memories of his and Adrian's car accident that he couldn't shake.

"It's not the same, Jake," Adrian tried to convince him. "Don't give into those memories."

Jake put his hand over his heart, which seemed to be beating faster than a broken kick drum.

"Trust me," Adrian said as she placed her hand over his. "It's not the same thing."

He sat back in his seat and took a deep breath, which got Cassie's attention.

"Jake, I'm okay. Really," Cassie said as she reached out to touch his cheek.

Jake took her hand and kissed it while his heartbeat gradually returned to normal.

"Now, c'mon," Jake told her. "Let's get in there before Charlie gets himself kicked out, if it hasn't happened already."

"Okay," Cassie agreed.

She knew something was wrong the moment her foot hit the pavement. She felt light-headed and would have collapsed if Jake hadn't reached her in time.

"Cassie!"

Chapter Thirty-Nine

EVERYTHING WENT DARK. THE NEXT thing Cassie knew, she was lying in a hospital bed.

"What happened?" she asked groggily.

"You passed out."

Cassie responded by trying to sit up and get out of bed.

"Whoa, whoa, whoa!" Jake objected. "Easy there, young lady."

"But we're supposed to be here for Charlie."

"Our main focus right now is on you," the attending female doctor said.

"I'm fine," Cassie said. "I was probably just dehydrated or had low blood sugar or something."

"I'm afraid it's neither of those things," said the doctor.

"So, what is it then?" Cassie asked her.

"Well, we ran some blood tests, and it appears that you're pregnant," the doctor answered as she stood back and smiled.

"Pregnant?" Cassie asked. "No, no way. Really?"

"Are you sure?" Jake chimed in.

"Yes, to both of you," said the doctor, chuckling.

"How far along am I?" Cassie asked.

"About six weeks."

"Six weeks," Cassie repeated solemnly.

The euphoria she felt faded fast because all she could suddenly think about were the two babies she had already lost. One at eight weeks; the other at four months.

"Well, I'll leave the two of you to process all of this together. The nurse should be in shortly with your discharge papers. And congratulations."

"Thank you, doctor," Cassie mumbled.

"Cass," said Jake, sitting alongside her on the bed after the doctor left. "I know what you're thinking, but," he lay his hand protectively on her stomach, "I've got a good feeling about this one. He's a fighter."

Cassie leaned forward and splayed her fingers out over her husband's. Then she replied, "I hope you're right about her."

"He is," Adrian said as she held both Cassie and Jake's hands together in hers.

Cassie knew it was way too soon, but she swore she felt something move inside her. *It's probably just indigestion or something.*

"I don't want to steal Charlie's thunder or anything," said Jake, "but this is huge."

The joy in his eyes couldn't be concealed, until his wife put a stronghold on his arm.

"We can't tell anyone about this yet," Cassie said. *Not until I know we're safe.* "Please. Promise me."

"But..."

"Jake, please.

He wanted to tell her she was overreacting—that this time would be different—but he couldn't.

"All right," he said while he brought her hand up to his lips and kissed it like a gentleman, "whatever you want to do is what we'll do."

"Thank you," she replied gratefully.

*

"Dude, it took you long enough," Charlie teased Jake.

It was early the next morning. Charlie looked drained, but he seemed to perk up at the sight of his best friend.

"I'm sorry, man, but I told you I had to get Cass home."

"How's she doing?" Charlie asked.

All Jake had told him was that Cassie had fainted.

"Better. She sends her love and this."

Jake handed Charlie a wrapped box with small green and gold bows on it. Charlie looked at his friend suspiciously before he opened it.

"Oh, man." Charlie laughed when he saw the Packer onesie.

"We had to make sure she was the best dressed baby in the nursery."

"For sure," Charlie agreed. "So, are you ready to meet her?"

"Well, I didn't get up this early just to see your ugly mug."

"Follow me."

Jake fell in line behind Charlie, who walked the halls to the nursery as if he lived there.

"Which one is she?" Jake asked.

"Second row, third one over," Charlie replied.

He caught the attention of one of the nurses. She moved swiftly to the glass bed, scooped Charlie's baby up in her arms, and made her way to the window where they waited.

"Jake, I'd like to introduce you to Miss Dominique Danielle Maxwell—Dee-Dee for short."

"Well, hello, Miss Dee-Dee. I'm your Uncle Jake."

Jake couldn't take his eyes off the tiny newborn who, as if right on cue, stretched her arms out above her head of curly black hair and let out a mouse-like cry.

"Isn't that the sweetest sound you've ever heard?" Charlie asked. He continued to swoon over his baby girl, until he realized he may have put his foot in his mouth.

"Ah shit, man. I'm sorry. I wasn't even thinking about how this may be hitting you."

"We're pregnant."

"What?"

"Cassie..." Jake turned to face Charlie. "She's pregnant. We found out last night."

"And you're just telling me now?"

"I'm not supposed to be telling anyone." Charlie looked confused. "She doesn't want to jinx anything. So don't let on that you know."

"My lips are sealed except for: Congrats, man! Now, back to my little girl...."

*

Cassie lay in bed at home and stared up at the ceiling while every bleak possibility raced through her mind.

"Stop it!" Adrian yelled at her. "You're going to worry yourself sick, and then something will go wrong with the baby. Is that what you want? You need to relax. Everything is fine. Your baby will be just fine."

Adrian's eyes connected with Kevin's, and what she saw in them angered her.

"Oh, no." She shook her head in contempt. "Don't even tell me."

"I wasn't planning on it," Kevin answered matter-of-factly.

"This is bullshit, Kevin, and you know it!"

"Adrian..." he tried to calm her down, but she wasn't having any of it.

"Complete bullshit!"

Adrian and Cassie were temporarily silenced by a crack of thunder that rocked the apartment building, while Kevin remained unphased.

"Whoa!" Cassie exclaimed. "We're in for one hell of a storm."

"Yes, we are," Kevin said with his eyes trained on Adrian.

"What?" Adrian asked him defensively.

"Nothing," Kevin said, "except that He wants to see you."

"He? Like Him?"

"Yes."

"How do you know?"

"Let's just say I've experienced it before."

Just then, an amazing multi-colored cylinder of lights descended upon Adrian, and all Kevin could do was watch.

Adrian couldn't move, but she wasn't afraid either. She shut her eyes to the blinding lights, and when she opened them again, she was treated to a spectacular view.

The cylinder of light receded and left Adrian standing at the foot of an old stone arched bridge. He stood in the middle of the bridge, not in a dazzling white robe but in khakis and a white cotton shirt.

The sun bled gold across the sky and highlighted His shoulder-length dark brown hair. He saw Adrian and beckoned her to join Him.

Her mouth went bone dry as she took a tentative step forward. All the confidence she had felt talking to Kevin was now long gone.

"So, Adrian," He said as he leaned back into the bridge, "I hear you're having issues with my plan."

"We-ll," Adrian stammered, her head down low.

"I believe the exact words you used were 'Bullshit. Complete bullshit'."

"Well," she tried again while her eyes slowly met his gaze, "that's because it is."

"Please, go on."

Adrian took a deep breath to calm her nerves. *I can't believe I'm about to argue with God!*

"It's not fair, what you've done to them already. Haven't they been through enough? All they want is a healthy child of their own. Is that too much to ask of you?"

"No, and they'll have one when the time is right."

Adrian couldn't help rolling her eyes.

"And it's your job as a guardian to convince them to keep believing in the plan I have for them, no matter how long it takes. Otherwise—"

"Otherwise, what?"

"Otherwise, I'll have to remove you as a guardian. Understood?"

Adrian swallowed hard. "Understood."

"Good. Now back you go."

Chapter Forty

"CORRECT ME IF I'M WRONG," Adrian said to Kevin, "but don't most expectant mothers have a glow about them?"

"No, you're right," Kevin agreed.

They were upstairs in Jake and Cassie's bedroom. Cassie sat on the edge of the bed and marked off another day on her pocket calendar.

"So, why isn't Cassie glowing? Where's your glow, girl?"

Cassie flipped the pages forward.

"Six more months to go."

She sighed as she tossed the calendar back into her purse.

"Well, don't sound so thrilled about it," Adrian replied before she moved closer to her friend. "This is a good thing, remember?"

"Look," Adrian continued as she knelt before Cassie, "I know you're scared, but you have to allow yourself to enjoy this; every single second of it."

Cassie responded with her hand over her mouth while she made a mad dash to the bathroom.

"Even that," Adrian said from her vantage point on the floor. "Which seems to be happening an awful lot lately."

A fact that didn't go unnoticed by Cassie.

Why am I so sick all the time? she wondered. *This can't be normal. Something's wrong.*

"Don't go there," Adrian told her.

But it was too late.

It's happening again. It can't be. I've been doing everything right this time. So cautious. I even promised Max I'd take it easy at work; go to a desk job without complaint, but now....

Her thoughts were interrupted by another wave of nausea.

*

"I have to agree; it's not normal to be as sick as you have been," said Dr. Rousseau over the phone.

Dr. Rousseau had come highly recommended by Benji. She was the best obstetrician in Brown County, according to him. He insisted on pulling strings to get his little sister in as a new patient with her.

Cassie didn't want everyone to know she was pregnant, but she'd had to tell Benji, and right now she was glad she did.

"I have an opening in my schedule this afternoon if you can make it," Dr. Rousseau said.

"We'll be there. What time?" Cassie asked.

She called Jake as soon as she got off the phone with the doctor. She needed him to be there with her, just in case...

...something was wrong.

Cassie didn't want to say it out loud because she didn't want to give it a life of its own. What she was thinking was bad enough. Which is why she needed Jake to talk her down off this wall.

*

Jake and Cassie sat in the waiting room of the doctor's office later that afternoon on the edge of their seats. They nearly jumped out of their chairs when the nurse called Cassie's name. Jake squeezed her hand reassuringly as they went inside.

"So, how are you feeling?" Dr. Rousseau asked.

"Well, I haven't thrown up in about an hour," Cassie replied.

"Let's get to the bottom of this, shall we?"

Cassie lay back on the table, her hand still clasped inside her husband's, her eyes diverted from the screen that showed her baby's ultrasound. Cassie didn't care what sex it was; she just needed to know her baby was okay.

"Doctor?" she called out tentatively after what felt like an eternity of silence.

"You've been trying to have a child for a while now, correct?"

"Long enough," Jake replied.

"Doctor, please," Cassie said, "just tell us what's wrong.

"How about I show you?"

Oh my God, Cassie thought, *it's that bad!* She turned to Jake, his shoulders already rolling back, his face stoic. *Damn it! I knew it. I just knew it. I knew something was going to go wrong. Why did I have to be right? Why couldn't we...?*

Cassie's thoughts drifted away when she heard the strong heartbeat beeping on the ultrasound.

"There's one," Dr. Rousseau said.

Cassie couldn't resist looking at the screen. The doctor moved the probe around her belly, then stopped.

"And here," she said, "is the second one."

"What?" Jake asked shocked.

"What do you mean, 'the second one'?" Cassie asked.

"I mean, you're pregnant with twins, which would explain why you've been so nauseous. It's a common symptom when you're carrying twins."

They both froze for the longest time while they processed this new information.

Jake eventually leaned over and said to Cassie:

"There's no way we're going to be able to keep this a secret."

Chapter Forty-One

"**M**OM," JAKE SAID, "I REALLY don't think this is a good idea." Jake sat across from her in a booth at Mama Jo's Pizzeria. He had stopped in after work and just confided in his mother how scared Cassie was, especially after learning she was pregnant with twins.

She was eight months pregnant, and Jake was still worried about her. It seemed like she was afraid to be happy.

He'd see her being fascinated by the babies moving around or kicking inside of her, and then, as if caught in the act, she'd switch gears and a wall would build up around her. Almost like his Riley stance.

God, I hope she didn't learn this from me.

He wanted to do something to convince Cassie to destroy that wall, but he couldn't come up with anything.

Laura suggested a surprise baby shower, which didn't go over well with Jake.

"C'mon," Laura said. "Who doesn't love a party?"

"Someone who's had two miscarriages and is terrified of having another," Adrian said.

"I really think we should ask her if she wants a party instead of springing one on her."

Laura waved her hand at her son like he was talking nonsense.

"The surprise will be the best part! Don't worry. I'll take care of everything; all you have to do is get her here."

Good. The less I'm involved in this, the better.

*

"I'm really not in the mood for this," Cassie said while she thumbed through her closet.

"I know," Jake replied, "but you know how stubborn my mom is. She won't take 'no' for an answer."

"How about we tell her I'm sick?"

"Then she'll rush over here to take care of you."

"You're right; she would. So I'm going to have to change out of my pajamas into something more presentable."

They pulled up to the pizzeria about an hour later. Cassie had to admit, one of Mama Jo's signature pizzas did sound really good to her and the babies right about now.

She thought Jake was just being chivalrous when he let her go through the door first. Then she got bombarded with shouts of "Surprise!"

Cassie gave Jake a look to kill over her shoulder before she turned back around and did her best to pretend she was thrilled with the party.

It wasn't a huge gathering. There was Sara and the girls, Maggie, a couple of friends of hers from work, and Julia and Kathleen.

Kathleen? Cassie thought.

"Well, she is her sister-in-law," Laura explained when Jake posed the same question out loud.

"Now shoo," Laura told him. "This party is for girls only. I can bring Cass home when we're done."

"Okay," he replied hesitantly.

"Have fun," Jake said to Cassie.

He leaned in to kiss her on the lips, but she jerked her head away at the last second so that he caught her cheek instead.

"Hey," he whispered to her, "this was all my mom's idea."

"Mmm-hmm," Cassie replied, unconvinced.

The next thing Cassie knew, she was being whisked away by her mother-in-law. Jake couldn't help snickering behind his fist when they adorned her sweater with safety pins and put a sash around her that said: "Mommy-to-Be."

She's going to kill me, Jake thought as he headed for the door, *but it'll be so worth it.*

*

Maggie always knew just what to do to distract Cassie. They sat together, far away from the children and Julia and Kathleen's judgmental stares.

Maggie insisted Cassie open her inappropriate gag gifts right then and there.

They did the trick. Cassie was laughing so hard she had tears in her eyes, until a sharp pain in her stomach took her by surprise.

And another.

And another.

Cassie was doubled over by now, and the focus of everyone's attention.

Maggie had a tight grip on her hand when Julia rushed over.

"Maggie!" Cassie called out desperately.

"I'm right here, sweetheart. I'm right here," Maggie replied.

"What's happening?"

"Well, I'm no expert, but I think your little bundles of joy are trying to make a special appearance at the party," Maggie said.

"What? No. They can't be coming. It's way too soon."

Painful memories flashed through Cassie's mind. She saw herself lying on the floor of the ice cream shop; sitting in the bathroom and feeling her child slipping away.

This can't be happening again. It just can't be.

"C'mon, sweetheart," Maggie said gently. "Let's get you to the hospital, okay?"

All Cassie could do was nod her head in agreement.

Then she thought of something that made her pause.

"Jake. We need to call Jake. He needs to know."

"I'm on it," Maggie said, her cell phone balanced on her shoulder with her other arm wrapped around Cassie.

Julia hung back and watched enviously while another woman guided her daughter out of the pizzeria.

That should be me, Julia thought.

"Hey, Mama!" Maggie poked her head around the corner. "C'mon; she needs you too."

*

Jake came flying into the waiting room as if the devil himself were chasing him. He was on the lookout for familiar faces and found Maggie's.

"How is she? Where is she?" he asked breathlessly.

"She's fine, but...."

"But what?"

"The babies are coming Jake, now."

"This isn't a drill? No Braxton Hicks false labor?"

"Nope, it's the real thing, Daddy," Maggie replied. "Now you go and give her my love."

Adrian was halfway down the hall, not far behind Jake, when Kevin called her back.

"What? We have babies to help deliver, don't we?" she asked.

"Come with me," Kevin replied.

"Why? The babies are going to be all right, aren't they?"

"Just come with me, please."

Adrian bit her lip while she glanced at the door Jake had just rushed through.

"Adrian," Kevin tried again, "please trust me."

She conceded to Kevin and followed him outside the hospital.

They weren't in the parking lot, but in a gorgeous flower garden in full bloom; in the center was the stone bridge Adrian had spoken to Him on.

"Oh, c'mon!" she protested. "What did I do wrong now?"

Kevin couldn't hide his amusement. "Nothing."

"But isn't this where we go when we've offended Him?"

"There are other reasons we come here."

"Such as?"

"Such as…for delivering babies."

Adrian's eyebrows wrinkled in confusion.

"You'll understand soon enough," Kevin promised.

Adrian sighed as she folded her arms and stared at the bridge.

Nothing happened for the longest time. Her eyes cut to Kevin as if she thought he were lying to her, and then He appeared bathed in a calming white light. Adrian was so mesmerized by His appearance that she didn't realize what He was holding in his arms until He reached them.

"Are those?" Adrian stammered.

"Yes," He answered, "and your job now is to deliver them to their parents."

She fell speechless when he placed a baby in her arms.

"She's so tiny," Adrian said.

"But they're both very strong," He said as He set the baby boy gently into Kevin's arms.

"What do we do now?" Kevin asked Him.

"Wait," Adrian interrupted before He could answer, "you mean you don't know what to do next?"

"No, this is my first delivery," Kevin admitted.

They both turned to Him for further instructions.

"Take the staircase," He told them. "That will get you back into the hospital."

"That's it?" Adrian asked.

"And you need to beware of the darkness," He said.

Ah, shit, Adrian thought. *The darkness, of course.*

Just then the sky turned blacker than night and the wind howled. Kevin and Adrian held their babies closer to them.

"Good luck," he told them before He vanished into the light.

"Luck?" Adrian scoffed nervously. "We don't need luck. This is my kind of weather."

But it wasn't just the weather they were up against. They heard voices as they descended the stairs. One Adrian instantly recognized as Cassie's. She was screaming obscenities that Adrian never knew Cassie knew.

"She's already in labor." Adrian sounded distraught. "Are we too late?"

"No," Kevin replied, his eyes intent upon the wisps of black wind that followed them down into the hospital room and hovered over Cassie. "I think we made it here just in time."

"C'mon," the doctor urged Cassie. "You can do it. Just one really big push."

"I can't," Cassie cried as her head fell wearily back onto the pillow and submerged in the darkness. "I can't do any more."

Jake gripped her hand tighter. "Yes, you can. I know you can."

Tears filled Cassie's eyes while she shook her head vehemently "no."

That's when Adrian stepped forward, prepared to do battle against the darkness.

She stared longingly at the perfect baby girl in her arms and knew exactly what she needed to do.

She kissed the infant goodbye before placing her in the crook of her mother's arm.

Adrian saw the fight reignite in her best friend's eyes; the darkness slowly began to recede.

"That's it," Jake said supportively. "You got this."

Cassie lunged forward and pushed with all her might, much to her doctor's approval.

"Here she comes," she told Jake and Cassie.

"She?" Jake was momentarily distracted.

His daughter crying pulled him back into the moment.

"Okay," the doctor said. "One more time, Momma. Here we go."

The obscenities—along with a threat never to let Jake near her again—came fast and furious once more, but the second baby wasn't coming yet.

Adrian motioned to Kevin to do as she had done and put the baby boy into Cassie's arm.

He did, but not before he held him up like baby Simba in *The Lion King*. Cassie summoned up all the strength she had left in her to push. She fell back exhausted after she heard her second child cry. And by then, the darkness had evacuated the room.

Chapter Forty-Two

CASSIE WAS WORN-OUT, BUT SHE became reenergized the moment the nurse brought her children to her.

She couldn't hold them close enough. Jake was hovering over them like the proud, protective father he was, when there was a knock at the door.

"Hey," Maggie said as she poked her head through the doorway. "Can you stand some company?"

"C'mon in," Cassie answered.

"Oh my God; look at these precious little ones," Maggie cooed. "Names please."

Jake and Cassie exchanged a look.

"Well," Cassie began, "we thought Adrianna Faith…."

"Oh," Maggie cooed louder. "And what about this little one here?" she motioned to the baby in the blue knitted cap.

"That," Jake sighed, "has been a little harder to decide on."

"I want a name with meaning, but not Jacob Jr.," Cassie said.

"How about Matthew?"

All eyes were drawn to the doorway where Julia and Benjamin stood. They were all silent as Julia continued on.

"It means 'gift from God'."

Cassie and Jake looked at each other. Neither of them seemed to object.

"Matthew Jacob?" Cassie asked Jake.

"Matthew Jacob it is," Jake agreed.

"Well, hello, Matthew and Adrianna," Julia said as she got closer to them. "I'm your Grandma Julia."

"Would you like to hold them?" Cassie asked her mom.

"I would love to," Julia replied.

Jake helped transfer the babies from Cassie to Julia. Kevin and Adrian stood on either side of Julia.

"Job well done," Adrian said to Kevin.

"Thanks, but our job is far from over," Kevin replied.

"What do you mean?" Adrian asked. "Julia and Cassie have worked things out; Jake and Cassie have their babies."

"And those babies are going to hit puberty and they're going to need us to help them through it."

"A guardian's work is never done, is it?" Adrian sighed, but deep down she was relieved their story wasn't over yet.

The End

About the Author

ANNE MILLER IS THE YOUNGEST of four children. She was born in West Allis, Wisconsin, and moved with her family to the Upper Peninsula of Michigan when she was two years old. Her passion for writing began at age ten when she wrote her first novel, *The Summer Murder*, and she hasn't quit since.

She attended the University of Wisconsin-Green Bay for two-and-a-half years where she majored in English-Creative Writing with a minor in Communications.

After college, Anne excelled at several different day jobs, including grocery store clerk, hotel night auditor, and hospital housekeeper. She is currently a customer service representative/bank teller at a local financial institution. All of her job positions have enhanced her storytelling skills.

Anne is also a die-hard Green Bay Packers fan. She enjoys reading, and her latest obsession is the Outlander series of novels. She lives in the same small town she grew up in. Anne is the author of *The Last Photograph* and its sequel *Having Faith*. She has many more books in the works.

You can visit Anne at her website:

www.MillersLastPhotograph.com

The Last Photograph

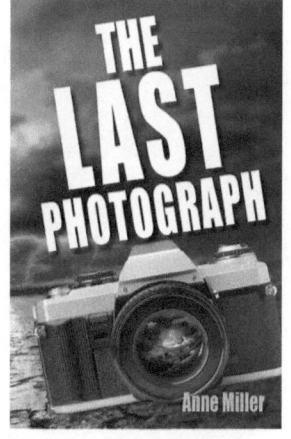

IF YOU ENJOYED *HAVING FAITH*, be sure to read Anne Miller's first book *The Last Photograph* where the story of Adrian and Jake first began.

Sometimes "Till death do us part" just doesn't apply to soulmates.

When Adrian Cattrel first met Jake Riley, she thought he was a conceited road crew worker whose only redeeming quality was his unnaturally stunning blue eyes. But the more she got to know him, the more she realized there was just something about him she couldn't resist. Four years later, Adrian is a budding photographer and happily married to Jake. They're on their way home from a family dinner one night when tragedy suddenly strikes.

Now Adrian is transitioning between two worlds and is concerned about how Jake will cope with her death. She knows he is not the kind of man to show his feelings—that's just not the way he was raised. His father taught him that real men—Riley men—never do that, but Adrian has tried to convince him otherwise right up until the night of her death.

Now the stakes are much higher. Can Adrian—with help from another unlikely guardian angel—change her husband's mind, or will he continue to live up to his father's expectations, which could ultimately destroy him?

As Adrian adjusts to her new role, she discovers that more than one person needs healing and that life still holds many surprises for her, even though she's no longer a part of it.

Available at:

www.MillersLastPhotograph.com
or your favorite bookseller